THE THEATRE
OF THE
MOMENT

A JOURNALISTIC COMMENTARY

•

GEORGE JEAN NATHAN

New Introduction By Dr. Charles Angoff

Fairleigh Dickinson

RUTHERFORD • MADISON • TEANECK

FAIRLEIGH DICKINSON UNIVERSITY PRESS

THE THEATRE OF THE MOMENT. © 1936 by George Jean
Nathan, © renewed 1964 by Mrs. George Jean Nathan. New material
in this edition © 1970 by Associated University Presses, Inc.

Library of Congress Catalogue Card Number: 75-120099

Reprinted 1970

Associated University Presses, Inc.
Cranbury, New Jersey 08512

ISBN 0-8386-7775-4
Printed in the United States of America

many of our theatrical critics, for all their theoretical admiration of high dramatic art, often actually derogate such examples of it as are placed before them and visit their esteem, instead, upon what is clearly and incontrovertibly second-rate, and sometimes third-rate stuff."

In the chapter entitled "The Histrionic Art," the author shows that he has no respect for Greta Garbo. ("It is quite possible that Miss Garbo is a great actress, but unfortunately for those of us who like a little verification of things, she has never given us any faintest proof of her alleged stunning virtuosity.") He is equally indifferent to the talent of Elizabeth Bergner.

Nathan reflects on the foreign theatre in New York, the producing gentry, and the progress of movies. He is not afraid to speak with vigor on the most controversial topics.

The Theatre of the Moment, with the originality, wit, impudent common sense and literary skill that belong to this master of the theatre, will help keep alive to the historians that raucous era of the 30s.

THE THEATRE OF
THE MOMENT
§ §

Another Book of the Theatre

Art of the Night

The Autobiography of an Attitude

Bottoms Up, An Application of the Slapstick to Satire

Comedians All

The Critic and the Drama

Encyclopedia of the Theatre

The Entertainment of a Nation

Europe After 8:15

Materia Critica

Mr. George Jean Nathan Presents

Passing Judgments

The Popular Theatre

Since Ibsen

Testament of a Critic

The Theatre Book of the Year 1942–43

The Theatre Book of the Year 1943–44

The Theatre Book of the Year 1944–45

The Theatre Book of the Year 1945–46

The Theatre Book of the Year 1946–47

The Theatre Book of the Year 1947–48

The Theatre Book of the Year 1948–49

The Theatre Book of the Year 1949–50

The Theatre in the Fifties

The Theatre of the Moment

The Theatre, The Drama, The Girls

The World in Falseface

1. *" Criticism today suffers from a lack of dignity."*
     — GEORGE SANTAYANA

2. *" The theatre today suffers from a lack of dignity."*
     — ST. JOHN ERVINE

Foreword

∽

It must be obvious even to the most loyal subjects and pertinacious admirers of Broncho Billy, Buster Keaton and Pearl White that the legitimate theatre, after its late attack of measles, is again rapidly getting back the rosy glow of health and is once more beginning to kick up its heels in the high, gay, old-time manner. It has been a long period since there have been such definite indications that the stage is again coming into its own, and not only in New York but, what is more significant, on what is known in theatrical lingo as the road. The reason is not particularly difficult to make out. When all is said and done, there is something about the theatre that all the moving pictures, radios, phonographs, automobiles, restaurants-with-entertainment, dance halls, free band concerts, and seasonal al fresco amorous impulses in the world cannot kill. It is the gilded and sometimes golden toy of the arts, and it has been that for centuries on end. It has behind it tradition, and the memory of countless nights of thrill and beauty, and some of the greatest literature ever written, and a thick album of tenderly remembered personalities — and each new year, whether it is healthy or whether it is ailing, it manages to recapture and to offer at least a snatch of its old glory. The public may at times desert it for other and newer amusement loves, but give the public a little time and always it will return to it.

Today, the public, which has grown homesick, is returning to it in sizable numbers. That public shows every sign of having become just a little tired of the overdose of films that endlessly repeat themselves and that continue with hardly any variation to bespeak its patronage and interest in stories every turn of which it by this time knows perfectly well five minutes after the first shot of the million-dollar penthouse, the airport with the mist rapidly settling down over it, or the train containing the adventurous female spy, the handsome young Englishman, and Stepin Fetchit, the comical porter. It also shows many signs of ceasing to believe that listening to radio advertisements of cathartics interrupted by a little jazz and the carefully expurgated joke about the farmer's wife and the book-agent constitutes a rich and emotionally satisfying artistic evening. And it shows even more signs that it has now at length got over its lingering prohibition passion for long guzzling evenings, and for night-time petting-party automobile excursions to dark suburban parking dells frequented by the more recherché hold-up men, and for band concerts with more disconcerting brass in them than a French premier, and for the prolonged imbecilities of backgammon, bridge, and indiscriminate couching. The public wants something better, something more greatly worth-while. And the theatre, it again has discovered, often offers it.

Contents

Introduction

By CHARLES ANGOFF

This book was published in 1936, an era of political and economic turmoil in the United States and the rest of the world. President Franklin D. Roosevelt was in his first term, trying to get some sort of normality into the body politic. American literature reflected this turbulence in every major form: the novel, the essay, poetry, and the play. It was the era of Proletarian Literature, of the Theatre Union, and of the Group Theatre. It was the era of the *New Masses* and the *Daily Worker,* and of the temporary immortality of their joint chief staff philosopher, Michael Gold. Maxwell Anderson and S. N. Behrman and Sidney Kingsley were writing plays, but the most noise was made by the plays of Clifford Odets and John Howard Lawson and Albert Maltz. It was, in large part, a raucous era, ridden with controversy and spattered with many colors. Now it is in oblivion that at times seems so distant as to challenge belief in its existence.

One thing is fairly certain, however. George Jean Nathan's books written in that time—he was a one-book-every-other-year man—will keep that era alive to the historian, in the realm of the theatre, of course, which was his main concern.

He begins, in typical Nathan fashion, by criticizing his fellow critics. He can't understand their lack of sensitivity to the value of, say, S. N. Behrman's *Rain From Heaven,* and their "ecstatic" praise "for such an unadulterated slice of Broadway pish as *Merrily We Roll Along.*" Then comes the chapter entitled "The Histrionic Art," and the man simply has no respect even for Greta Garbo: "It is quite possible that Miss Garbo is a great actress, but unfortunately for those of us who like a little verification of things, she has never given us any faintest proof of her alleged stunning virtuosity." He is equally indifferent to the talents of Elizabeth Bergner.

Nathan's pet dislike in *The Theatre of the Moment* is Clifford Odets, prince of the Proletarian playwrights. Only one of his plays, he says, has appreciable merit: "*Waiting for Lefty* . . . , a mere prolonged one-acter utilizing the audience-actor device familiar to popular audiences for several decades but with the kick of new passion in it." *Awake and Sing,* about Bronx Jews, has "some interesting character drawing . . . , but on the whole a play at once defectively composed and toward its conclusion not a little bogus." Odets "has a share of real talent," he is capable of pity, "But he can also—and at times close upon heel—write counterfeit theatrical dialogue; he can feel and convey a grease-paint passion; he can sophisticate character to stage ends; he can be spuriously eloquent and he can smear pity like mustard on what is essentially dramatic ham." As a dramatist, Odets is "much like a pianist who has learned much more about the loud pedal than he has about harmony." Even as a pleader for the cause of the downtrodden, Odets is deficient. His "propaganda, in short, is for those who are already convinced of its subject matter before the curtain goes up."

Nathan pays his respects, as the saying goes, to Maxwell Anderson (his *Valley Forge* "is largely declamation that essays to warm itself into theatrical life" and Anderson as a whole still has to make up his mind whether he's a poet or a dramatist), Robert Sherwood (writer of "intellectualized melodrama"), Sidney Kingsley (a playwright with "first-rate dramatic ideas and a second-rate dramatic equipment"), Lillian Hellman (he likes her, chiefly because, it appears, she's a good dramatic carpenter), George M. Cohan (a man of "real native humor and merit . . .

the most surefooted and proficient actor in the whole American theatre"), and George S. Kaufman (his plays have "an infinitely greater affinity with life reflected in *Variety* than life lived away from the world of Tony's Hollywood studios, the company of the metaphysical Marx Brothers, and the concomitant ferocious, indefatigable repartee. It is, in short, gaggery) ."

The foreign theatre in New York? Nathan liked little of what came here in the mid-thirties. Jacinto Benavente? He is, "as you know, the foremost living dramatist of Spain. He is also one of the foremost living bores in or out of Spain." Federico Garcia Lorca is only "additional proof that the Spanish drama is no longer welcome to the American stage." Lorca offers this additional proof "with a vengeance."

At times, alas, Nathan is more brilliant than just in the light of hindsight wisdom. But his percentage of "rightness"—in so far as "rightness" applies to drama appreciation—is phenomenally high. And his style carries one along for page after page. Of what other dramatic critic in all American history can this be said?

Fairleigh Dickinson University
Rutherford, New Jersey

THE THEATRE OF
THE MOMENT

CHAPTER I

The Literary Drama Returns

To the student of theatrical phenomena, it becomes more and more evident that the critical tendency of the present-day American stage is toward the literary drama. By literary drama is not meant the dramatic hybrid which confuses the library with the stage, nor yet the drama whose composition suggests the man of letters who regards the theatre as a medium beneath his lofty dignity. What is meant by the phrase is drama, sound in its theatrical self, that at the same time has in its web and woof the silken threads of literature and that, apart from its purely stage appeal, merits the consideration of publication as literature.

Two elements have contributed to this increased theatrical predilection for the species of drama in question as opposed to the erstwhile all too insistent drama of unadulterated greasepaint. One, of course, is the motion picture. The motion picture, by ridding the theatre of its demi-emotional and demi-intelligent audiences, has created a residual audience that, both emotionally and intellectually, is more or less a unit, and that, unlike the former

[3]

miscellaneous audience, may be approached by a producer upon recognizable and at least partly anticipated and understood terms. The disappearance of what is loosely to be designated as the old gallery and rear balcony trade — the present backbone of the motion picture audience — has been a critical godsend to the reputable theatre and to reputable drama. The second item is the increased sophistication of the residual audience itself, its discontent with the kind of plays upon which it often formerly looked kindly, or with a passive kindness, and its avid search for drama of a more exalted nature. The epiphany of the more literary drama is the result.

The three outstanding American dramatists of the present-day theatre, it is doubtless safe to say, are Eugene O'Neill, Maxwell Anderson and S. N. Behrman. They are also among the most successful at the box-office. All three fall under the heading of literary dramatists, that is, literary dramatists by our prefatory definition. O'Neill, for some time now at work on a cycle of nine full-length plays that will comprise the study of an American family against the changing background of American life in the years from 1779 to 1932, was not represented in the theatre this last season, although the first three plays of the cycle will probably be ready for production in the not far future. Anderson contributed *Winterset,* a drama of murder and vengeance in the underworld wrought in the rhythms of broken verse. Although not always too ably articulated and although here and there fuddled in its gallant effort

[4]

to break through to vigorous beauty, it was relatively the most estimable literary-dramatic exhibit of the year and was properly given the Critics' Circle's blessing. What is more, in the reading it plays out its drama in the theatre of the imagination quite as effectively as it acted it out on the stage of actuality.

Behrman is the most cultivated and literate of the American comedy writers. His latest play, *End of Summer,* while considerably beneath the quality of his previous season's *Rain From Heaven* or his *Biography* and *The Second Man* of the seasons before, despite its dramatic lapses at least indicated again a flavor of mind, a skill in literary grace and a dexterity in the business of putting well-chosen words together that many of our overly hymned prose writers might envy. From the very first day, many years ago, that he sent in his earliest short story writing to the magazine of which I was at the time co-editor, there has been discernible in him that combination of cultured European view of life and American directness and humor which, in these later years, has shown an increased maturity of expression. His plays, also, are quite as much at home in the library chair as in the orchestra seat.

Among the popular successes of the season were two dramatizations of novels, one of Edith Wharton's *Ethan Frome,* by Davis *père et fils,* the other of Jane Austen's *Pride and Prejudice,* by Helen Jerome. Dramatizations of novels, for no good or sound critical reason, have long been suspect in the theatre. Any number have confounded the criticism which contends, in the face of fact, that no worthy novel may be converted into a satisfactory stage play and yet retain what is most valuable in the novel. The two dramatizations in point, the latter in particular, confounded such criticism further. While the dimensions of dramaturgy restricted the scope of the Wharton novel in the latter passages of the stage play, enough of the original remained to hold the mirror accurately up to literature. In the case of the Austen dramatization the essence and air of the novel were duplicated to a nicety within the proscenium arch.

Laurence Housman's *Victoria Regina* falls, by common critical consent, much more pointedly into the category of literature than of stage drama, yet it was one of the most prosperous attractions of the year. Even the fact that its thirty episodes, as published in the printed version, were for theatrical purposes necessarily reduced to a mere ten did not interfere with its wholehearted reception on the part of audiences. Its lack of drama (in the usual and passé sense) was freely tolerated for its proportionate presence of luminous and tender English prose. *Parnell,* by the late Elsie Schauffler, also coming under the head of approximate literary drama, found such favor with audiences that its closing week brought in more than twelve thousand dollars at the box-office and a return engagement was called for. The revival of *The Taming of the Shrew* not only packed the Guild theatre but the theatres out of New York as well; the revival of *Ghosts* by Madame Nazimova surprised even the most hopeful ticket vendors; and the prosperity of the dramatization of Erskine Caldwell's *Tobacco Road,* in its third year in the New York theatre and doing a land-office business with several companies on the road, was still another straw which suggests the way the theatrical wind is blowing.

Lynn Riggs, whose plays have borne in mind some literary and even poetic quality and who until this last year, despite the very modest success of his *Green Grow the Lilacs* in a Theatre Guild production, has been unable to find his audience, now at length found it with *Russet Mantle,* a play often sadly defective but one which listed sincerely toward poetic expression. And *Lady Precious Stream,* Dr. S. I. Hsiung's paraphrase of the classic Chinese drama idea, while perhaps debatable as to any true literary quality, at least exercised a certain particularized audience appeal, for all the play's botched performance, and attracted interest in its published book form.

That the theatre public is no longer frightened by drama which makes an approach to literature thus becomes apparent. And it becomes just as apparent, from the sales statistics on published plays, that to that present theatre-going public there is rapidly being added a public of considerable proportions that, unable to see the plays because of residence away from the theatrical centers, is welcoming them in book form. Surely when one looks at the current publishers' lists and compares them with those of, say, a decade ago, one must be astonished to note the great number of plays that in these later years have been vouchsafed book covers. Moreover, there must be an equal astonishment over the favor that many of these published plays have found and are finding with readers as distinguished from theatregoers. That the plays of Bernard Shaw, for example, have in the ten years in point enjoyed a reading reception of increased and very considerable magnitude is, to be sure, not too surprising, since from almost the beginning Shaw's drama has happily bridged the library and the stage. But there is a very definite and very satisfactory surprise in the almost unbelievable success of the literary-dramatic product of an American like O'Neill, whose published plays have sold, in certain cases, like a Sinclair Lewis best-selling novel and, in others, to a figure that never previously had been reached even remotely by an American dramatist. Think of a single published play selling more than 110,000 copies! Yet that is the record of O'Neill's *Strange Interlude.*

There is no space here for an extended record of the sales figures of the published plays of various other dramatists, both American and foreign, but that there is a steadily growing library audience for drama of some literary worth is unmistakable. The published plays that pretty generally fail to find a reading audience are those that lack any literary quality. Their theatrical success alone is not a sufficient reading magnet. Even the worst stage failure of a literary-dramatic writer like O'Neill — *Dynamo* or *Days*

Without End for an example — appeals to infinitely more book buyers and infinitely more readers than the biggest stage success of a non-literary playwright like the widely discussed Clifford Odets or the Pulitzer prize-winning Sidney Kingsley. The Laurence Housmans and the Maxwell Andersons may generally be relied upon to capture more readers than the Dodie Smiths and the Philip Dunnings.

Just as present-day theatre audiences have gained a taste for the drama that approaches literature, so have they synchronously achieved a happy and safe discrimination between what is more or less authentic in that direction and what, for all the reputations of the specific authors in the field of literature, is plainly bogus. No longer will they accept the fraudulent literary-dramatic play because of the literary standing of a writer. Thus, when a Priestley gives them something like *Eden End,* which is three-quarters novel and but one-quarter drama, they gag at it even as the professional drama critics, fully appreciating that on such occasions it isn't that Priestley writes plays like a good novelist but rather that he writes them like a bad dramatist. And thus, also in this same last season, when a Clemence Dane produces something like *Granite,* which is a mere pretentious pseudo-literary thrust at the stage, they laugh it promptly into the discard not only because it is bad drama but because it is even worse literature. As things stand in the American theatre today, the literary drama has every chance to come into its successful own. But it must be literature and drama at one and the same time. It cannot, finally to arrive in the library, proceed *from* the library. It must move, with the pace of drama, *toward* it.

CHAPTER II

Sex in Greasepaint

ↄ ↄ

The stern pronunciamento of Der Reichsführer designating the sexual side of life as a petty business unworthy of the austere consideration of any true nationalist and demoting it, especially in the arts, to a level with Bismarck herring and the music of Mendelssohn, brings the ignoble and useless theatrical critic to meditate the greatly altered contemplation of sex not only in current German but in almost all of international drama. It was not so very long ago, as everyone knows, that sex occupied the major attention of drama, and that the aforesaid sex was customarily treated with so grave and even tragic an air that one had difficulty in naming more than a few plays in which the sex act, however casual, did not lead haplessly either to sudden death and disaster or at least to very painful stiletto wounds and the criminal courts. This was the period when the phrase, " a fate worse than death," echoing from countless stages, made it impossible for fear-struck virgins to sleep o' nights and when sex was vested solely in the hideous person of a low scoundrel with a fierce black moustache and a stinging riding crop or of a lecherous old roué, usually a duke or the head of the Czar's secret police, given to copious brandy drinking and to toying with the sharp edge of a sinister paper-knife. This was the period deplored by Mr. Walter Prichard Eaton as being sadly lacking in playwrights who were aware that a bed may sometimes be used for sleeping purposes and by Dr. Rudolf Kommer as containing only plays that ended either in the grave or in bed and usually and simultaneously in both.

That a large change has come over the dramatic attitude toward sex needs no re-statement, but a scrutiny of that change may interest the historian of theatrical phenomena.

The inaugurators of the changed attitude were the English. Themselves, along with the playwrights of other nations, guilty of long lugubriosity in the reconnaissance of the sexual relations of men and women, they suddenly — almost over-night — began to view the erstwhile tragedy with a light and sardonic eye and to offer the opinion that it might even be possible for a male and a female to indulge in an anatomical peccadillo without consequences more dire than being embarrassingly caught in the rain on the way back home from a private supper room at *The Pig and Whistle* or driving a cuckolded husband to the consumption of an additional whiskey and soda. (Reference, of course, is to the so-called more serious playwrights of England and the various other countries as distinct from the open-and-shut farceurs, although even in the latter quarter it was chiefly the French who successfully capitalized the saucy sex slant.) Despite the progress shown by the Englishmen, however, the old waters passed under the bridge with considerable reluctance, and in England and on the Continent the main current of drama still persisted in emphasizing the 1895 scoops that a woman who had had an affair before marriage, were she otherwise soever irreproachable, was inevitably doomed to wreck her husband's and children's lives and to end up in the gutter; that a young woman's single past misstep was sufficient to prevent her from getting any kind of job in the future, especially one of governess with any household in a village containing an active curate or even one of stenographer or amanuensis to a voluptuous, if somewhat elderly, marquis; and that the young scion of a good family who so much as cast an eye at a pretty maid servant could be saved from a calamity that threatened his career as a potential leading barrister only by shipping him off instanter to a sheep ranch in Australia.

The French, strangely enough, were even more backward than the English in allowing new values to the cerebration of the sex business and their plays steadfastly continued to identify the boudoir with the undertaking parlor. The slightest extra-indulgence in the world's oldest amateur sport was still the occasion for dramatic Gettysburg addresses on behaviorism and morals, and it remained difficult for even the more enlightened audiences theatrically to dissociate a mere amorous *faux pas,* even one recorded as having come to pass long since amid the rose bushes of Provence, from something closely approaching a world catastrophe involving the disruption of the Chamber of Deputies, the overthrow of the French government, and the discovery that the impromptu child of the horticultural contretemps, now grown to manhood, was his own mother's current lover. The Germans, of course, maintained in the main their old established attitude, to wit, the conviction that sex — apart from connubial duty and routine — was something reserved for the trumpery and inferior French, and that its place in Teutonic drama was accordingly gratuitous, save perhaps as a bogy wherewith to scare precocious children, flippant Berliners who had made a poisonous trip to Paris, and the more suspect patriots in Alsace-Lorraine. There were exceptions, to be sure, but they were few and far between and even they achieved their highest degree of independence in the species of drama that succeeded in flustering dramatic critics with ten children with some such bombshell as attributing an undue bigotry to a family whose Magda, on her return home, was denied her share of the Senfgurken and sauerkraut because of her fall from grace, or contending that there were Beatas and Marikkes in the world who might sin from an excess of passion and who could explain their delinquency to the complete and even rapturous satisfaction of the fatter ladies in the audience. And as for the Italians and Spanish, sex continued to be a golden gloves contest conducted by the counterparts of the Messrs. Lincoln J. Carter, Harry Clay Blaney and Sullivan, Considine and Woods.

Just as it always takes the drama at least ten years to catch up with any philosophy already freely accepted by the generality of people and at least twenty or thirty to catch up with any freely accepted and already long dismissed as outworn and banal by the slightly more intelligent, so it has taken what we are pleased to refer to as the modern playwright an inordinate amount of time to find that there is something more phallic than a needle in the average modern haystack. The Italians and the Spanish are in the aggregate still Victorian Desperate Desmonds in the matter of sex, confirmed in the belief that whenever a man and a woman come together in a blaze of passion something pretty terrible is bound to happen to them by All Saints' Day. But the playwrights of other nations — even the quondam Gloomy Guses of Russia — have gradually come to see the light, the light o' love that was placed in the window by the Viennese to guide the sad and wayward sons of drama back to the warmth and happy contentment of life. A truth and a humor have come in turn to the stage's consideration of humanity's anatomical didoes and where once the drama's sex was mainly either bogusly romantic or bogusly ominous and tragic we now discover it to be pleasurably treated with the same realism, on the one hand, that is accorded to war and fashionable society and with the same humor, on the other, that is accorded to democracy and God. Dramatists who continue to look at sex in the old way have suites reserved for them by the public in the poor-house, whereas dramatists of the new order are resplendent in the latest modes in neckties and platinum perfecto cutters. And not only in the western world but in the eastern. "Vassily Vassilovitch Shkvarkin," announced the Russian correspondent of a London newspaper a short time ago, " is reputed to be the richest man in Moscow today, and he is neither a banker nor an industrialist. He is a dramatist who until recently was relatively unknown. So popular has his rollicking sex farce, *Another Man's Child,* become that he is reputed to have earned approximately one million roubles in royalties in less than a year." And right here at home there is a much burlier bank account in the humorous sex of a *Personal Appearance* or the unromantic sex of a *The Children's Hour* or the realistic sex of a *Tobacco Road* than in all the *Spring Freshets, Roman Servants* and *Living Dangerouslys* that you can shake a lumber-yard at.

The English playwrights, especially the younger men, have gone so far as practically to abandon the bed as a somewhat too rococo article of amorous furniture and have saved their producers considerable money on the old prop by substituting for it either the floor, which costs nothing, or a settee, which costs probably less than half. The Germans, despite Hitler's unremitting frown, have followed suit and while, because of an ingrained homey aversion to mussing up the company room, they still look askance at employing a floor for purposes other than a cuspidor and a settee for purposes other than a depository for the posterior of the visiting family pastor, they have at length qualified sexually such hitherto sanctified acres of Jehovah as apple orchards, cornfields and barn-yards. The French, the most old-fashioned people in the world when it comes to sex, God bless them, persist in championing the bed, as their fathers and grandfathers did, but nevertheless often no longer wait until the third act to focus upon it and periodically even go to the extent of putting it in the prologue. Sacha Guitry himself, up to only a few years ago the *chaud bébé* of Gallic theatrical sex, fearing now, what with youthful competition, that he is losing his old audience kick, will try to recapture box-office attention in his next play, report hath it, with an exhibit containing four beds in each of its first two acts and five in its third, all of them, save for a few minutes when apéritifs are being served, in constant use. The newest play of one of the leading American dramatists, due to be produced in New York during the coming season, has as its heroine a Paula Tanqueray who has just celebrated her sixteenth birthday, and there are tidings from Vienna and Buda-Pesth that the season will see, in the former capital, a production of Wedekind's *Awakening of Spring* with a jazz band accompaniment and, in the latter, one of Ibsen's *Ghosts* with an induction and epilogue, something after the manner of Shaw's *Fanny's First Play,* in which actors representing five of Hungary's most eminent medicos will sardonically thumb their noses at old Henrik and Mrs. Alving.

CHAPTER III

The Critics

       ഗ *ഗ*

Do They Prefer Second-Rate Plays?

In the last half dozen years we have had considerable evidence that many of our theatrical critics, for all their theoretical admiration of high dramatic art, often actually derogate such examples of it as are placed before them and visit their esteem, instead, upon what is clearly and incontrovertibly second-rate, and sometimes even third-rate, stuff. This appears to be true despite the fact that theatrical reviewing has improved at least fifty-fold in more recent seasons. But although it has advanced as greatly as it has, it still would seem to have some distance to go before its appraisals, in certain quarters, become intelligible to the layman who, without being paid for it, can distinguish the difference in values between the Brothers Minsky and the Brothers Karamazov, to say nothing of the Warner Brothers and the Quintero Brothers.

To argue that there must always exist differences of opinion is to evade the point. It is properly to be expected, even demanded, of any reputable critic that he recognize fine drama when he sees it. Or that he recognize it, if not completely, at least partly. But we often find such otherwise reputable judges not only not recognizing it but actually dismissing it with a gesture of faint contempt. It is small wonder, therefore, that those of our theatrical producers who occasionally have attempted to produce something daringly beautiful and out of the ordinary have skeptically scratched their heads and proceeded thereafter safely to put on easily digestible dishes of hokum.

Consider three plays produced in the last few seasons: Gordon Daviot's *Richard of Bordeaux,* Denis Johnston's *The Moon in the Yellow River* and Sean O'Casey's *Within the Gates.* Here, certainly, whatever one's prejudices as to drama, was a trio of dramatic exhibits that individually and collectively represented something infinitely finer than our theatre is usually accustomed to. Each of the plays had many qualities that lifted it far above the general run and that stamped it with the mark of relative dramatic distinction. Yet a considerable number of our critics dismissed the three plays as being of little consequence, and whooped it up instead for other plays that were little more than filchings from the old Broadway garbage barrel.

Although, as has been duly noted, play reviewing in our midst has improved remarkably, there would still seem to be times that recall the older day when Barrie's *Peter Pan,* upon its first performance in America, was denounced as contemptible childish drivel, when Porto-Riche's *Amoureuse* was waved aside with wisecracks, when George Birmingham's *General John Regan* was declared an inferior grade of humor to that purveyed by Roi Cooper Megrue, and when Augustus Thomas, that dean of the American dramatic platitude, was almost unanimously voted a dramatic genius superior on all counts to the most illustrious dramatists of Europe.

It thus does not require much digging into the critical files to find S. N. Behrman's sensitive and beautifully written *Rain From Heaven* disparaged by critics who raised their voices ecstatically for such an unadulterated slice of Broadway pish as *Merrily We Roll Along*. Nor does it require much more to find a play like Pirandello's *Right You Are If You Think You Are* treated with a lofty condescension while loud cheers were reserved for such piddling imitations of the O'Neill drama as Owen Davis' *Icebound* and *Detour*. And there are any number of other examples, including the recent ballot of three members of the Critics' Circle for Robert Sherwood's feather-weight *Idiot's Delight* as against Maxwell Anderson's *Winterset*. Even the now generally accepted idea that that dose of arch-claptrap known as *Abie's Irish Rose* was announced to be such by all the New York critics is completely false. A few, to be sure, did announce it to be just that, but there were a number who allowed that it had its points!

That such plays as *Tobacco Road, The Commodore Marries,* and certain of Vincent Lawrence's comedies may not constitute absolutely first-rate drama, anyone will admit, but that at the same time they constitute drama of some real merit it would be pretty difficult to deny. Yet we have had sufficient critical instances of that denial, which might not be so confounding if the same critical nay-sayers had not simultaneously bestowed their laurels on out-and-out trash. The future historian of modern American drama will have to read much of modern American criticism with his fingers crossed if he wishes to derive a true picture of modern dramatic worth.

The day when critics discerned in the Harvard melodramas of Edward Sheldon genuinely important contributions to the American stage is past. The day when the yap-traps of Charles Klein and George Broadhurst were accepted with critical solemnity is also past. But the day seems to be yet occasionally with us when something like Sidney Howard's *They Knew What They Wanted,* with its stale echoes of earlier German drama, may be accepted as a masterpiece of dramatic art, while something like O'Neill's *The Great God Brown,* freely allowing for its defects, is consigned to a place six or seven rungs lower on the critical ladder.

There are certain good plays, it is true, about which a difference of opinion is quite understandable. Such plays, for example, as Bahr's *The Master,* Zoë Akins' *Papa* and *A Texas Nightingale,* and the like. For they deal with themes that require a certain specialized experience in life and literature for their wholehearted sympathy and appreciation. The aforesaid difference of opinion as to them is accordingly more or less intelligible. But there are other plays, fine plays, that should sweep intelligent criticism as a unit into their embrace, and it is such plays that often find criticism strangely deaf and dumb.

The fault, to be overly generous in the matter, does not lie so much in that deafness and dumbness, grieving as it is, as in the rapturous praise that, on the other hand, is bestowed by the same critics upon inferior plays and in those critics' endorsement of the inferior plays as magnificent works of art. Surely there is something wrong somewhere with any critic who seriously believes and states, as a large number of our critics have, that a play like *Reunion in Vienna* constitutes top-notch drama, when everyone in any way connected with it clearly and honestly perceived, when it was first shown out of New York, that it was utterly feeble and rather junky stuff and when only the pleas of Alfred Lunt and Lynn Fontanne, its stars, that they be allowed to convert it into a burlesque shambles by jumping over sofas and rolling around on the floor subsequently succeeded in making it passable.

Producers, Playwrights and Critics

There is, accordingly, something to be said for our theatrical producers and playwrights who have lately been inveighing in the public prints against the drama critics. It is a pity that, for all their lush verbosity, they haven't been able to say it for themselves. To contend, for example, as Mr. Elmer Rice has, that certain critics are alcoholics and in the last stages of senility may — let us agree for the sake of argument — be sound enough truth in itself, but it has nothing to do with their competence as critics, however much it may have to do with what the police and their wives publicly or privately, as the case may be, think of them. Strindberg, who was not only a boozer and senile but commonly reputed to be downright insane, confected dramatic criticism that makes that of such a relatively youthful teetotaler as myself, for example, look like a child's scribblings. Coleridge, grantedly one of the finest critics that ever lived, was a dope fiend, and Hazlitt, Lamb and Steele, certainly all worthy fellows, as Mr. Rice would allow, were under the table night after night. Poe and Whitman, the latter senile by Mr. Rice's definition, were galoots for rum, and Saintsbury — as everyone knows — could drain a magnum in nine and three-quarters seconds flat. Huneker's beloved nose was often mistaken by strangers from out of town for a Rubra Superba peony, but Mr. Rice wouldn't argue that, even when Jim was in his latest years, it diminished the brilliant color of his critical writings. Some of the profoundest asses who ever have mussed up type pages with criticism, on the other hand, have been and are comparative youngsters or total abstainers. (Let us politely refrain from mentioning names.)

For a reason that is hard to make out, dramatic criticism is the only profession concerned with the arts in which a man of increased years is supposed to know less than he did in his earlier years, and in which a practitioner is supposed to be *non compos* if, like Shakespeare or Thomas Huxley, he likes a drink now and then. Such animadversions as Mr. Rice's, accordingly, are blood cousins to stupidity. They are as hollow and empty, indeed, as the recent plays of Mr. Rice himself, who is neither senile nor a dipsomaniac. The arguments against the critics, which he and his fellow playwrights and producers seem to be unable to think up, are quite different. Not against all the critics, to be sure, but against a sufficient number of them to lend their statement a reasonable justice. In view of the fogginess of these critic-baiters, let one himself a critic come professionally and hospitably to their assistance.

The first objection the producers and playwrights might rationally make against much of current dramatic criticism is its confusing habit of praising certain inferior plays and denouncing others that are equally inferior. Under such circumstances, it is no wonder the producers do not know where they stand so far as the critical press reaction goes, and gradually go crazy.

A second objection is to the kind of critic who lambastes the tar out of a play and subsequently, by way of attesting to his magnanimity and freedom from personal prejudice, hypocritically and self-insultingly (albeit he doesn't seem to recognize the fact) allows that he " hopes it succeeds anyway and makes a million dollars."

A third objection is to the kind of critic — usually one with punditical overtones — who justifies his endorsement of a cheap farce and his condemnation of an ambitious piece of dramatic writing with the ancient critical·claptrap that a piece of work must be accepted on its own terms and that the cheap farce, which pretends to be nothing more than what it is and sets out only to be amusing, is deserving of greater praise than the ambitious play which sets out to reach the moon and on the way stumbles over a few stars. If a play is always and inevitably to be accepted critically on its own terms and the success with which it meets them, *Boy Meets Girl* — as every such contending critic must agree — is three times as critically commendable as Shakespeare's *Cymbeline* or Rostand's *Chantecler*.

A fourth objection is to the species of critic who gabbles loudly for beauty in drama and who, when at length he is vouchsafed just a little of it by some aspiring and uncommercial producer, loudly objects to the whole enterprise because there wasn't more of it — and declares the occasion, consequently, a total failure.

A fifth objection is the benevolent habit of praising a leading actress or actor in ratio to a play's lack of merit. The worse a play, the better notices the leading actress or actor seems bound to get.

A sixth objection is to the critics' constant plea for a finer and nobler theatre, a theatre of authentic dramatic art, and their unwitting discouragement of any producer or producers who might have ambitions in such a direction with their periodic hysterical eulogies of the ordinary products of the present commercial theatre. Think of the producer who hopefully dreams of instituting a theatre of uncommercial dramatic splendor and then picks up a newspaper and reads such endorsements as these: " *Dods-*

worth is one of the greatest plays I have ever seen "; " *The Distaff Side* is a masterpiece of our time "; " *Lost Horizons* is one of the most notable dramatic experiments, and one of the most moving, of our times "; " *Merrily We Roll Along* will surely make history in the American theatre "; " *The Farmer Takes a Wife* is just what our theatre has been longing for and so badly needs "; " *Judgment Day* is one of the modern theatre's most thrilling and stirring plays "; " *Merrily We Roll Along* is a play which proved its power to blow its first official audience's heart into particles of sheer gratitude "; " *Divided By Three* is one of the theatre's superior items "; " *Roll, Sweet Chariot* is a remarkable achievement "; " *Small Miracle* is exactly what the theatre has been crying for "; " *Spring Freshet* stems from that inner urge which is the source of any author's finest work "; " *A Ship Comes In* brings the kind of brave intelligence into the theatre that the theatre needs "; " *Lost Horizons* is a stimulating and imaginative play, arresting in conception and engrossing to the end "; and — in the somewhat higher quarter — " *L'Aiglon* is one of the world's plays magnificent! "

Even if the producer in question sought to put such stuff down to a critical charity in an off season, what would he think when he reflected that the same deplorable absence of standards is visible year after year? Where would be his desire to risk something really fine when, after reading such confounding tributes, he turned to the journals of a season before and again encountered such disheartening critical news as this: " *Come of Age* is a rare adventure in the theatre "; " Don't waste a minute. Run and buy tickets for *Ten Minute Alibi* "; " *The Dark Tower* is a real treat for literate and intelligent playgoers "; " *The Dark Tower* is a lavish experience in the theatre "; " *Theodora, the Quean* glows with life as a drama "; " *By Your Leave* is truly witty, often truly touching; it will be one of the pet plays of the town "; " *They Shall Not Die* is a masterpiece "; " *No More Ladies* is a comedy masterpiece "; " *Men In White* is one of the theatre's more magnificent dramas "; " *She Loves Me Not* is what the theatre must have more, a lot more, of "; " *The World Waits* is in many respects triumphant drama "; " *Double Door* is a gem "; and " *The Shining Hour* pretty well represents all that is best in the theatre."

Note On Memory

Memory, albeit sometimes defective, is often cruel to players who, however talented, follow the originators of rôles. It is the habit of critics, over which they honestly have no control, to remain more or less subconsciously in sentimental thrall to the first performance they have seen of a part, save only in Shakespeare, in which case many of them go completely off the enthusiastic handle at intervals of every five or six years, particularly when some relatively young actor or actress makes an appearance. But otherwise the newcomer, even though he or she be first-rate, has a hard time of it with them.

[28]

What Is a Play?

It is the expressed conviction of our critical *Opistharthri,* very emphatically delivered, that Laurence Housman's *Victoria Regina,* which consists of ten episodes in the life of the Queen extracted from the sum total of Housman's original thirty, is not a play. Just what it is, they do not make any too clear, but that it isn't a play they are certain. Without taking sides for the moment, maybe if it isn't a play that is just what the audiences who crowded the Broadhurst theatre liked about it. Perhaps the show business has been hurt by too many plays and what the public wants when it goes to the theatre is something that isn't a play, or at least something that the critics decide isn't a play. This is not the only time that plays-declared-by-the-critics-not-to-be-plays have drawn a deeply relieved and enchanted trade. From the day of Shakespeare's *Much Ado* to Schnitzler's *Anatol* and from the day of Kaiser's *Gas* to Shaw's *Getting Married* and Toller's *Hoppla, We're Alive!,* the critics have been telling the public that what it is seeing and enjoying are not plays, and the public has been eating it up nonetheless.

It may be quite true that *Victoria Regina* is not a play in the sense that *Satellite* or *Truly Valiant* is a play, but that, surely, is not much against *Victoria Regina.* It may also be quite true that *Victoria Regina,* while it has a beginning, a middle, an end and several other such elements so dear and vitally necessary to the critic-pundit heart

[29]

(even though that heart has apparently here overlooked the fact), is technically a mere series of episodes, but so, technically, are two of Shakespeare's historical-chronical plays, so is Schnitzler's *Reigen,* so is Drinkwater's *Lincoln.* Many so-claimed not-plays — without being in the least alecky or paradoxical about it — are a heap better on all counts than many professorially endorsed are-plays. It would take a pretty balmy person to contend that Shaw's *Misalliance,* for instance, which the critics insist isn't a play at all, isn't surely a whopping lot better than any six gross of *Moons Over Mulberry Street* which, even as the critics denounce it as claptrap, they yet freely allow is a play. But you simply can't please some of those boys. When something like *Victoria Regina* isn't, to their way of looking at it, a play, they complain and demand a play. Then when you give them something like O'Casey's *The Silver Tassie,* they complain that it isn't only a play, it's *two* plays. And when you give them something like Odets' *Paradise Lost,* they complain that the trouble with it is that it's four or five plays!

Critics As Actors

Last year, at a banquet of people interested actively in the theatre, John Mason Brown was listed as one of the after-dinner speakers. Following him came Miss Laurette Taylor. In the course of her remarks she slyly observed that, for one who undertook to criticize actors, Brown's acting performance incidental to his speech, what with its awkward physical comportment, fumbling with table props and monkey-business with the back of his chair, was not only inadequate but downright incompetent. To which Brown, with a low bow, politely replied that all he could say in extenuation was that he had learned his acting from watching the actors on the New York stage.

Mr. Brown, who was foresightedly named after John Mason, the well-known Frohman actor of twenty years ago, is not the only critic who has plainly learned his acting from studying the players on the local stage, as may be appreciated from a contemplation of the performances given by critics when, for the nonce, they turn actors. Take Mr. Brown's supporting company in the one-act play by Marc Connelly that was presented in a Broadway theatre as part of the program of an Authors' League benefit. The said support included, among others, John Anderson, who was named after John Barrymore, Gilbert Gabriel, who was named after John Gilbert, and the much lamented Percy Hammond, God rest his good soul, who was named after Percy Haswell, one time leading woman for William H. Crane. If it hadn't been for Brown's prompting, the play would have been a pantomime. Not only did Gabriel and Anderson emulate handsomely their professional mentors in forgetting lines, but Percy, who had a single small line to repeat at intervals throughout the action, got temperamental, like Richard Bennett, after he had spoken it once, decided, like Lou Tellegen, that his dignity as an histrionic artist had been imposed upon by giving him such a restricted part, took matters into his own hands, like Arnold Daly, and began to stick in the ode to the sun from *Chantecler* and the big speech from *Mrs. Dane's Defence,* like Louis Mann.

Mr. Brown, the star of the occasion, was very wroth. " They're just a bunch of hams," he growled. Apprised of the low reflection upon their art, his colleagues retorted that Brown was just a destructive critic who tore down without building up and that he was prejudiced against them because they hadn't sent him the usual telegrams of good wishes and congratulations before his opening.

Also in Mr. Brown's company on this occasion was Robert C. Benchley, who was named after Robert Mantell, Robert Edeson, Robert Loraine, Robert Hilliard, Robert Warwick and Lionel Atwill. Mr. Benchley is the best actor among the reviewers, as he reviews fewer plays and as his pure art is hence not so greatly influenced and corrupted by professional actors. The only time Mr. Brown had to prompt Mr. Benchley, accordingly, was at five o'clock on the afternoon directly preceding the performance, when he prompted him that the show was to take place not in Wilmington, Delaware, as Benchley loudly insisted, but in New York, and that, anyway, no actor worthy of the profession of Coquelin and Salvini should take more than thirteen Side-cars before a performance.

Mr. Benchley, who has acted in various revues, as well as in the movies, is the only critic who is a member of the

Actors' Equity Association and who looks like W. C. Fields.

Alexander Woollcott, who was named after George Alexander, Ross Alexander, Alexander Carr and Alexandra Carlisle, practically gave up play reviewing to become an actor, at which profession he has made a large success. Like Mr. Benchley, he does not confine his art to the legitimate stage, but has also made a name for himself in the films. His first starring appearance, in S. N. Behrman's *Brief Moment,* under the direction of Guthrie McClintic, tested the character of his former critical colleagues who, patently envious of his greater histrionic competence and good fortune, might have been expected to let him down with a bang. But so *sympathique,* so replete with delicate nuances and so emotionally *irrésistible* was his performance that even critical prejudice was helpless before it, and Mr. Woollcott scored a triumph. His more recent appearance in the Hecht-MacArthur talking picture, *The Scoundrel,* solidified his reputation. Just as in *Brief Moment* he stole the show, as the vulgar phrase goes, from all the other actors on the stage, including the surprised and abashed Miss Francine Larrimore, so in *The Scoundrel* it took all of Noël Coward's considerable diplomacy and cunning — Mr. Coward was the nominal star — to persuade Woollcott volitionally to under-act so there wouldn't be any danger of his repeating the trick.

[33]

George S. Kaufman, who was named after George Arliss, George Bickel, Grace George, George Holland (*père et fils*), George Cohan, George Fawcett, George Grossmith and George, the porter on Maude Adams' old special Pullman, is another former play reviewer with histrionic propensities. When a professional actor in one of his plays falls ill or demands two dollars a week more, Mr. Kaufman jumps into the rôle. Mindful of his own old critical penetration, however, it is his practice on such occasions to bar all critics. As a consequence, Mr. Kaufman's acting gifts must remain a matter for speculation. Professional actors who have played with him say that he is lousy, but any such derogation may be put down, perhaps, to the notorious jealousy of the genus actor. Whatever may be said against Mr. Kaufman as an histrionic artist, it still cannot be denied that he has more hair than Brian Aherne.

Robert Garland, who was named after Hoot Gibson, has thus far not deigned to appear on the New York stage, although his performances in his native Baltimore with the Paint and Powder Club have been favorably commented upon by critics who have gone out of town to cover the shows. Mr. Garland's forte is character acting, chiefly in folk drama. It is his proud boast that, in all his histrionic career, he has never interpreted a rôle that didn't call for whiskers. And he attributes his success as an actor to the fact that whiskers have all but disappeared from the modern drama and that consequently his art has not suf-

fered from any imitation of professional acting performances.

Walter Winchell, who reviews plays for the *Mirror* and
who was named after Walter Hampden, is so positive an
acting personality that professional actors imitate *him*. In
twenty-seven plays and forty-three moving pictures during
the last four years there have been actors who have pat-
terned themselves after Winchell in characters representing Winchell. It has got so that Mrs. Winchell doesn't
know any longer whether she is married to Winchell or
to Lee Tracy, Jack Oakie, Lew Ayres, Ted de Corsia, or
any one of three or four dozen other actors who in their
various rôles have realistically winchellized themselves.
It has also embarrassingly got so that when Winchell himself appears in a moving picture everybody thinks that it
is somebody else imitating him. As he has a great artist's
natural vanity, this makes him so angry that he insists
upon being paid two salaries: one for himself and one
for the actor he is mistaken for. (This accounts for Winchell's wealth.)

J. Brooks Atkinson, who was named after J. Harry
Benrimo and J. Edward Bromberg and who is a lineal
descendant of J. Baruch Atkinsohn, founder and chief
actor of the Habima Players troupe, was a mime of considerable repute in the years directly preceding his entrance
into the profession of dramatic criticism. Although he tries
to deny the fact, attributing the confusion to an actor
named Brooks J. Atkinson, a Negro, the records disclose

that he toured the Middle West in 1912 with the company reviving *Ben Hur* and the following season made a tour of the South with the road company of Paul Dickey's and Charles W. Goddard's *The Ghost Breaker*. (In the latter company, he appeared under the name of J. Joseph Schildkraut.) His work in both plays, particularly in the former, wherein he had the important rôle of a chariot driver, was highly commended by the provincial critics. The one and only qualification noted by them was his tendency always to carry a cane. The provincial critics, doubtless due to sheer provincialism, seemed to think that a cane was not *comme il faut* in the portrayal of a chariot driver.

The lure of the stage is a well-known thing and critics appear to be able to resist it no more than other bad actors. The late J. Ranken Towse was for a number of years a Shakespearean actor in his native England and through the whole of his long critical career in New York admired only Shakespearean actors — the worse they were, the more he admired them. Nor does the Towse histrionic impulse ever die. Scratch a critic and you'll find an actor. The chief and only difference between critics and actors, as I once impolitely made bold to venture, is that the latter do most of their acting on a platform.

Heywood Campbell Broun, who was named after Thomas Heywood, the seventeenth century actor, and Mrs. Pat Campbell, the sixteenth century actress, is another quondam theatrical critic who has adopted the sock and buskin. And not only during his critical incumbency but afterward. Mr. Broun's peculiar talents lie in the direction of the revue and musical comedy. As a *compère* or as a monologist he has been seen in various productions. His first appearance was on the old Century Roof, under the sponsorship of the Shuberts. I hope that no one will read an implication into the remark that all his succeeding appearances have been under his own sponsorship.

Mr. Broun is an actor-manager of sorts. He intermittently produces a revue or musical show in which, to the envy of the other critic-actors, he surrounds himself with beautiful girls. His own act in the various exhibits, which after long training he has perfected, is to come out on to the stage at five or six periods in the evening and loftily pretend, in lines which he has written for himself, that the beautiful girls don't mean a thing to him and that he hopes the *audience* is having a good time.

Mr. Broun's great appeal to the theatrical trade lies chiefly in his personal appearance. Surfeited with actors who look like tailors' dummies, the trade welcomes Broun, who hasn't had his pants pressed since 1910 and all two of whose 1912 shirts caustically decline to remain hidden from view beneath his 1908 vest.

The general critical mind in respect to acting was best betrayed by Percy Hammond when he was rehearsing for the Marc Connelly drama, *Custard's Last Pie,* the outstanding feature of the *Post-Depression Gaieties,* to which reference has already been made. During the rehearsals, Percy was excessively sour, muttering his displeasure and discomfiture in having been hornswoggled into playing in the show. On the day of the performance, he was given his costume, a magnificent affair of fancy braid, silk fringes and gleaming cloth. He put it on and gazed at himself in the mirror. " Say! " he beamed — and his infinite satisfaction with himself was almost Vesuvian — " Say!," he repeated. " Acting is swell! "

Critical Prepossessions

The last season continued to witness a persistent and stubborn critical adherence to various long-established, yet perfectly bogus, theatrical and dramatic doctrines. First and foremost was the condemnation of at least four plays on the ground that if one of the characters paused even momentarily to ask a single intelligent question the plays in point would immediately come to an abrupt and wholly satisfactory end. It is true that the plays thus denounced were poor plays, but it is equally true that the criticism of them in the direction named was both foolish and eminently unfair. Some admittedly very good plays would, if the same contretemps occurred in them, come similarly to a sudden termination. Two illustrative cases will perhaps suffice. If one of the characters in Miss Hellman's *The Children's Hour* were to ask the maliciously influenced brat to particularize exactly *what* and *all* she saw when she spied into the room occupied by the two women teachers, it is reasonable to suppose that, at that tender age hardly privy to the intimate details of Mytilene vaudeville, she would promptly convince everyone that she was a liar, and that the play, accordingly, would immediately stop dead in its tracks. If, secondly, to reach into a somewhat higher dramatic altitude, Othello were to ask his under-officer, Cassio, a single significantly direct question about the fateful handkerchief, to which Cassio obviously would honestly respond, Othello would grab a pillow without further delay, smother Iago in Desdemona's stead, and so end the play at least three-quarters of an hour earlier.

On three occasions we were again vouchsafed the stenciled critical decision that as many plays were complete miscarriages because they failed to persuade audiences of their truth. Since when, we may ask, has it been vitally necessary for a play to persuade an audience of its truth in order that it may be successful? What audience, save perhaps one composed of D'Annunzio's old sweeties, was ever persuaded of the truth of, say, *The Dead City,* or of the truth of Wedekind's (not Strindberg's) *The Dance of Death,* or of the truth of any number of such varied and highly prosperous lulus as *Turn to the Right, East Is West, Within the Law, The Shanghai Gesture, The Witching Hour, Children of the Moon* and *Abie's Irish Rose?* This very last season a revival of Ibsen's *Ghosts* played to paying and enraptured audiences not only in New York but in the other larger cities. Is there such an audience today which, if it stops to meditate for even so long as ten seconds, isn't impelled to chuckle derisively at the "truth" of a drama that contends hereditary syphilis would drive a

[39]

boy insane at a still relatively green age, that his half-sister could not conceivably have been affected by the disease, and that his mother, though the author clearly states she returned to bear the cross of her contaminated husband, miraculously came through with what is currently known as a negative Wassermann?

Another contumacious legend in materia critica, aired again this last season by local practitioners of the profession, has to do with the resentment of audiences at being fooled by a playwright and with the successlessness of plays that attempt such deception. Although the legend lives in the critical mind with full-bodied strength, it is basically spurious, for all its occasional support from plays so bad otherwise that their deceptive natures, considered apart, have utterly nothing to do with the audience resentment of them. Certainly George M. Cohan, to name a single example, found no audience that resented his fooling it in the case of either *Seven Keys to Baldpate* or *The Tavern,* both of which, and the former in particular, proved great popular successes.

With the production of the play called *Night of January 16,* there came duly into print once more the critical allegation that nothing is so destructive to a play and to its good fortune as an inconclusive ending. Despite the conviction of the critics, it should be noted that the play in question, evidently believing differently, enjoyed a long and very prosperous run. One speculates as to how these critics who are determined that plays with inconclusive endings are bad plays and cannot possibly engage the sympathy of audiences reconcile their obstinate certainty with such plays as Galsworthy's *Strife,* Gorki's *Night Refuge,* Hauptmann's *The Weavers,* and even Shaw's *Too True To Be Good.* It seems, furthermore, that the last Nobel prize for literature and drama went, if we remember rightly, to the dramatist who has written more plays with inconclusive endings than all the other living dramatists rolled together.

The revival of *Romeo and Juliet* brought with it again, as was to be expected, all the time-honored critical descriptive phrases: " the world's greatest love story," " the most lovely of the drama's heroines," " the greatest lover in literature," etc. Occupying ourselves primarily with the last phrase, we wonder if those critics, as well as laymen, who endlessly parrot the unparalleled stature of Romeo as a romantic lover have ever studied the character closely. It seems more likely that their picture of him has been derived largely, if not solely, from the superficial gloss and sheen contributed to the rôle by the various matinée idols who have played it. And it also seems likely, accordingly, that their evaluation of Shakespeare's hero as lover has been influenced less by Romeo himself than by his stage creators, with their six-foot altitudes, their sleek thighs, their velvety larynxes, their God's-gift-to-women profiles, and their hot sex appeal.

Even one of these very Romeos by proxy, Mr. Leslie Howard, lately discerned the truth which appears still to be beyond the ken of the critics. "Though the name has come down through the language and even into our slang to mean a lover, definitely *the* lover, I don't think Romeo a great lover," he is quoted. "He is just part of a tragedy, caught in the toils of it. Juliet all but makes the first advance, completely giving her feelings away before the man has a chance to speak. Surely, this isn't the way of a lover, great or small."

To the close analyst of Romeo, there are any number of points that stamp him as a second-rate lover, and not only as a second-rate lover but as a first-rate amorous pickle-herring. When we first hear about him from his friend, Benvolio, and from his father, we are told that he is so absurdly addle-pated, weak and sentimental that he walks in the woods before dawn crying wet tears that "augment the fresh morning's dew" and sighing deep sighs, and that later in the day he petulantly locks himself in his room, pulls down all the blinds, and sits around groaning to himself. And all, it develops, because his best girl, Rosaline, has had a tiff with him. What is more, it also develops that though he, Romeo, the theoretical incalescent lover, has done everything in his power to persuade her to give in to him, even to the bounderish extent of offering her "saint-seducing gold," she will have none of him. In fact, she declines even to listen to his "siege of loving terms" or to "bide the encounter of assailing eyes." Romeo, "a sick man in sadness," whiningly confesses himself licked.

Nevertheless, when Romeo hears that his girl is going

to sup at the Capulets', he makes a monkey of himself by accepting an invitation to the party and thus giving the hussy a second chance to give him the cold shoulder. No sooner does he arrive at the party, however, than he — who swore he could never so much as look at another woman — claps an eye on Juliet and again promptly goes cuckoo, like a Hollywood movie actor meeting still another platinum screen star. But even as a kisser he is evidently no great shakes, since Juliet reproves him with the criticism, " You kiss by the book."

Comes the celebrated balcony scene. Romeo, the great, brave, dashing lover, laments that, in his simple act of standing beneath the balcony and hoping to speak to Juliet, he is " too bold." It is Juliet who has to make all the first passes. In point of fact, Romeo is so bashful and hesitant that Juliet has to apologize for her eagerness to loosen him up — " If thou think'st I am too quickly won, I'll frown and be perverse and say thee nay." She even has to bait her doltish gallant with the promise that " I'll prove more true than those that have more cunning to be strange." And she is driven by his awkwardness to give him her love's faithful vow " before thou didst request it." But she takes no unnecessary chances. If the cluck Romeo is going to get her, the price plainly must be matrimony. " If that thy bent of love be honorable, thy purpose marriage," she warns the faltering dud, " send me word tomorrow."

In the same balcony scene, Romeo boorishly tells Juliet

how beautiful his own voice is and then employs it in a mere chill and passionless " My dear," followed by a commonplace remark on the hour of their next morning's date. It is Juliet again who has to do the love work. When Romeo satisfies his inner man by telling Juliet that he would he " were her bird," Juliet must turn on the necessary and missing heat by breathing, " I should kill thee with much cherishing."

Coming to Friar Laurence's cell, we find Romeo cadishly derogating his ex-girl, Rosaline, in favor of his new one, whereupon the Friar critically rebukes him that his much-heralded love equipment must be pretty shallow as it seems to lie chiefly in his eyes. In his scene with Tybalt, wherein the latter challenges him to combat, our great lover is so cowardly and full of equivoke that Mercutio, disgusted, is impelled to denounce his attitude as " dishonorable, vile submission." Subsequently, when Mercutio shows up Romeo for the poltroon he is by taking up the fight with Tybalt in his stead and is mortally wounded, Romeo seeks to wave the whole business aside by superciliously telling Mercutio, who is dying, that " the hurt cannot be much," and even when Mercutio is led off to die Romeo thinks first of himself and of his " reputation stain'd." He admits openly that Juliet has made him " effeminate." His subsequent duel with Tybalt — " Here comes the furious Tybalt back again," Benvolio warningly shouts — he could not possibly avoid; it was Tybalt's life or his own. Even so, it was necessary for him to goad himself on by steaming himself up with emotionally flagellating phrases.

That Romeo was a feeble jester and pathetically weak at repartee we need listen only to Mercutio's ribbing of him in Act II, Scene 4 — "Come between us, good Benvolio; my wits faint" — fully to appreciate. That he uttered no single unembroidered thought and had no single unembroidered idea much above the intellectual quotient of the average actor who plays him is clear to anyone who studies the text. That he was a talker, a fellow of words, rather than an active, virile lover we need no more than the scene in Capulet's orchard in Act III, with his urging of Juliet to prolonged chatter, to convince us. And that he was satisfied with one kiss on his painful farewell to Juliet is equally embarrassing to the legend of him.

So it is from the beginning to the end. Can this be the sorry clown whom women and critics esteem as the symbol of the world's truly great romantic lover?

Radical Critical Technique

The outstanding idiosyncrasy of the younger radicals amongst us who look upon Stalin as the one savior of mankind is their apparent inability to argue their case with the calm and poise displayed by even a Chinese laundryman into whose rear trouser neighborhood urchins have inserted a lighted firecracker. Their idea of a triumphant joust, it seems, is to dismiss all replies based even remotely upon their opponents' logic, or occasional lack of it, and

loudly to belittle the latter and call them names. Let someone observe that there are conceivably some flaws in the realistic practice of Communistic doctrine and, instead of
quietly endeavoring to prove him in error, the boys seek to
confound him by alleging that his great-uncle was once ar-
rested for stealing a ham, that his grandfather on his mother's side shined J. Pierpont Morgan's shoes, and that he
himself had to pay his own way when he last visited
Russia.

I have read about nine-tenths of the stuff printed during
the last year by the fledgling Marxes and I think I report
only the bare truth when I say that the great bulk of it
consisted, not in cool, dispassionate and attemptedly per-
suasive statements of radical opinion, but in violent personal abuse of everyone who did not happen to believe in
all that they believed. The Sovietissimos, indeed, regard
as lèse-majesté not only any skepticism as to their espoused
governmental, economic and social convictions but, even
more greatly so, any skepticism as to themselves personally
as world-beating geniuses and supermen.

The writer, accordingly, who ventures that even one of
their pet ideas is perhaps not so entirely sound as they believe it is is forthwith delegated to the cloaca maxima of
humanity on the ground that he is an odoriferous skunk.
But the writer who ventures that they themselves are
maybe not all Lenins and Marxes is not only denounced
as the odoriferous skunk in question, but is accused, in addition, of being an odoriferous skunk suffering from a

variety of Freudian and Stekelian inflictions ranging all the way from algolagnia and autoerotism to a somewhat degenerate zoöphilia, and of being, further, the man who taught the former Kaiser the gustatory delights to be found in Belgian babies.

The business goes so far as an attempt to discredit individuals who haven't even opened their mouths the one way or another about the radical boys themselves or about their Soviet polemics. Let an author write a novel, and a good one, that doesn't somewhere in it at least once grow indignant because coal miners have to work in coal mines instead of at the St. Regis and the Leftist critics as one man proceed violently to denounce him as a foul stain upon the art of literature. Let a playwright write a play, and a good one, that, whatever its theme, neglects to list capitalism in the same category as smallpox and nodular leprosy and the same critics derisively proclaim him a rococo ass in no way fit to mingle with the intellectual aristocracy of Webster Hall.

It is by the exercise of such tactics that the boys hope completely to dismay and rout their disputants, and it is in that hope that they reveal themselves doubly as optimists plus. Their practice of attacking not an opponent's ideas but the opponent himself defeats them for two reasons. In the first place, the technique of successful personal attack is a very subtle and often even occult business; it takes years of literary experience, training and prayer to master the art; and the simple fact is that the young radical critics are not privy to its tricks. The moment you call a man names, however justified, a dozen men, even if they do not themselves particularly relish him, will come in one way or another to his defence, for that is the strange quirk of human nature. In order to do the dirty work up in auspicious style, you must so skilfully word your attack upon him that the names in question will be visited upon him by your reader. In other words, the attack must be so couched as to suggest the opprobrious terms to the reader without specifying them, much as, in the parlor game based on Dr. Hugo Münsterberg's psychological inquiries, a word is spoken and the others present are bidden immediately to answer it with something which the word suggests or connotes.

The adroit writer has a prevision of such connotations and, in his personal demolition of an opponent, is aware of the proper words and phrases to evoke them. If he wishes to denounce a man, say, as a cheap and contemptible liar, he appreciates that to do so in so many words may prejudice his reader in favor of his enemy and against himself, so he allows the reader to do the job for him simply by designating the man, with at least a surface show of amiable politesse, wholly bogus, as either a pushcart vendor of Canterbury tales or a Scapin with his shirt tail flapping in the noses of all Gérontes. Or, if he believes it more effective to be less allusively literary, he will describe the foul, filthy, loathsome liar, hypocrite and bum in some such metaphorical and relatively less spleenless manner as the only man on earth whom the Blarney stone itself ever kissed, which accounts for the dirt on it, or one whose congenital fear of hatchets is perhaps due to the circumstance that he was conceived under a cherry-tree.

It is the misfortune of the young Redicals that they have not learned that successful propaganda is not to be achieved with brass knuckles, but with a dexterous mixture of laughing gas and poisoned perfume. Propaganda is simply another phase of diplomacy and, like diplomacy, it hardly achieves its best results with obloquy and insult but rather with shrewdly calculated low bowings from the waist (the right fist concealed in the coat-tails) and with a suave drawing-room pretence of give-and-take.

The second reason for the radicalissimos' defeat is their failure to be completely upright and honest with themselves. In their secret hearts, as they only too clearly show, they are full of misgivings as how to explain certain of their public acts to their private selves. Apparently unable to, and bewildered and wroth as a consequence, they seek a protective coloration and a defence mechanism either in doubly violent attacks upon those who show them up for the anomalies they are or in various pathetic and easily penetrable excursions into a mock-expansive jocosity which is designed to reduce their critics to a more genial attitude. Thus, when Clifford Odets, to whom capitalism is ostensibly so much fetid gum-resin, was lately approached by a newspaper columnist in Hollywood, where he is pulling down several thousand pleasant dollars a week from the movies, and was ironically asked to explain what a man like himself could like about the capitalistic movies, he sought to soften his interviewer's attitude toward him with the Jack Benny wheeze, " The money." And thus when radical playwrights like Albert Bein, radical novelists like James T. Farrell, radical poets like Isidor Schneider, and radical critics like Granville Hicks greedily accept fellowship money from the capitalistic Guggenheim family upon which to live luxuriously and pursue their enterprises — when, indeed, certain of the radical boys accept the money year after year — when they do this self-insulting thing, their hatred of and contempt for those bourgeois writers who make their own pens earn their own livelihoods, without benefit of either capitalistic or anti-capitalistic charity, show an increased virulence and bitterness.

As artists, some of these radicals, it must be emphasized, are not without some merit. But as honorable radicals, sincere in their deepest anti-capitalist convictions, their merit is decidedly questionable.

CHAPTER IV

The Histrionic Art

∽ ∽

The Buncombe of Acting

More supreme bosh continues to be written about acting than about any other topic under the sun, except perhaps Communism, Napoleon brandy, American opera, the gustatory splendors of crêpes Suzette, the profound meditations of Senator La Follette, Hollywood art, Enzo Fiermonte, and the wonderful work being done to rehabilitate the defaulted guaranteed mortgage certificates.

Acting is one of the few subjects on which everyone, especially those who believe that *Three Men on a Horse* is a greater play than *Iphigenia in Tauris* — " well, anyway, better entertainment, if you know what I mean " — constitutes himself an authority. There are consequently more unconstrained critics of acting in the United States than in all the other countries of the globe rolled together, and those who get professionally paid for the job are often not much more excessively luminous than their lay confrères. Although Coquelin was doubtless the only actor who ever lived who proved that he had a critical mind in the appraisal of acting, one nevertheless must sympathize with even the rank and file of actors themselves who are often dumfounded to read tributes to their histrionic genius after performances which they privately, and quite honestly and correctly, have considered eminently lousy — or at least not up to their standard.

That there is such a thing as fine acting, we of course know. But just what it consists in and what it is we certainly have a lot of difficulty in finding out from what we read and hear. We are assured, for example, both by linotype and by word of countless mouths that Greta Garbo is a great actress. Now, it is quite possible that Miss Garbo is a great actress, but unfortunately for those of us who like a little verification of things, she has never given us any faintest proof of her alleged stunning virtuosity. All that she has thus far in all her movie career done is to play isolated thirty second or, occasionally, minute-long bit-scenes in a cinematically satisfactory manner, but that she can steadily and continuously sustain a rôle, as a real actress must, we none of us have been privileged the slightest hint. Surely the ability effectively to play little snatches of drama doesn't constitute an actress. If it did, the late Amelia Bingham, who for years tore down the roofs of vaudeville houses shooting the works in an act called *Great Moments From Great Plays,* would have been one of the most magnificent actresses in America, whereas, in sad fact, she happened to be one of the worst of her time.

In the theatre, consider the case of Elisabeth Bergner.

Although she has played many plays in her native Germany, she has been seen in America in but a single one, a slice of tripe entitled *Escape Me Never*. On the score of her performance in that single play and that single rôle, she was promptly hailed by most of the professional critics and by the larger share of the playgoing public that saw her as the greatest genius among living actresses, domestic or imported.

Without going into an appraisal of her European repertoire, let us scrutinize the details of this single local performance and try to discover the reason for the Bergnerian hallelujahs. Her rôle in the play was that of a lovable little gamine who was endeavoring to win back the love of her seducer and simultaneously to retrieve a father for her illegitimate baby. The gamine phases of the character Miss Bergner indicated with a grease-paint coyness and cuteness of such ferocity that Shirley Temple herself seemed in comparison like an eighty-year-old Mrs. Whiffen. Without let-up, she tossed her bobbed hair about like a mop agitated by a simoon; she archly pulled up her stockings at intervals of every few moments; she scratched her legs as if a victim of a particularly acute case of eczema; she scratched her head as if a victim of something that isn't customarily mentioned in refined society; she bounced about the stage like a ballerina full of vodka; and she periodically dejected herself abruptly upon her rear with the gusto of a circus clown.

On the strength of such ignominiously stale and mouldy

monkeyshines, which, if practised by an American actress would have been booed out of countenance, Miss Bergner was enthusiastically touted both by the critical professors and the paying customers as the last word in acting talent.

We are so regularly entertained by such absurdity hailed as acting genius that we no longer recognize real acting when we see it. Any actress who can play a duchess very badly one week and a scrubwoman equally badly the next is acclaimed for her remarkable versatility. Any actor who can read a rôle in a play by a thinking dramatist with sufficient clarity to make himself understood is allowed to be a very intelligent actor. Any actor who has a decent speaking voice, who lifts it so he can be heard in the back rows, and who can stand firmly on his feet without wobbling, is praised as an actor of authority. And any incompetent actress who can get somebody to back her in a series of Shakespearean and Ibsen plays, all of them staged and performed with a woeful amateurishness, is sure to be given a banquet by some imbecile stage society and to be presented with a gold medal or silver cup attesting to her great pride in the noble arts of acting and drama.

The phenomenon takes strange and mysterious forms. Sometimes an actress is regarded by both the critics and the public as a poor actress but the legend that she is, in some inscrutable way, none the less a good one persists. Nance O'Neil is a case in point, and Bertha Kalich is another. The critics have roasted them and the public has stayed away from their performances, but still the idea of their theoretical fine talent hasn't downed. Figure that one out and you get a free round trip to Bermuda.

The buncombe about acting spreads, naturally enough, to actors themselves. The late Henry Miller, a good actor, as a young man was in the same Boston repertory company with the late John Mason, a decidedly indifferent one. Miller, in the second play in which they appeared together, one night vaingloriously tried to steal a scene from Mason. The latter said nothing, bided his time, and the next night, when the scene came around, suddenly let go with his booming voice and completely killed the effect of Miller's speeches. Simply on the ground of Mason's idiotic bull roar, Miller for the rest of his life steadfastly considered Mason a sterling artist!

There was a day when any ham could get the reputation for being an histrionic nonesuch by appearing in a so-called protean rôle, one wherein he played, say, two brothers — one a paragon of all the virtues and the other an ignoble bum — and the difference between which he indicated by playing the paragon standing up erect, with his coat collar turned down, and the bum by slouching, with his coat collar turned up. That day is with us no longer — although we can't be too sure. But the day is undeniably still with us when hams not much better earn handsome reputations by speaking old-time rousing go-to-hell melodrama lines in quiet, well-mannered tones, the meanwhile nonchalantly lighting cigarettes and flicking imaginary dandruff off their coat lapels, or by the simple device of playing Hamlet in a way that he never before has been played, or by the even simpler device of ingratiating themselves with jay critics and audiences by sacrificing their relative youth and good looks to rôles which call for makeups presenting them as venerable and obscene dodos of one sort or another.

Bergner

The outstanding defect in the previously mentioned and much discussed Elisabeth Bergner's art is that she is unquestionably one of the most highly perfected technical actresses on the stage of the western world and is unable to conceal the laudable fact from her audiences. This is not to say, contradictory though it may seem, that she is not popular with audiences — she was, before Hitler sniffed the poisoned blood of Rachel and Bernhardt in her veins — the favorite of German theatregoers as she became subsequently the overwhelming favorite of British. It is simply to say that the aforesaid popularity, along with the critical estimation of her, is of a piece with the popularity and, in collateral critical circles, the estimation that are the portion of the mechanically perfected, or what is more generally called the "well-made," play. She is a Pinero of histrionics, a sure and finished craftsman and a very fine technician with an inner insubstantiality and with an acting heart that is chill as a cucumber. She is like a soundly constructed, fully appointed, beautifully frescoed, perfectly run, soulless hotel. She is, in short, an actress for one's aloof respect and esteem if not for one's warm admiration and affection. And that, in this critic's definition, is not what goes to constitute a complete and really great actress.

True art, in the old phrase, lies in a concealment of art, and Bergner not only parades hers but literally hits her audiences in the face with it. Never for a moment, even when she is at her technical best, is she able to achieve the valuable and all-vital air and sense of spontaneity. She does not, on the whole, overact, but she so lingers over and fondles the smallest details of a rôle that one gets that impression. Like a college professor given to the literary art, she so assiduously, scrupulously and indefatigably polishes her compositional performance that it comes out in the end as perfectly manicured, as superficially flawless, and as augustly chaste as a suburban real estate development garden, and as artificial, unnatural and lifeless.

Observing Bergner's performance in drama (as well as in the cinema), one thinks of Maugham and his reasons for the greater entrancement we find in El Greco than in Titian, in the incomplete achievement of Shakespeare than in the consummate success of Racine. Perfection of technique in the emotional arts may be carried to a point where effect and feeling are largely blotted out by the heavily overlaid skill. In this way, Bergner constantly suggests to us, in one and the same body and person, a thoroughly competent and often even brilliant director painstakingly guiding his pet pupil through every turn and facet of her rôle. Worse, though it is possible for Bergner on occasion to immerse her personality in a rôle, at least to a degree, it seems to be impossible for her to divorce her own mind from the mind of the character she is playing. One feels always that what she is saying is what the character would say, but that what the latter is thinking is what Bergner herself is thinking. She should recall the dictum of Réjane, also an intelligent woman, who confided that she used to the utmost every last ounce of intelligence she possessed during rehearsals but, on the rise of the very first curtain, promptly and entirely dismissed it.

Mr. Charles Cochran, one of the foremost of British producers and the man who introduced Bergner to English audiences, has noted in a statement to the American press that for the life of him he cannot understand any such insistence upon Bergner as a purely technical actress, as Reinhardt, who directed her in pre-Swastinka Germany, found her difficult to handle because — so Mr. Cochran says — she would periodically allow a sudden inspiration to change the previous flow and character of her performance. The first truth is that Reinhardt found it difficult to direct her because, as those close to him know, he happens to be ridden by a peculiar personal idiosyncrasy that makes it almost impossible for him sympathetically to direct any woman who has red hair, which was the color of Bergner's at that time. And the second and more proper critical truth is that, while it is doubtless a fact that Bergner had such periodic seizures of inspiration during rehearsals, she subsequently so made them slaves to a technical exactitude, so disciplined them out of their easy and spontaneous birth that, when the curtain went up on her public performance, they issued from her histrionic machine as strictly calculated and as coldly precise as so many symmetrical ice cubes.

Bergner is, to repeat, an actress who knows infinitely more about her craft than the great majority of living actresses, but she lacks what some of her vastly less competent sisters possess. What she lacks is the precious and convincing quality of naturalness, or, better still, the even more precious and convincing gift of successfully counterfeiting it.

Is Movie Acting Acting?

It seems to me that the people who believe in great moving picture acting are the same people who believe that if one goes without eating the first day at sea one will not become seasick, that the entire population of the state of Montana is bow-legged from excessive horseback riding, that poor folk who do hard manual labor and eat plain food, if any, live much longer than the idle rich, that a child can learn a foreign language in two weeks, whereas an adult is lucky if he can learn one after many years' study, and that men who live on the open plains and prairies have eyes set wider apart than those who live in the crowded cities. It also seems to me that those who believe that successful movie actors and actresses are at the same time great actors and actresses are the same who believe that a bottle of fifty-year-old champagne would constitute a delicious drink, that if one were to try to break an egg-shell on the bridge of one's nose one would break the bone of the nose instead, that steel ships float because they contain some wood, that the Spanish and Italian languages have such simple spelling systems that not even the most ignorant Spanish or Italian peasant ever makes a mistake, and that it requires the combined efforts of a mattress maker, a pillow manufacturer, a couple of upholsterers and four watermelon growers to give Mae West that bathycolpian and steatopygous look.

That there are a number of very effective movie actors and actresses — some of them splendiferous of face and figure, to boot — no one can deny. But that even the best of them are actors and actresses in the true dramatic sense of the word only an excessively exuberant film fan can believe. Miss Helen Hayes, a stage actress who knows what real acting consists in, lately hit off the difference nicely in these words: " At the end of 1931 the movies beckoned me. The play *Lullaby* was selected as my first vehicle. I thought that the picture was terrible, and that my acting was worse. I was all prepared to take the next train to New York. But Irving Thalberg, to my surprise, saw merit in the picture. He insisted that I stay and make a few retakes. Then I left post-haste for New York to do a play. Before the play opened there appeared in New York the picture called *The Sin of Madelon Claudet*. I dimly recognized it as *Lullaby*. The critics raved, fans gushed —

and I pondered. What had brought about the change? Then I realized that a few retakes . . . the expertness of people who cut and paste film together . . . had changed *Lullaby,* a draggy, weepy picture into *The Sin of Madelon Claudet.* I was called ' a big film star — potentially the biggest.' I couldn't understand what was meant by ' potentially.' I felt that my efforts had little to do with the success of the picture."

Miss Hayes added that several years later she had an idea that she would like to do a film version of Barrie's *What Every Woman Knows,* that she thought it would really give her an opportunity to do some real acting, if that were at all possible on the screen. " It was after that," she concluded, " that I realized I wanted to remain on the stage. All of it (my Hollywood work) seemed so disjointed and pointless, although later on the screen and after leaving the cutting-room it was far from that."

Motion picture acting, as Miss Hayes was brought sadly to appreciate, bears the same relation to dramatic acting that a hamburg steak bears to a cow. It derives from dramatic acting (at least now that the talkies have finally triumphed completely over the silent films) quite as a hamburger derives from Old Bess, but it is made up of so many chopped up bits that its mother hardly recognizes it.

The best actor on a movie lot, as everyone should know and as Mr. Sidney Howard apparently took four years in Hollywood to discover, is the man in the cutting-room. It is he who points and safeguards a movie actor's climaxes, edits his physical comportment, assists his tempo, and otherwise heightens his best points and conceals his weakest. If you have ever seen the so-called " rushes " of a picture and then at length the finished product, you will realize that the ten best motion picture actors and actresses of any year are the ten best cutters. Someday the movie magazines are going to give them the credit that is due them, and print their photographs on the covers in eighteen colors.

This all is not to say, as I have already carefully specified, that there are not some extremely effective movie performances. There are. But there is all the difference in the world between such performances and authentic dramatic acting. The competent dramatic actor must go out on a stage and, after due preparation and direction, stand or fall on what he shows to an audience. The competent movie actor, on the other hand, may do all of his failing and falling in the studio before an audience gets so much as a peep at him, and he may subsequently stand proudly before his public with all his defects and deficiencies edited out of him by shrewd and clever studio lieutenants and with only his virtues accordingly remaining.

The dramatic actor or actress, further, must lay hold of a rôle when the first act curtain goes up and must sustain it until the third act curtain comes down. The screen actor or actress needs only to sustain a rôle for a relatively few moments at a time: his or her performance consists in playing isolated snatches of a rôle out of which the pic-

ture, when finally assembled, creates the mechanical illu-
sion of a sustained histrionic performance. The dramatic
actor, in other words, is like a juggler who must keep half
a dozen balls in the air for two straight hours, whereas the
film actor is like a juggler who keeps one ball in the air
for a few minutes but whose audience is made so dizzy
with rapid trick photography that it sees six balls where
there is only the single one.

The truth of these animadversions, as Miss Hayes has
hinted, is borne in upon us when a stage actor or actress
enters the movies. And it is often borne in upon us doubly
when a movie actor or actress enters the theatre. In the
former case, the stage actor finds that much of his valuable
dramatic acting technique is utterly useless, indeed, slightly
objectionable, to the screen — and he is frequently a fish
out of water. In the second case, the movie actor often
finds that the stage is as uncomfortable to his peculiar
Hollywood art as the so-called hot seat, and he squirms
helplessly and grotesquely under its prickly histrionic demands.

The moving pictures are valuable to an aspiring actress
in only two ways. First, they can teach her how to walk,
move and comport herself gracefully and, secondly, they
can teach her how to make herself physically and facially
more comely than she previously was. But otherwise I
doubt that they can do much for any talent she may possess, except ruin it. That is, unless she regards the screen
simply as a makeshift on the upward road to a dramatic

acting career and uses it cautiously as a minor and transient means of experiment. Then, it may safely serve its modest purpose. Then, it may help her to learn how to do her hair, dress her body, move her legs, master some of the intricacies of makeup — and learn generally some of the things *not* to do when she deserts the studio for the theatre. But beyond that it can make only a one-finger piano virtuoso out of two hands that might someday, with other training, play beautiful and thrilling melodies on the keyboard of the drama.

What I have here set down is intended as no reflection upon screen players as such. In their own way, peculiar as it may be to the discriminating artistic eye, they serve their purpose fully and satisfactorily. But real and true and authentic acting is quite another matter. " Nevertheless," one of them loftily asserted not long ago, " what we do on the screen will, unlike acting on the stage, be perpetuated irrevocably through the centuries." To which Miss Katharine Cornell very quietly and effectively made rejoinder: " Well, how many five-year-old pictures have *you* seen lately? "

Our Best Young American Actress

Who is she? Is she Helen Hayes, who has many champions for the honor? Is she Lynn Fontanne, who also is not lacking in admirers of her art? Is she Ina Claire, heralded by many as our foremost comédienne? Or is she Katharine Cornell, proclaimed by a considerable number

of the critics to be the First Lady of the American theatre?
In view of the seeming confusion, a careful investigation
and appraisal of the four ladies may be of some help in arriving at a decision.

Let us consider them in the order named. First, Miss
Hayes.

The earlier activities in the theatre on the part of this
actress were devoted to light and for the most part insignificant ingénue comedy rôles, in all of which she gave a
sufficiently satisfactory account of herself. Her best performance in these years, and by long odds, was that as
the scrambling, bawling, young get-in-the-way in Booth
Tarkington's amusing *Clarence,* in turn the best of the
comedies in which she appeared. Though the play was
wild, moonstruck foolery, she invested her rôle, while
keeping it strictly in key with the shambles tone of the
exhibit, with a shrewdly calculated eye to recognizable
reality. In the following years she proved herself a delightful Cleopatra in Shaw's *Caesar and Cleopatra,* incidentally
a very much better performance on all counts, save perhaps pictorially, than that given by Gertrude Elliott in the
original American production of the play — a performance that caught the Shavian quasi-child quality to a
nicety; an equally delightful Maggie Wylie in Barrie's
What Every Woman Knows, a surer performance in almost every way than that given by Maude Adams — there
was in it an achievement of womanly warmth that Miss
Adams failed to negotiate; and a decidedly mediocre per-

[65]

formance purveyor in the self-miscast heroine's rôle in the dramatization of *Mr. Gilhooley* — it amounted to little more than stock company histrionics embroidered with the faintest hint of an Irish accent.

There was also a rather poor performance in the poor comedy called *Petticoat Influence* — the kind of acting that almost any less experienced comedy actress could have dished out without straining a muscle; a first-rate performance in *Coquette,* expertly worked out to the last detail and here and there actually converting intrinsically dubious material into something relatively real and moving; and a workmanlike, if not particularly inspired, performance in Molnár's uninspired *The Good Fairy.* In the last named instance, Miss Hayes, as a reverse-English Viennese Pollyanna, simply took a leaf out of her early comedy acting and accented its obvious phases by way of putting over the play — which needed considerable putting over — at the box-office. Then came *Mary of Scotland* and, last season, *Victoria Regina,* both still fresh in the memory of theatregoers. In the former, her limitations in a physical direction — she is too small a woman to fill out the tall robes of Mary — and in the reading of what approximated heroic blank verse operated against her, although here and there she contrived, out of her sharp knowledge of acting trickery, to make her audience partly oblivious of her shortcomings. In *Victoria Regina* she gave what was unquestionably her best and most considered performance to date, one all the more noteworthy because of the almost motion-picture choppiness of a script that had been cut down from its original thirty episodes to a mere ten, with the resulting blank spaces between and the comparative lack of fluid dramatic continuity and mounting force.

Secondly, Miss Fontanne. Introduced into the American theatre by Laurette Taylor, she made her appearance, after a start in minor and unimportant rôles and a lively performance in *Dulcy,* in a succession of plays produced by the Theatre Guild. In Shaw's *Arms and the Man* she failed to distinguish herself, and neither in his *Pygmalion* nor in Werfel's *Goat Song* did she do much to stimulate the critical pulse. There was an affectation, a forced quality, to her performances that tried sorely an audience's sympathetic reaction, and her habit of listening lovingly to the sound of her own voice contributed further to critical discomfort. This was equally evident in *The Brothers Karamazov.* In all of these exhibits she revealed herself as hardly above the general actress run; she was fairly adequate, as the college boy critics put it, nothing more nor less. Then, turning to light comedy, there was a sudden change for the better. In Molnár's *The Guardsman,* she took over the part played in the original American production by Rita Jolivet and played in so wrong a key that the play went quickly to the storehouse, and delivered herself of so slyly humorous a performance in the rôle of the wife who theoretically cannot penetrate her husband's childish disguises that she helped to lift the piece into a

[67]

profitable run. In S. N. Behrman's two comedies, *The Second Man* and *Meteor,* she provided similarly a satisfactory light account of her talents, although neither rôle imposed the demands upon her that the Molnár rôle did. In *Caprice,* in the rôle of a coquettish cleverosa, she turned in a first-rate and entirely captivating comedy performance — what she did with vocal trickery was immensely cajoling; and her rough-and-tumble farce-comedy cabotinage in *Reunion In Vienna* was, in its way, equally effective. Her scenes of physical roughhouse with Lunt were, as the musical show lyric has it, tops.

In *Design For Living,* the Noël Coward comedy, a portion of her performance in the rôle of the woman divided by two men was excellent and a smaller portion patently strained, particularly in those scenes wherein she was called upon to be jovially airy about promiscuity. A kind of moral qualm seemed to be hidden in her larynx and her lines sounded as if, for the moment, she were histrionically holding hands with Will Hays. Her Jennifer in Shaw's *The Doctor's Dilemma* was one of the best things that she has done — it had a depth and womanly understanding that caught beautifully the innards of the character; though her talents were only in a very, very faint degree up to the demands of O'Neill's Nina Leeds in the long and difficult *Strange Interlude.* The scene between Nina and the three men she read convincingly enough, but the rest of her performance was, in the main, save for a few moments at the end, largely a mere recitation. In *Strange Interlude,* she

[68]

was, to tell the simple truth, pretty bad. As Elizabeth in Maxwell Anderson's *Elizabeth, the Queen,* some feeling crept periodically into what was another recitation, but on the whole her performance was projected with too studied an air to galvanize the rôle. In Coward's rubbishy sex melodrama, *Point Valaine,* she was perhaps as good as any actress could be with such base and idiotic material; a sister-act composed of Duse and Bernhardt couldn't have saved the rôle from refractory burlesque; poor Miss Fontanne was to be pitied for having to play such stuff, which at bottom was old Theda Bara vampire nonsense. And in last season's revival of *The Taming of the Shrew* she was, except for a careless and rather slipshod reading of the long speech at the play's conclusion, commensurate. In many of these exhibits she has played opposite her husband, the highly gifted Alfred Lunt, and has benefited, even when she has not met up with a rôle, from the juxtaposition.

Thirdly, Miss Claire, who has devoted her career almost exclusively to light comedy rôles. When she has briefly essayed a rôle of somewhat tougher fibre — as in the case of *Children of Darkness* — she has sensed her own discomfiture in it and has volitionally withdrawn. Like Marie Tempest, the best comédienne on the English-speaking stage, Miss Claire began in musical plays, in which she acquitted herself very happily. She was drawn to the dramatic stage by the late David Belasco, her first appearance being in a fluffy little comedy, hardly more than a potential book for a musical comedy, called *Polly With a Past*. She was successful in this initial enterprise — as success goes in such negligible exhibits — and then moved on to another similarly empty comedy affair called *The Gold Diggers,* also under the Belasco direction. Her rôles in both these doses of claptrap were little more than those of 10–20–30 soubrettes dressed by Lucile and offered to the public at three dollars top. Thereafter she appeared successively in the comedies *Bluebeard's Eighth Wife, The Awful Truth, Grounds For Divorce, The Last of Mrs. Cheyney,* and a revival of Maugham's bitter slice of irony, *Our Betters.* In all of them — the last named alone being of any pretensions to quality — she was in the main up to the demands of the rôles. Save in the Maugham play, which called upon her for a bit of acting beyond what was customary for her and which here and there she had some slight difficulty in adapting herself to, her comedy performances were delivered with that sure sharpness of reading, that sure sense of pace, and that physical gaiety that, as a comédienne, she enjoys to a most fortunate and gratifying degree.

Then, after several years spent in the picture studios, she gave a performance in Behrman's *Biography* that, with a maturity gained paradoxically and almost mythically in Hollywood, of all places, captured a variety and finish that had not completely been in her work before — it even suggested the mark of a competent dramatic actress and of one close to the acting secrets of depth of emotion; and,

[70]

following that excellent performance, a performance in the adaptation from the French called *Ode To Liberty* that was Hollywood plus. In the rôle of a sex-saucy woman — a rôle, incidentally, that had been so monkeyed with by various hands, including her own, that the original author would never have recognized it as his — she overplayed to such an extent not only in a deportmental but in a sartorial direction that Mabel Barrison, of the old Al Woods farce school, would have blushed for her. Her most recent appearance has been in Behrman's *End of Summer*, in which her playing of the rôle of the flighty, middle-aged Leonie Frothingham, while occasionally highly dexterous, suffered often from that common comédienne ailment, a straining for what the critics call " brilliant verve."

And now, fourthly, to Miss Cornell. A scrutiny of her major performances on the local stage results in the following estimates. In *A Bill of Divorcement*, in one of her earliest performances, she presented herself, in the not very difficult rôle of a young girl who finds herself the center of a disordered household, as an attractive and competent ingénue, little more. Various novices since, Margaret Sullavan, Sylvia Sidney and Barbara Robbins, for instance, have done every bit as well — some of them, indeed, better — in rôles somewhat more trying. In the other two Clemence Dane plays, *Will Shakespeare* and *The Way Things Happen*, she gave what were mainly routine and orthodox performances. In the former, a physical awkwardness, due to the unaccustomed ·costumerie of her rôle, added to her embarrassment; and, in the latter, a tendency to work an arbitrary tragic tone into her voice, whatever the immediate nature of the situation, contributed to critical nose-scratching. In *The Enchanted Cottage,* the Barrie play written by Pinero, she had one of those sweet-sweet rôles that offer less challenge to acting than to look and personality and managed to do pretty well by it. In *Casanova,* in the second-grade part of a lady of station who is not averse to a loose wink now and then, she wisely centered her efforts largely on the pictorial side and succeeded, with the aid of handsome costumes and efficient stage lighting, in projecting a very fetching picture. In *The Outsider,* a *Barretts of Wimpole Street* plot in which the invalid heroine is cured by faith and a handsome medico instead of by love and a handsome poet, she first caught the attention of the more acute critics with a performance that combined tenderness with strength and resolution with beauty, though the rôle, imbedded in hokum, was anything but onerous, as other occupants of it have sufficiently attested.

In the melodramatic and somewhat unintentionally humorous *Tiger Cats,* a dose of Scandinavian Minsky, she found herself in the position of a Metro-Goldwyn lion growling majestically in behalf of a pie farce; though she acted sincerely, even desperately, the dialogue constantly sneaked up behind her and tied tin cans to her art. And the same thing was true, though to a considerably less embarrassing extent, in *The Letter,* in which the usually most estimable Maugham for the nonce went Harry Clay Blaney, with overtones of Bartley Campbell. Finding the script in the way of any honest acting, Miss Cornell resorted to such a display of histrionic fireworks that even Nance O'Neil might have looked around in alarm for the nearest exit. As the heroine of Shaw's *Candida,* however, she turned in a really excellent performance — delicate in its strength and lovely in its manner — and I hope I will not seem to detract from that performance when I note the obvious fact that most performances of Candida have a way of being surprisingly good. It would be foolish, of course, to say that the rôle is actor-proof — it surely is not — but nevertheless it seems to be decidedly pro-actor.

In *The Green Hat,* in the Laura Jean Libbey rôle of Iris March, the Ostermoor romancer, she was first-rate. Considering the awkwardness of the material, her performance in lifting a servant-girl heroine into some faint semblance of romantic dignity (grease-paint dignity, that is) was all the more critically interesting. In *The Age of Innocence,* she was entirely charming in a rôle artfully manufactured for nostalgic reaction and, in addition, her physical comportment began to take on a considerable ease and grace. And in *The Dishonored Lady* — what a trio of scripts! — she was, save for one greatly overplayed melodramatic and silly scene in which she acted the New York *Mirror* idea of a woman murdering her lover, about all that any critic who could manage to stay awake had a right, under the circumstances, to expect or demand. Her handling of the scene mentioned, however, what with its Louise Glaum snaky sneaks around the darkened room, its wide-eyed intense Boris Karloff glarings into space and its Wednesday matinée Dorothy Donnelly bosom heavings, was, to put it politely, ham.

Coming down to more recent years, we find Miss Cornell at her best as Elizabeth Barrett, in *The Barretts of Wimpole Street,* a truly admirable performance in every detail, and doubtless too familiar to most readers to call for amplified comment. Her Lucrèce, in the Obey play of that name, was a sorry botch and proved, if nothing else, that, like the majority of our younger American players, she is sadly deficient in the art of pantomime. In *Alien Corn,* a trashy script about gamy doings in a Western college town, she comported herself, as in *Tiger Cats* and *The Letter,* with so overly tragic an air and so monotonously dirge-like a speaking voice that the impression, considering the play, was of a lady embalmer having breakfast with Mr. Samuel Shipman. In *Flowers of the Forest,* in the rôle of a woman whose lover calls to her from beyond the grave, she gave a smooth but undistinguished performance of an undistinguished part. Uncertain direction in this instance was doubtless responsible for her somewhat undue repression which, as the evening ran its course, became naturally confused in the audience's mind with histrionic inertness. Her recent Juliet, widely acclaimed by the younger reviewers as the top Juliet of all time, or at least from 1608 to 1935, inclusive, seemed to one older critic happy enough on its pictorial side but otherwise largely technicalized and calculated out of emotion, and in the aggregate rather chill. We come to *Saint Joan,* her latest offering.

That our theatrical critics go to, as well as come away from, Miss Cornell's various exhibits heavily prejudiced in her favor and ready and eager to give her the benefit of every doubt has been pretty clear for some time now. What is more, it is understandable, for in recent years she has become the one actress in our theatre who, in everything that she does, shows a high pride in the theatre as an institution, who alone has rejected every attempt of the movies to meddle with her dignity, and who has abjured consistently and determinedly — now that she has enough money — the facile temptations of the popular box-office. To this extent I string along with my colleagues in at least their cordial approach to anything she undertakes. I want her to succeed, as we all want thoroughly honest, intelligent and exceptional aim to succeed, and I, too, I think, have a secret and uncritical heart which is on her side. But neither my large respect for her nor that uncritical warm heart has yet made me oblivious, as seemingly with my graciously less critical colleagues, of her shortcomings as an actress when those shortcomings are placed plainly on view.

Her revival of Shaw's *Saint Joan* is a case in point. It was splendidly and without stint set upon the stage. To its performance she brought the very best company of actors that she could find. To its direction she as usual called her husband, Guthrie McClintic, who lately has demonstrated himself the most skilful director we have. In its approach to the dramatic text it was well-reasoned and judicious. But in the performance of the leading rôle it was, while here and there amply satisfactory, scarcely all that might have been desired. That, judging from her performances of Juliet and of Joan, Miss Cornell seems to be quite unable to articulate, suggest and project the vital mood of inspiration and exaltation which she feels is, save one be so prejudiced in her favor that black is white, wholly obvious. In the early phases of the Shaw play she was excellent, albeit her indefatigable Ziegfeld ballerina smile was a trifle disconcerting to the picture of Joan, whether Shaw's or anyone's else. And in the deplorably unnecessary and absurd epilogue, as in the earlier portion of the antecedent fine trial scene, she was beyond cavil. But in the several great moments of the play when the hot passion of faith and resolve rapturously consumes her and when in turn it should rapturously consume an audience's emotions she was, with her voice battling vainly to soar out of her throat to the heavens without aid from her diaphragm and with her constricted little parlor gestures, little more than an Iris March in armor. Often during Miss Cornell's performance it was easy to believe in Miss Cornell. But equally often it was not at all easy to believe in her Joan. Her Joan, in short, while it had occasional praiseworthy contacts with histrionic criticism, at only widely isolated moments was in any way believable as the Maid of Orleans.

These, then, the critical statistics on the four ladies. What do we discover from them?

We discover that in any attempt to single out the most important of our younger actresses Miss Hayes must figure in the consideration with Miss Cornell. To Miss Cornell, however, must go the balance in favor on the score of her much wider variety of rôles. That Miss Hayes is an actress soundly grounded in her craft is hardly open to question. As one of her directors, Mr. Miller, recently expressed it to me: " She knows all the acting tricks that Elisabeth Bergner knows, only the difference is that, where Bergner lets an audience detect them, Hayes is skilful enough to conceal them." I doubt that Miss Cornell has Miss Hayes' shrewdness in this respect, although she enjoys a natural equipment the superior of Miss Hayes'. Miss Cornell has a sweep and inner something (all right, if that is too irritatingly vague a word, I take the blame) that Miss Hayes seems at times to have to struggle for. Miss Hayes, on the other hand, has a vocal trickery, most cajoling, that Miss Cornell, in turn on the other hand, often has to struggle for. Miss Hayes has seldom given a distinctly inferior performance; Miss Cornell on occasion has. Miss Cornell has a natural stage presence that Miss Hayes must create by artifice. That Miss Hayes is able to create it is doubtless to her further acting credit.

Miss Claire is unquestionably a talented comédienne, but she has never challenged the heights of any such talent with anything more than what in the main have been run-of-the-pack and facile box-office exhibits. Miss Fontanne improves very greatly with the years; she has given some good comedy performances, if not so good, so sure, so brightly edged as those of Miss Claire; and she has indicated a variety of dramatic skill far in advance of Miss Claire. But neither of these ladies is in the class with Miss Cornell and Miss Hayes.

When the adjective " young " is employed in the instance of certain of these actresses it is employed, obviously, in a purely relative sense. While Miss Hayes, according to the statistics in the latest *World Almanac,* was born in 1902 and is therefore thirty-four years old and while Miss Cornell, according to the same authority, was born in 1898 and is therefore thirty-eight, we discover from the same source that Miss Claire was born in 1892 and is therefore forty-four and that Miss Fontanne, if we are to believe such things, first saw the light of day in 1882 and is hence fifty-four. As a gentleman, I doubt it; as a commentator, I simply quote from the impolite records. But, whatever the facts, it remains that the adjective " young," as noted, is used merely as poetic justice.

There are admittedly older actresses, Margaret Anglin is one and Grace George perhaps another, the quondam Ethel Barrymore and Laura Hope Crews are others, and Nazimova, Effie Shannon and eighty-odd year old Mrs.

[78]

Whiffen are still others, who could give our selected quartet cards and spades in many directions. And while we are about the business of qualifications, let us not overlook the fact that Judith Anderson, a dexterous actress and one of considerable versatility, is still this side of forty, that Mary Ellis, who has offered several excellent performances, is only thirty-seven, and that Jane Cowl, the best Juliet, to this critical mind, of the latter-day American theatre, and Pauline Lord, highly esteemed by various critics, are just forty-six.

However, taking our arbitrary and questionable premise as we find it, it remains a toss-up between Miss Cornell and Miss Hayes, with the favor, at the moment, just a shade Miss Cornell's.

Footnote on the Cornell Juliet

In an effort to make her Juliet obediently youthful to the text and properly in key with the teensful Shakespearean spirit, this Miss Cornell, that otherwise most charming and most valuable asset to our stage, leaned so far forward that the performance often took on the aspect of F. Scott Fitzgerald's début as Little Eva with the Princeton Triangle Club. Such was Miss Cornell's unremitting insistence upon the externals of virginal girlhood and the theoretical deportmental concomitants thereof that of Shakespeare's Juliet there remained little more than an impression of Louisa M. Alcott's Jo.

Why is it, one wonders, that of all the youthful rôles

[79]

in the higher drama Juliet is the single one which in more recent years has induced in our mature actresses the idea that only by converting themselves into a behavioristic diaperdom can they effectively play it? The great Juliets of the theatre have not made that mistake. They have realized the complete absurdity of any attempt to play the rôle in terms of a sapling when their Romeos, nine times out of ten, are and must be played by actors obviously and emphatically in their late thirties and forties. The dramatic contrast, they have appreciated, becomes increasingly ridiculous as the visualization of Juliet goes lower in the age scale. What is more, these wiser actresses have understood that, if — like the fourth wall — a dramatist's stipulation of a heroine's age is taken by audiences more or less for granted, or at least with a politely remitted judgment, in the case of the realistic drama, it certainly may be accepted doubly in the poetic drama. If forty-five-year-old actresses may easily pass muster as twenty-nine-year-old Hedda Gablers, if thirty-five-year-old actresses may convincingly play twenty-two-year-old Hilda Wangels, and if a forty-year-old actress could play the youngster Peg in *Peg o' My Heart* to the complete and wholesale intoxication of three years' paying audiences, there doesn't seem to be much critical sense in an actress of thirty-eight or so (herself sufficiently lovely and attractive) who imagines that the best way to play Juliet is to make her a sister to Emilie Dionne. What, one speculates, would Miss Cornell do with such a rôle as Hermia — "Thou hast by moonlight at her window sung," or such a one as Cordelia?

Another point. Assuming that what is indited above is deficient in sound critical sense, where still is the sound histrionic interpretive sense in imagining that a very young girl in love — or out of love, for that matter — comports herself, as did Miss Cornell, after the excited, jumpy, gurgly manner of a white Topsy? Is not such a conception in direct line with the old stock company idea and direction of ingénue rôles? Where but in tender youth does one find, even under poetic stress, a natural, artless and often very confounding and embarrassing poise, dignity and skeptical reserve?

The New Talents

A contemplation of the new, or relatively new, young talents, among both the girls and the boys, which appeared upon the New York stage last season disclosed the following appraisals, the girls considered first. Doris Nolan, in *Night of January 16,* although the recipient of some pretty blooms from the critical gentry, seems to have a modest equipment for obvious melodramatic rôles but, beyond that, not much. She may develop, but her performance was corrupted by that spurious physiognomic intensity favorite of Wampus Babies in their first rôles showing them anticipating something worse than death at the hands of some night club gangster or Fu Manchu, and also by a self-consciousness equalled only by that of a dramatic critic at *Stevedore* in a tail coat. Doris Dalton, seen at the end of the previous season in *Petticoat Fever* and this last season in *Life's Too Short* and one or two other exhibits, has an excellent stage presence, a considerable deportmental and physical grace (particularly when sitting, which is a rarity with our young women players), and a pleasant speaking voice. Her height may be a handicap, as many of the better younger male actors, to say nothing of some of the older ones, are considerably this side of six feet.

Julie Haydon, the very lovely young anti-febrifuge who appeared in *Bright Star,* plainly needs more experience. She is still nervous and ill at ease on the stage, all clearly demonstrated by her constant uncertainty as to what to do with her right foot when in a standing posture. She needs, more than anything else — and far more than personal study — a director who will dismiss her indisputable beauty as of second importance and who will talk to her like a Dutch uncle. One can feel a talent in her that may one day blossom, but it needs a directorial walloping to give it the right course. Tucker McGuire, which is hardly a name after the Hollywood glamour school, was revealed to us in *Substitute For Murder* and indicated an unusual naturalness in speech and comportment. There is, too, a fresh and artless manner about her that reminds one of the young English actress, Jessica Tandy, in her earlier performances. But she should diet. Mary Rogers, daughter of the late lamented Will, not only has much of the same naturalness and ease but an added sense of inborn theatrical spirit. Thus far, she has had the misfortune to appear only in cheap and trashy stuff. And nothing can so quickly ruin a promising young player as cheap and trashy stuff. She will have to watch out.

Elspeth Eric, in *Dead End,* has emotional intensity but doesn't yet know how to handle it. She begins a scene of violent emotion at such a pitch that when it is three-quarters over she is able to do nothing more with it. Barbara Robbins, seen most recently in *Abide With Me* and perhaps not legitimately to be included in this catalogue of newer players — she has been acting hereabouts for several years — has proved in previous performances that she has a talent above the general younger run, especially in rôles bordering on the tragic. Something of a studied chill, however, seems to have crept into her playing since then, which is to be deplored, as she is an actress who, if properly handled, should have a future. Marie Brown, who made her bow in *How Beautiful With Shoes,* is apparently a sensitive little thing but one who will need a wealth of training before she is ready for anything important in the way of dramatic rôles. Dorothy Hyson, the young English girl who appeared in *Most of the Game,* has a number of qualities that fit her for polite drawing-room comedy, among them poise, style and the suggestion of the feeling that, as a youngster, she must have had a good governess.

Margo, the young Mexican girl who has already achieved a reputation as a dancer, and also as a screen player under the guidance of those two Astoria sons-of-Lubitsch's, the MM. Hecht and MacArthur, indicated in her first dramatic rôle (*Winterset*) that she has in her the stuff of a potentially authentic actress. She has the inner temperament and slumbering flame that most of our young Broadway Nordics so completely lack; she has that vocal sullenness that is so strangely compelling in the theatre; and, through her training in the dance, she knows what to do with her body and her hands. With more experience, a still missing shading and variety in the reading of lines should come to her. Beatrice de Neergaard, of *Squaring The Circle,* has evidently fallen so greatly under the spell of Elisabeth Bergner's performance in *Escape Me Never* that, if she doesn't look out, the Gerry Society will get her, and Fraye Gilbert, in the same exhibit, while possibly available material for some painstaking director, was so arbitrarily disposed to adopt the air of a tragédienne, whether the immediate occasion called for it or not, that the effect was sometimes of Bertha Kalich playing footie with Jimmy Durante.

Polly Walters, late of *She Loves Me Not* and more recently in *The Body Beautiful,* has become the the rubber-stamp Hollywood baby ingénue. Hancey Castle, in *A Touch of Brimstone,* reads clearly, has an agreeable stage manner, and suggests the lady, but what she can do in the way of acting remains still in doubt, as the two feeble plays she has been in have offered her neither help nor resistance. Doris Dudley seen in *The Season Changes* and

[84]

End of Summer, hints of a future and has a full quota of personal elixirs.

As for the boys, Burgess Meredith, in *Winterset,* again indicated that his is by all odds the best talent among the younger male actors. Myron McCormick is another lad who shows promise, his work in three successive plays last season — *Substitute For Murder,* in which he had a comedy rôle, *Paths of Glory,* in which his rôle was straight dramatic, and *How Beautiful With Shoes,* in which he played the character of a demented dreamer — proving that he has an equipment unusually varied for a player so youthful. Elisha Cook, Jr., who gave a creditable account of himself in *Ah, Wilderness!,* went completely ham in *Crime Marches On.* Joseph Downing — I don't know his age, but he is new to me — gave an admirable performance, exact in the smallest detail, as the gunman in *Dead End.* Theodore Newton, in the same play, showed nothing the one acting way or the other in the rôle of the cripple. Jules Garfield, in *Weep For the Virgins,* indicated that he is worth some critical watching, and James Mac-Coll, by virtue of his performance in *Boy Meets Girl,* rates as an available candidate for future young romantic rôles. Shepperd Strudwick, who started out ably a few seasons ago, in *Let Freedom Ring* still showed a certain amount of talent but also an increasing artificiality. The youngster, Frankie Thomas, who appeared in *Remember The Day,* has much that is commendable for one so young but also a suggestion of precociousness that his father, the experienced Frank Thomas, Sr., who was in the same play, should promptly spank out of him.

And then, of course, there was that truly remarkable set of kids, all under fourteen, in *Dead End*. Their names are Gabriel Dell, Billy Halop, Huntz Hall, Bobby Jordan, Charlie Duncan and Bernard Punsly, and they make one wonder just a little about this whole business called the art of acting.

The New Pulchritude

One of the pleasantest phenomena of the last season was the increased pulchritude of the stage in a feminine direction. In the previous five or six years our stage had revealed some talented young women, but those who constituted available cigarette-picture material might have been counted on a few fingers. I duly appreciate that the subject of actresses' looks is considered much too trivial for the consideration of any true professor of the critical art, but I still somehow agree with the late and deeply lamented Huneker that good looks, so far as he could make out, never gravely hurt any actress. This last season would have encouraged Jim. Aside from the question of talent or lack of talent, just as in the older theatrical days when Jim and Percy Pollard and Vance Thompson and all that gay critical crew enthusiastically drew one another uptown from the Brevoort to the Hoffman House bar in open barouches, Jim would have been gratified by the fairness of a considerable number of the stage's young ladies.

[86]

He would have deposited a pleased eye, for instance, on the delicate champagne loveliness of the slender Julie Haydon, in *Bright Star,* on the George Lederer blonde beauty echo in the face of Marie Brown, in *How Beautiful With Shoes,* on the natural, early autumn leaf soft light brown hair above the fresh, bright face of Mary Rogers, in *Crime Marches On,* and on the dark, brooding, hypnotically warm Mexican decorativeness of Margo, in *Winterset.* He would have drunk a couple of seidels of Pilsner to the smart young English air of Dorothy Hyson, in *Most of the Game,* to the pale licorice Anne Brown, in *Porgy and Bess,* to the dancing Ziegfeld memory that shone through the blue-eyed blondeness of June Knight, in *Jubilee,* and to the tall, slim, cocoa-haired, light-footed Eleanor Powell, in *At Home Abroad.* He would then have ordered up another round in celebration of the youthful, untinted Martha Hodge, in *Remember the Day,* the black-haired and intense-eyed Margaret Rawlings, in *Parnell,* the sharply chiseled, fair haired Elissa Landi, in *Tapestry in Gray,* the billboard cigarette-model contours of Claire Carlton, in *The Body Beautiful,* and, most assuredly, the slim, delicate and rare Oriental loveliness of Mai-Mai Sze, in *Lady Precious Stream.*

To continue to contribute to Jim's overflowing cornucopia, the record would have vouchsafed to him at least fifty percent of the girls in *Jumbo,* including Mary Jackson, the target of her whip-snapping brother, Harry Jackson, Jr., and the sombrous Chicago girl who performed with her brother, in turn, above the open cage of lions. Also, he would have experienced something of a pleasurable jounce over the post-débutante ensemble that goes by the name of Hancy Castle, in *A Touch of Brimstone,* over the younger edition of a smaller-nostriled, less sinewy and more engagingly feminine Katharine Hepburn named Doris Dudley, in *The Season Changes, Stick-in-the-Mud* and *End of Summer,* over the brooding Latin cloudiness of the visage of Fraye Gilbert, in *Squaring the Circle,* and over the relatively unspoiled Hollywood aspect of Barbara Weeks, in *Satellite,* God forbid! And, to bring up the procession, over the Bartholdi sculpturing of Whitney Bourne, in *O Evening Star,* over at least one of the nine or ten young Sisters in the convent play, *Few Are Chosen* (it is difficult to identify a stageful of maidens all in the same costume, particularly when the author doesn't provide distinguishing dialogue), over the colored, gleaming-toothed, earthquakey Avis Andrews, in *Smile At Me,* over the tall, slim-bodied, aloof Edith Atwater, in *This Our House,* and over the especial — most certainly the especial — brunette perturbation of Helen Trenholme, in *Victoria Regina.*

That the previous shortage in ornamental women had hurt the box-office, it did not take an auditor to prove, because for every devotee of beautiful drama there are, and always have been, a dozen customers of beauty in some other and perhaps less formal direction. Ask the average old boy what he remembers about the drama of yesterday and you'll generally find that he gets William Vaughn Moody mixed up with Teresa Vaughan, Arthur Pinero with Julia Arthur, and Bronson Howard with either Florence Howard or Mabel. As for producers, he has to scratch his head to recall George Edwardes, although he can describe Paula Edwardes to her last toe-nail; A. M. Palmer he remembers only vaguely, but Minnie Palmer is a cinch; and as for George Tyler, all he knows is that maybe he was some relation to Odette Tyler. And while *Faust* may have been an opera to Oscar Hammerstein, it was a honey named Lotta to him.

Lillian Russell did more for the commercial prosperity of the American theatre than any half-dozen esteemed pie-faced dramatic actresses of her day. If there is any record of the horses of Madame Janauschek's carriage having been replaced by delirious stage fans, I haven't heard of it. And people don't change much. What the mob wants — let us critics cry into our beer all we wish to — is not so much good actresses as good-*looking* actresses. When a theatre has them it prospers, and when it doesn't have them it loses a lot of its trade. If the movies suddenly decided to stop hiring merely pretty girls and to go in for real actresses, it wouldn't be long before the Messrs. Goldwyn, Schenck, Mayer, *et al.*, would be on the public relief rolls.

[89]

Gazing At The Stars

Some years ago, on the opening night of a comedy called *The Consul,* the author was horrified when in the middle of the third act the star of the occasion, Louis Mann, suddenly stopped short in his tracks and interrupted the course of the play to recite a lengthy soliloquy on love and homesickness that had no more to do with what the play was about than a saw-mill scene has to do with *The Merry Wives of Windsor.* Rushing back stage the moment the curtain fell, he indignantly demanded of Mann what he meant by it. Drawing himself up to his full height, the late Louis loftily informed him that the soliloquy in question was from a play in which he had acted five years before, that it always had got a response from the audience, that it was therefore his belief that it might be used profitably in any other play, and that, besides, wasn't he a big theatrical star and couldn't he do as he damned pleased?

If you are so unacquainted with things theatrical as to believe that Mann was a ridiculous exception to the general star actor rule, you do not know star actors. What is perhaps more to the point, you do not know star actresses, for the ladies are often even more exuberantly hoddy-doddy than their male confrères, if we are to put faith in footlight chronicles. Joseph Verner Reed, quondam theatrical producer, relates for example in his charmingly frank book, *The Curtain Falls,* how Miss Jane Cowl, whenever things at rehearsals didn't suit her fancy, was in

the habit of prostrating herself flat upon the floor of the
stage and of issuing from that bizarre position loud, lugu-
brious critiques of everyone connected with the enterprise,
and how Miss Mary Ellis, under similar circumstances,
was given to tormenting the feelings of any co-player who
threatened even for a moment to give a good acting account of himself at the expense either of herself or of Basil
Sydney, her spouse. Yet these two stars were and are little
angels compared with certain others whose antics have become affidavits in the modern theatre.

In the last seven or eight years I have in the course of
my play-reviewing duties observed with the rest of the
audience no less than four celebrated lady stars on opening nights so wobbled from an excessive imbibation of
ethyl buttermilk that one of them on attempting to make
an exit mistook a bookcase for the door and essayed with
great aplomb to promenade through it; that another became so entangled in a negligée into which she was endeavoring to insert herself that she ripped it in two and
then tripped over it and landed with a crashing boom
against the side of a bed; that still another, appearing in
a gentle fantasy by a famous British dramatist, periodically had to be kept from falling on her face by the other
actors on the stage (the play had to be withdrawn after a
few days); and that a fourth got so completely balled up
with what she was doing that she read her third act
speeches in the first act. A spirit of old-fashioned chivalry,
combined with pity, precludes mention of them by name,

though they are readily identifiable by anyone who follows the New York stage.

Miss Elsie Ferguson would sometimes delay her first stage entrance for so long, in order to whet an audience's applause against the great moment of her sweeping appearance, that it would thereafter take at least fifteen minutes to work the play's action back into its proper and even tempo. This same star actress, appearing in an exhibit called *Scarlet Pages,* became so wroth over the success of a pretty young novice, Claire Luce, in a secondary rôle, that on one occasion, unable longer to conceal her displeasure and chagrin, she smacked the girl a smart one across the nose.

Richard Bennett's impulse suddenly to interrupt a play, stride to the footlights and vituperate any audience whose response to his art was not entirely to his liking eventually compelled at least one manager to insert a clause into his contract specifying that he must refrain from such impromptu elocutionary divertissements and content himself and his audiences with the lines the playwright provided for him. Among other male stars who have been given to a passion for telling audiences just what they thought of them were Nat Goodwin, who saw red every time he spotted any man out front who looked even remotely like a critic; Willard Mack, who at least retained some tonic humor as a balance to his indignation; and Lowell Sherman, who once overheard someone in the audience at the Hudson theatre reflect on the style of a doggy new dressing-gown he was wearing and who, upon the fall of the act curtain, came out and denounced not only the grievous offender but everyone else in the house as a low and highly smelly polecat, of illegitimate birth to boot.

Miss Margaret Rawlings, the talented English-Australian leading actress, two years ago was cast by a well-known London producer for a rôle in a drama laid in Victorian times, the elaborate costumes for which had been made with a nice eye to modest exactitude and at a very considerable expense. Imagine the producer's feelings, accordingly, when at the final dress rehearsal the actress came upon the stage with the bodices of her costumes cut so very low that even a Bali débutante might have been slightly embarrassed to wear them. The producer let out a yell. "This is the Victorian period!" he shouted. "What's the idea?" Whereupon the actress demurely informed him that she had taken the costumes to her own dressmaker and had had them cut away in front in order to reveal her luxuriant charms, as she believed that the aforesaid charms should not be denied to her admiring audiences.

Miss Rawlings' solicitude for her audiences was at least somewhat more commendable than Miss Ethel Barrymore's on her late tour of the South, if we are to trust the newspaper accounts of her peccadillos in certain communities which she visited. Thus, for example, Burch Lee, Jr., reporting on her performance in Shreveport, La., in the *Times* of that city: "Ethel Barrymore, supposedly one of the greatest actresses ever to speak a line from an American stage, played in the Municipal Auditorium Friday night and walked out of the lives of nearly 2,000 Shreveporters, perhaps forever, leaving them with a poor taste in their mouths because of a performance far below her publicized ability. Miss Barrymore apparently had no control over herself during the performance. In the first act her footing was not secure and she slurred her first lines. Later she pronounced her lines more distinctly, but for the most part she could hardly be heard beyond the first six rows. It was particularly disheartening to an audience that had come to witness a stellar performance. Surrounded by a cast that did all in their power to make a successful performance, Miss Barrymore seemed not to care and went blissfully on her way, rubbing her arms as an occasional cool draught of air struck her. And as the climax to her performance she haughtily wiped the famed nose and strode from the stage after she had cast a disdainful look about an audience that had brought her out for a bow, because they thought it their duty to a trouper. As the lights came on in the huge auditorium a stunned crowd moved slowly out. They had come to see a member of the royal family of the stage and they left having seen the shell. Perhaps it was her age and then again perhaps it was something else. It might have been that Shreveport was too small to bother about, but comments of the homegoers indicated that Miss Barrymore's next appearance, if ever again, will be when it snows in June."

From the circus tantrums of Mrs. Pat Campbell to Mrs. Fiske's well-known penchant for turning her back to her audience and reading her lines to the rear wall of the stage and from Miss Julia Marlowe's unwritten back-stage rule that the actors in her company shouldn't bother her with their presences or speech save during performances to the very recent Miss Katharine Hepburn who, when headlined in *The Lake,* put up a screen leading from her dressing-room to the stage in order that Miss Blanche Bates and Miss Frances Starr, celebrated stars of an earlier period who were appearing in the same drama, wouldn't get in her august way — from the beginning to the end, the story seems to be much the same. Once an actor or an actress becomes a star, even the peacock hides his head in relative modesty.

Note on Folk Plays

The so-called folk play customarily has something of a whimsical tussle with the kind of actors hired for its folk rôles. It is, of course, entirely possible that absolutely first-rate actors, whatever their personal and private composition, may be able to interpret the characters of an alien folk drama, be it of a species however bizarre. But with the average run of the actor pack it proves to be a disconcerting job. Thus, to find, as in the case of something like *Let Freedom Ring,* that the rôles of Carolina hill-billies like old Grandpap Kirkland and his tribe are to be played by actors and actresses whose several fortes, according to the statistics in the back of the program, have been Mrs. Fiske comedies, farces laid in Brooklyn, English war plays, detective and mystery melodramas, plays of fashionable society, movie burlesques, Robert Mantell repertoire and *Sailor, Beware!,* is never too reassuring.

CHAPTER V

The Cinema

∾ ∾

A Drama Critic Looks At the Movies

The movies suffered their first great setback when some now forgotten press-agent, in his cups but yet foxily privy to the susceptibility of his *nouveau ritz* boss, dubbed them an Art. And they suffered their second when the aforesaid boss, after breathlessly rushing to telephone the unctuous news to his wife, proceeded forthwith to conduct his business upon the press-agent's theory.

The movies, in their entirety, are no more of an art than the theatre in three-quarters of its manifestations. Like the theatre in its lesser phases, they are purely and simply a gesture toward unimportant pastime. But, unlike the theatre, when they aim at a higher star they are vainglorious, quite silly, and just a little embarrassing.

The pictures have, with the progress of the years, improved upon their own particular brand of entertainment. Various clever inventions, the introduction into the business of more advanced minds, the hiring of more competent writers, and other such phenomena have succeeded

[97]

in bettering the celluloid product. But with all their progress and all their betterment the films remain still, even at their very best, a mere spotty mirror held up to the mirror that the drama in turn holds up to nature. They are to an art, in short, what the photograph of an artist is to the artist himself, in person.

There are numerous supporting grounds for such a contention that indicate clearly the deep chasm between the cinema and the theatre. The better an actress is on the stage, for example, the worse she generally finds herself to be in the films. She finds, as Bernhardt once found and as Bergner now finds, that while the stage is the place for compositional acting, the screen is simply the place for isolated moments snatched from a compositional performance, and that a screen performance hence bears the same relation to a stage performance that a hiccup bears to Camille's tuberculosis. A Helen Hayes, as already noted, discovers and freely confesses that, despite box-office favor with the fans, she cannot be satisfied with her performances in the films, and a George M. Cohan, the best actor in the American theatre, similarly discovers with something of a shock that the George M. Cohan on the screen is evidently some other fellow from Providence, R. I.

The opposite is also very often true. The worse an actress on the stage the better she is in the pictures. The late and much loved Marie Dressler was a low comédienne in theatrical music-shows; of dramatic acting she knew utterly nothing. Yet she became the most admired of movie dramatic actresses, and was awarded a magnificent gold cup by her Hollywood confrères for her cinema histrionic virtuosity. Without impolitely mentioning living names, there are no less than eight actresses in Hollywood today who, though they could not get jobs in even inferior plays in the theatre, are now among the films' elect.

Art — whatever its kind — is a permanent thing; it isn't here today and gone tomorrow. But in the movies we engage the constant spectacle of great Hollywood artists, all acclaimed as geniuses, who enjoy their little day in court and are then summarily dispatched to the ashcan. Look over the list of actors and actresses since the early days of the pictures and then look into the aforesaid ashcan. Look at the favorites of the last fifteen years and see how many have lasted. Look even at the record of the last five years. In the theatre, an actor or actress of talent, provided only he or she keeps off the gin bottle, persists until old age and arterio-sclerosis set in. In the movies, a five-year career is something to be pathetically grateful for, and a ten-year career something to be embalmed in the pages of history.

Maurice Chevalier a year or two ago got into an altercation over a scenario with his studio heads. " You listen to George Arliss, why don't you listen to me? " he wanted to know. They told him that they considered Arliss the superior artist. Chevalier let out a derisive hoot. " Just you watch! " he yelled. " I'll last twenty years longer in pictures than Arliss. *He* can't sing! " (Chevalier is already out of pictures, save for an occasional French-made quickie, and is back in his native French music halls.) As for Arliss, the superior artist, I take the liberty of quoting a report made to me by one of my confidential agents in Hollywood. It provides an illumination not only of Mr. Arliss but of the picture business at its presumable best.

When *The Iron Duke* screen play was completed, so goes the report, Mr. Arliss, as usual, fished out his quill pen and set himself to the task of building up his rôle. This is an invariable practice of his, and while it always serves to make him look quite pretty, it usually plays havoc with both history and story. But the outstanding contribution he made to *The Iron Duke* was, according to my *amicus curiæ,* a scene in which one of the great ladies of the play enters a room, comes suddenly on Mr. Arliss as Wellington for the first time in her life, and swoons.

"But why?" asked the puzzled authors.

"Because I have had some experience of hero worship," Mr. Arliss explained with his gentle and modest smile, "and no one knows more than I what a powerful emotion it can be."

The movies are an amalgam of the histrionic philosophy of Chevalier and the personal and dramatic æsthetics of Arliss.

In the matter of slapstick or bawdy comedy and of shoot-'em-up melodrama, the films are at home and on safe ground. In these departments they succeed in providing satisfactory entertainment. Moreover, actors are equally on safe ground when they perform in such films. A Cagney in melodrama, a Hugh Herbert and an Allen Jenkins in slapstick, a Mae West in sporting-house drama — all are good and sufficient unto their mediums. And for a readily discernible reason. Melodrama is light-the-fuse-and-jump drama; slapstick comedy is hit-and-run drama; and the Mae West species of exhibit is the snapped-line-and-so-long-baby drama. All consist in spasmodic, quick-trigger, on-again-off-again stuff. They do not call for sustained acting, but for a rapid succession of bit performances on the part of a single player. Their rôles are to the rôles of stage drama what a snapshot is to portrait photography. They are a series of quick clicks rather than time exposures.

The all-vital emphasis of the motion picture is, naturally and appropriately enough, upon motion, which is a dramatic synonym (at least in the movie mind) for action. The drama of the screen is the drama of the stage placed arbitrarily in a squirrel cage. To allow it to be as relatively static as it is in its stage incarnation is to court wholesale box-office failure. To do *Rosmersholm,* say, on the screen exactly as it is played in the theatre would be to put the entire movie audience to sleep in fifteen minutes' time. To do it at all on the screen (heaven forbid!), it would be necessary to jounce the inaction with scenes showing Rebecca battling her way to the home of the Rosmers through the perilous fjords, other scenes showing a hair-pulling contest between Rebecca and Beata, and all kinds of post-

D. W. Griffith spectacular melodramatic shenanigan with the mill-race.

The movie's insistence upon purely physical action as against the stage's increasing insistence upon cerebral action, or at least action that stems from character, markedly differentiates the one from the other. The drama of the movies is the drama of the theatre in its pre-puberty stage.

But there is a simpler and more significant difference. The drama of the movies is the drama of scenes; the drama of the stage is the drama of acts. The former is — indeed, has to be by reason of its aim at exaggeratedly wide appeal — contrived for audiences without the education for sustained thought and reflective attention. Hence it must be devised in terms of short ocular and dramatic startles and shocks, all leading up, with painless assimilation, to a normal gathered-skein ending. There can be no dawdling on the way, no time for philosophical comment, character analysis or any other such item that the more leisurely constituted and meditative theatrical audience delights in. The drama of the better modern stage considers all those things most worth-while which the cinema has no use for. The drama of the inferior modern stage, on the other hand, is simply movie drama. And it is this movie drama, masquerading as stage drama, that latterly and often conspicuously has discouraged theatre attendance.

Champions of the films will seek to pick holes in this discourse by nominating a few exceptions to each of the several arguments which it advances. That there are minor exceptions is quite possible; indeed, I can think of a number myself. But the general canvas remains, I believe, intact. The strongest points of the cinema, whether in drama or in acting, are by and large the weakest points of the theatre. The movies admire most greatly those very elements that the theatre has contempt for, and vice versa. The movies are the diversion of the uneducated masses; the theatre is the diversion of the educated few. The former have to pay the artistic penalty of their large, undiscriminating audiences; the latter has to pay the financial penalty of its small, discriminating audiences.

A person of the slightest culture and experience finds that the motion picture, even the far-above-the-ordinary motion picture, does not satisfy him as the theatre, even in its lesser flights, does. For all the circumstance that he may be amused or diverted while in the movie parlor, he experiences a sudden feeling of complete emotional, mental, physical and spiritual emptiness, of time frittered away and wasted, when he emerges. He finds that he takes with him into the open no after-feeling, no after-image, no after-thought (save maybe of some animating cutie), as in the case of the dramatic theatre. He leaves his mood and his reaction inside.

The test of any art is the lingering impression it leaves. Upon a well-tuned, well-trained and sensitive mind the movies leave no impression other than one of having spent an hour or so in a spiritual vacuum.

The cinema, like the detective story, hard liquor or the

gentle art of wenching, serves its purpose as a distraction
from routine and as an aimless, haphazard, easy, and
meaningless diversion. That, at least, may be said in its
favor. Nor let it be too riled and disgruntled. It may
proudly, if it wishes, recall that Theodore Roosevelt,
Woodrow Wilson and Calvin Coolidge, those immortals,
reveled in detective stories; that General Grant and Huey
Long had a rich taste for straight hard liquor; and that the
great Kings of France raised merry hell in the haystacks.

Till Holly Wood Remove to Dunsinane

Those persons who early in the 1935-6 theatrical season
began wringing their hands and weeping loudly over the
stranglehold that the moving pictures were about to get
on the dramatic stage may, now that the season is past history and the returns are in, recompose themselves. Not
only did the picture folk fail, whatever their intention, to
make the slightest indentation in that stage but it becomes
increasingly evident that, if there is any indentation to be
reckoned with, it is the stage that more and more is making it in the pictures.

Looking over the season's records, we find that the chief
and most obnoxious thing that the movies did to the
theatre was the contribution of a considerable fortune in
the way of money toward the production of plays. That
ignominious act, it seems to me, may hardly be viewed
in the light of a particular outrage. For among the plays
which the very welcome money made possible were some

of the most estimable and thoroughly interesting of the year. If movie money was occasionally behind such dishes of scrapple as *The Body Beautiful* and *Play, Genius, Play,* it should not be overlooked that it was, at the same time, also behind such worthy productions as *Winterset* and *Ethan Frome.* And if Hollywood boodle here and there offered itself as backing for such litter as *Sweet Mystery of Life* and *Good Men and True,* it should not be forgotten that it also made possible the production of such plays as *Pride and Prejudice* and *Boy Meets Girl.* Furthermore, while Hollywood is being denounced for putting its theoretically filthy money into the theatre and bringing into the theatre various doses of trash, thus contaminating the proud art of drama, let the indignantos pause and reflect that such great masterpieces of that art as *Satellite, Truly Valiant, Alice Takat, The Devil of Pei-Ling, This Our House, Moon Over Mulberry Street, Mulatto, Strip Girl, Triumph, If This Be Treason, Pre-Honeymoon, Crime Marches On, The Fields Beyond, Lady Luck* and a lot of similar exhibits were put on with pure and holy theatrical money that was not in the least tainted with the fingerprints of Louis B. Mayer, Sam Goldwyn, the Warner brothers, or any other such low lens swine.

Surveying the gloomiest side of the picture as painted by the arbitrary anti-Hollywood howlers, we are confronted by the uneasy fact that while Hollywood's Irving Thalberg put up the money for Philip Barry's *Bright Star,* neither he nor any other sniffed-at movie mentality put up even a counterfeit dime for Laura Walker's *Among Those Sailing*. And we are simultaneously confronted by the doubly uneasy fact that, though *Bright Star* was far from being reputable drama, only a thirty-third degree moron would argue that it wasn't one hundred and thirty-three times more reputable in every respect than *Among Those Sailing*. In the same way, while it was the combined æsthetic mentality of Hollywood's Messrs. Schulberg and Gering that discerned a high and beautiful dramatic quality in Martin Flavin's pretentious drool, *Tapestry In Gray*, it was the great solo æsthetic mentality of that eminent theatrical-dramatic darling, Mr. Walter Hampden, that discerned an even higher and more beautiful quality in the same Mr. Flavin's even more pretentious drool, *Achilles Had a Heel*.

The Warner family may have backed *The Body Beautiful*, but it was sacred theatrical money that backed *Strip Girl*, which was just as bad. The Paramount company had money in *There's Wisdom in Women*, but even *There's Wisdom in Women* was considerably better than *Mother Sings* or *I Want a Policeman*, in which neither it nor any other movie company had a cent. *The Puritan*, poor as it was, at least more soundly merited the decency of movie money investment, which it enjoyed, than such gimcracks as *Fresh Fields*, *Black Widow* and *Mainly For Lovers* merited what theatrical money was wasted on them. I don't seem to be able to work up much critical indignation over the circumstance that *Libel!*, *Paths of Glory, First*

Lady and *Jubilee* owed their production to Hollywood backing, nor do I seem to work up much critical enthusiasm, on the other hand, over the circumstance that *The Ragged Edge, The Sap Runs High, Mother* and *Smile At Me* owed their production purely and solely to spotless theatrical backing.

Thus, when it comes to Hollywood's evil lucre in the theatre, I fear that I must remain aloof from the spitball blowers. At its worst, it isn't any worse than the kind of money that is and often in the past has been contributed to the theatre by angels of one sort or another, most of them with a bigger personal ax to grind than even Cecil B. DeMille's property man himself ever thought up. If I were a theatrical producer I should as lief have Darryl Zanuck's or Joe Schenck's money in my shows as that of some Wall Street broker whose idiotic wife wanted to bask in what she fancied was an arty atmosphere, or of some Second Avenue graduate cloak-and-suit magnifico who relished himself in evening clothes and in the company of opening night Broadway celebrities, or of some fashionable round-the-town boozer whose girl had to get her chance to be an actress, or else. And I would sooner have Metro-Goldwyn back my musical revues than the gangster, Waxey Gordon, who backed a couple of them for as many theatrical managers when he was in the money, and I would sooner be annoyed any day — or any night — by the Twentieth Century-Fox or Columbia movie outfit's bank account, even if I occasionally had to have dinner with the worms who signed the checks, than by the money of any one of two or three well-known theatre owners who throughout their careers have been the aggressive debasers of almost everything theatrical that has come their way.

When we consider the so-called invasion of the theatre by film actors or actresses, there seems, in the light of the season's statistics, even less to worry about. Investigated closely, the big invasion appears to have been confined to exactly seven conceded screen players so far as the dramatic stage was concerned and to exactly one so far as the musical stage was concerned. That makes a grand total invasion of eight against something like six or seven hundred actors of the old legitimate line who appeared on the same stages. Investigated even more closely, it appears that several of these screen players were pretty good and that one or two who were pretty bad had nevertheless received all their early training in the legitimate theatre. Look over the list. The movie's sole invader of the musical stage was June Knight, a very attractive song and dance girl who helped out *Jubilee* considerably. The six invaders of the dramatic stage were Richard Barthelmess, who contributed a very fair if somewhat too literate and undeveloped performance to *The Postman Always Rings Twice;* Margo, who had appeared in only a couple of pictures, one of them made in nearby Astoria by Hecht and MacArthur, and who, in this, her first appearance on the stage, brought to *Winterset* precisely the personality, tone, look and performance that the rôle called for; Martha Sleeper who, in both *Good Men and True* and *Russet Mantle,* gave a quite passable account of herself; Barbara Weeks, who did all that any person could do with a rubbishy rôle in the rubbishy *Satellite;* Julie Haydon, who had previously appeared in but a single picture, also made in nearby Astoria by Hecht and MacArthur, and who at least contributed a very considerable beauty, if a nervous inexperience along with it, to the rôle in *Bright Star* which, in the year before she entered pictures, she had tried out on the road under Arthur Hopkins; Elissa Landi, who five years ago had made a decidedly favorable impression in the dramatization of *A Farewell to Arms* and who, in *Tapestry In Gray,* indicated that the intervening years spent in front of a camera had done much to corrupt her as a stage actress; and, lastly, Jobyna Howland, who had spent fifteen or more years on the stage before going to Hollywood and who, like Miss Landi, showed in *O Evening Star* that Hollywood had put its curse upon her.

So much for the big frontal stage attack of film players.

Coming to the actual direction of plays, we find that two and only two movie directors stole up on the dramatic muse from behind and that, for all the circumstance that they had had considerable theatrical directorial training in other years, both were hooted into the storehouse with trigger-like alacrity. Marion Gering, who produced *Tapestry In Gray* for Benjamin S. Schulberg (the single movie mogul whose name was permitted to appear on any season's playbill), was one, and William C. DeMille, who directed *Hallowe'en,* was the other.

We now turn to the plays conferred upon the season's stage by writers for the films, most of them — and let it be clearly remembered — backed and produced not by Hollywood intruders upon the theatre but by persons removed from the movies and more or less definitely associated with the theatre. Dismissing those plays written by more or less recognized playwrights who have now and then gone into scenario writing as a side-line, we engage the following straight screen-writer exhibits: *Blind Alley,* by James Warwick, a serviceable and rather exhilarating psychoanalytical melodrama; *The Body Beautiful,* by Robert Rossen, twaddle which was removed after a few days' display; *Hell Freezes Over,* by John Patrick, Grand Guignol melodrama that went to the ashcan in short order; *Co-respondent Unknown,* written in part by a Hollywood literatus named Goldman, a feeble comedy; and *Come Angel Band,* by Dudley Nichols and Stuart Anthony, a poor attempt at Southern sex drama. In other words, just five plays by professional scenario writers, one of them, to boot, not bad and the other four, at their worst, hardly more odoriferous than at least twice their number written by persons who had never been anywhere near Hollywood.

That Hollywood has apparently put the Indian sign on such once mettlesome playwrights as Zoë Akins, Arthur

Richman, Sidney Howard, *et al.,* who tried vainly to return to the theatre during the season, is true. But that Hollywood doesn't seem thus far to have done anything in particular to the talents of Maxwell Anderson, S. N. Behrman and the Spewaks, judging from *Winterset, End of Summer* and *Boy Meets Girl,* must be recorded in the same critical paragraph.

We return, finally, to the question of Hollywood money as it affects the theatre. So long as Hollywood is willing to pay out to reputable theatrical producers annual sums running into hundreds of thousands of dollars for the mere screen rights to such plays as *Dead End, Pride and Prejudice, Winterset, Ethan Frome, Parnell, Russet Mantle* and the like, and through such payment encourage, however obliquely, the production of better-grade drama, just so long will Hollywood money be hardly a dose of poison but rather a veritable godsend to the theatre.

So let us stop listening to all the nonsense about Hollywood's rape of the stage.

The Two Censorships

That, judging from the more recent antics of public officials and private busybodies in various American municipalities, the day is perhaps not far distant when the drama outside of New York will be subjected to a general censorship beside which the widely protested present censorship of the movies is negligible, begins to seem likely. Already has O'Neill's *Strange Interlude* in at least one city been declared unfit for performance because of its sexual philosophy, and already in several cities has Lillian Hellman's *The Children's Hour* been forbidden a showing because it deals with the subject of abnormality in sex. Already have O'Casey's *Within the Gates* and the Kirkland-Caldwell *Tobacco Road* been banned because the former comments on religion and because the latter is allegedly sacrilegious and vulgar in speech. Already has Odets' *Waiting For Lefty* been denied a hearing on the score of its radicalism, and already has there been protest against Maxwell Anderson's *Valley Forge* as a WPA presentation because, in its picture of the soldiers of the Continental army, it employs some profanity. Any number of plays have been allowed production only after heavy excisions have been made in their texts, Noël Coward's *Point Valaine* and the Nicholson-Robinson farce, *Sailor, Beware!,* being two examples out of many. On the lower levels of theatrical entertainment, vaudeville has been packed off to the bone-yard because of its demanded wholesale purification and burlesque has been subjected to such rigorous police scrutiny that it has become indistinguishable from a one-night-stand musical turkey. As for the musical shows and revues themselves, the outlying American cities have periodically imposed so tart a blue pencil upon their lines and sketches that little has remained in them but a moon song, an adagio dance (fully clothed), and a couple of blackout skits in which the bed has been replaced by a piano.

Even in New York itself, that theoretical Gomorrah,

censorship of one brand or another has in late years exercised its holy will upon the stage. The case of *The Captive* is still readily remembered. The political censor shenanigan that made things difficult for the play *Merry-Go-Round* when it was brought uptown from the little Provincetown Playhouse is also fresh in the memory. The dispatch of Mae West to the Bastille for offending the delicate sensibilities of the Broadway cloak-and-suit æsthetes and the police raid upon her play, *Pleasure Man,* need no recalling. The much more recent commanded deletions in the dialogue of Sidney Kingsley's *Dead End* are still green in the recollection. The police and license commissioner activities and suppressions in the matter of burlesque are in the records. And Earl Carroll's troubles with the constabulary are also there. Surely all this intimates that the American stage is not always so exempt from interference as we are sometimes led to believe.

That the movies, for all the talk about the drastic censorship imposed upon them by the MM. Hays and Breen, are in general still pretty free from non-Papal censorship of any great importance must be obvious to anyone who takes the trouble to give them even a cursory glance. It is perfectly true that they are subjected to a steady blue-penciling, but that blue-penciling seems to operate, except in a very few cases, upon what are, after all, only insignificant and unimportant details. In the way of themes, the screen is surprisingly untrammeled. The occasional abandonment on the part of one of the movie companies of some such purchased story as Sinclair Lewis' *It Can't Happen Here* or the occasional discontinuance of further showings of some such film as the Marlene Dietrich Spanish picture are not the result of any Hays-Breen censorship but simply the result of a disinclination of one or another of the companies to lose the good-will of certain of its foreign markets, with the coincidental loss of a lot of future good money. It is shrewd business rather than censorship, and it should not becloud the issue. That even such films as the Spanish one in question were freely passed by the movie censor organization is not to be forgotten.

While movie censorship frowns in a general way upon pictures that treat of religion in a manner that may offend certain sects, it yet does nothing to stop Mae West from appearing in a picture called *Klondike Annie* which does that very thing. If the Metro-Goldwyn-Mayer company itself privately concludes that it would be an unwise commercial policy to film the Lewis novel and offend its markets in fascist Italy and Germany, the Hays-Breen blue-pencil cops are still perfectly willing to let it make the picture if it wants to or to allow it or any other company freely to make some such picture as *Robin Hood of Eldorado*, which must arouse enough animosity on the part of Mexicans toward Americans to start a war, if the Mexicans had even a couple of thousand dollars left to buy ammunition. Charlie Chaplin is permitted, in *Modern Times*, to release a picture so Communistic in intent that the boys down in the Fourteenth Street dramatic Little Red Schoolhouse must consider themselves rank amateurs. Pictures inducing so wholesale a contempt for Americans that, in the case of at least one of them, *Convention City,* even St. John Ervine was constrained to devote his leading article in the London *Observer* to deploring such shortsightedness, are a common occurrence.

Pictures are regularly endorsed by the movie censors — not only by the Hays-Breen organization but by the various censorship boards throughout the country — that make mock of China and the Chinese, that stultify French morals and decency, and that treat every present-day Russian either as a bomb-thrower or a walking repository for cooties and bedbugs. Although censorship may forbid the display of some foreign picture like *Ecstasy* on the ground that one of its scenes shows a woman swimming under water in what seems to be the altogether, it does not forbid the free showing of any number of other foreign pictures like *Tempest,* in which the ebullition of the sex act is conveyed to the customers with a realism, despite some sly hocus-pocus, that the stage has not yet approached. Mr. Lubitsch has been allowed to get away with such murder in his bed and boudoir scenes that Al Woods himself is reduced to crimson blushes. Mae West's *She Done Him Wrong,* if shown as a play in the theatre, would undoubtedly have found Mae again in the patrol wagon. And though the screen was compelled to deodorize *The Children's Hour,* the movie called *Mädchen in Uniform,* first rejected and then passed by the local censors, was, for all its several deletions, three times more Lesbianly vivid than the stage version which was put on at the Broadhurst theatre.

Motion picture censorship hits mainly in the direction of dialogue and bits of business and hence is not too concernful even to the few remaining donkeys who still look upon the screen as an art. But theatrical censorship, as it appears to be spreading about the nation, is mainly in the direction of themes, and hence a matter of deep concern to everyone who hopes to safeguard the art of the drama. When a trashy themeless film like *Hollywood After Dark* is rejected by the movie censors, it is of no more importance than when a trashy themeless play like *Sex* is suppressed by the stage censors. Both, being garbage, have no place either on the screen or the stage, and when the arbitrary bellowers against the evils of censorship suppression yell themselves hoarse with indignation they only make fools of themselves. When the movie censors censor off the screen something like *The Informer* on the ground that it is offensive to the Irish or on any other ground, it will be time enough for the movie anti-censorship shouters to make their racket. But when, in the theatre, a thrillingly beautiful theme like *Within the Gates,* a moving and life-throbbing theme like *Strange Interlude,* a dignified and soberly considered theme like *The Children's Hour,* and a true and biting theme like *Tobacco Road* are all, in the small span of a few years, denied a hearing in many American cities, surely then is there some justification for the present concern over a censorless, free and unhindered American stage.

The forced excision of a few cuss words, a few bits of business and a few nude hussies is of no more moment to the drama — or even to the revue — than to the films. It may be too bad that there still exist persons so bogusly moral as to quake lest the great body of humanity be contaminated by them, but it still doesn't matter. The presence of the ejaculation *sonofabitch* never made a bad play good, nor can the enforced absence of it ever make a good play bad. A scene showing a man buttoning his nether habiliments may bring an extra hundred francs to the box-office of the Palais Royal, but it never buttoned or unbuttoned the artistic standing of a Tristan Bernard, Hennequin or Veber. A woman's uncovered epidermis may be valuable to a painter or a sculptor, but it has never alone succeeded in making a playwright an artist. Let fool censors do what they will in these directions and no one, except possibly the boy in the box-office, gives a hoot. But when censorship, whether exercised by a mayor of Boston, Chicago or Detroit, by municipal police, by an official board of blue-pencilers or by unofficial but influential private bluenoses, seeks to clamp down the lid not merely upon a few incidentals to an important subject but upon the important subject itself, then is the time for all good men to come to the aid of the tar-and-feather party.

That time, as I have observed, is doubtless — judging

from the way the wind is blowing—not far away. If a dramatist is to be denied the right of any other citizen, the right to stand upon a platform that in his case is the stage, and from it to exercise his privilege of free speech on any subject he chooses, whomsoever it may irritate, offend and even outrage, the integrity and honor of our theatre are to be despaired of. If dramatists like O'Neill, O'Casey and Anderson are to be forbidden their say, whatever it may be, and if plays like *Tobacco Road* and *The Children's Hour* are to be forbidden a hearing, God help not merely Boston, Chicago, Detroit and other such backward burgs, but the future of the entire American stage.

CHAPTER VI

The Producing Gentry

∽ ∽

They Who Produce Your Play

As every other person in the United States is said either to be planning to write a play, to be writing one, or already to have completed the job, a brief description of the men to whom hopeful playwrights must entrust their brain-children should have a wide appeal. Just what are the leading managers and producers in the American theatre like? What sort of men are they? What are their extrinsic interests and their personal predilections?

Gilbert Miller is the son of the late Henry Miller, an actor, and of the late Bijou Heron, an actress. He says of himself that he once remarked to his estimable father that somebody had said he was a chip of the old block. " Rather say," drawled his father, " a slice of the old ham." But Papa was unfair to his enterprising son, for the latter — while himself an off-stage actor of considerable nuance — has an unhistrionic appreciation of good literature and good drama, even if he does consider Robert Sherwood's *The Petrified Forest* the best American play of all time.

" O'Neill has never touched it," is his somewhat alarming conviction.

Miller speaks and reads French and German as fluently as he does English. Although he has the good taste aforesaid, he nevertheless lacks courage when confronted by any new and truly distinguished piece of dramatic writing; he prefers to play safe at the box-office. He spends part of his time producing plays in London, where he owns a charming house; he vacations in Le Touquet, on the French coast, where he has another charming house; he is fond of the fashionable social life; he prefers the work of established dramatists, chiefly foreign, and takes little interest in new playwrights; and he is the first humorously to criticize and to admit his own shortcomings.

Arthur Hopkins, unlike Miller, has since his earliest days in the theatre had a deep interest in new playwrights, despite his wholesale passion for golf. He is a taciturn fellow and if he so much as grunts it is the eloquent equivalent of a two-hour speech by Mr. Norman Thomas. He believes that competent actors should be able to act a play with a minimum of direction and consequently spends most of the time that a play is in rehearsal at the Astor Hotel, eating a series of lunches and discoursing on drivers and niblicks with any fellow-producer who happens to be around and who is willing to listen. An occasional highball is to his taste and he rides about in a splendiferous pea-green automobile. He believes in the finer things of the theatre, even if in more recent years much of his old discernment seems to have forsaken him.

The directors of the Theatre Guild are Lawrence Langner, Theresa Helburn, Philip Moeller, Maurice Wertheim, Lee Simonson, Helen Westley, and Alfred Lunt, the actor. Langner is one of the leading patent lawyers in the country and is reported to derive a very handsome income from his profession. It was he who drew Bernard Shaw into the Guild fold and worked for O'Neill's acceptance in the face of his colleagues' hostility. He sweats hard to write plays himself, has written a number of peculiarly bad ones, and has had them produced outside of the Guild. Theresa Helburn is the executive of the board. She has until lately been spending much of her time working on the Hollywood lots. Philip Moeller does most of the actual direction of the plays selected and is perhaps the hardest worker in the crowd. Like Miss Helburn, he also has been casting sheep's-eyes, similarly not too successfully, at Hollywood. Maurice Wertheim is the financial brains of the organization. He is a Wall Street banker and last year bought the controlling interest in the liberal weekly, *The Nation*. Simonson, the board's sharpest intelligence, attends mainly to the scenic details. Miss Westley is an actress who performs in various Guild productions when she isn't engaged in Hollywood film work. She is the frankest and most outspoken of the sextette.

Jed Harris, once a strikingly original producer and a

man of resource, seems, at least for the time being, to be in sad eclipse, although he continues to announce large and handsome producing plans which have a way of never coming off. He, too, has unsuccessfully flirted with Hollywood. He started out as a press-agent with one shirt and then came into the sweet money with *Broadway, The Front Page, Coquette,* and *The Royal Family.* Thereafter his luck seemed to go back on him and — save for *Uncle Vanya* — his record became one of failures. Sam H. Harris (no relative) began as a prize-fighter's manager, became subsequently the successful producing partner of George M. Cohan, and has lately, as a solo producer, put on a succession of hits, chiefly musical. He is a modest, withdrawn, generous fellow who is reputed always to keep his word. He is, furthermore, moderately hospitable to experiment. His diversion is playing golf with Arthur Hopkins and investing in hypothetical gold mines in California and elsewhere. William Harris, Jr. (no relation to either) rounds out the Harrises. Although once a producer of an acumen and resolve above the ordinary — he was Vincent Lawrence's sponsor for years through thick and thin, chiefly thin — he has in recent years been disposed to dream of the box-office as opposed to sound dramatic merit.

Max Gordon, one of the most successful of current producers, began as a slave in Martin Beck's vaudeville booking office and subsequently handled vaudeville acts himself in conjunction with another erstwhile peon. Like

Gilbert Miller, he is chiefly fascinated by " names " and, also like Miller, has an eager eye to potentially prosperous plays and casts from England. He is a great admirer of the Noël Coward species of playwriting; he bought himself a *soigné* new black overcoat for his first meeting with the Rockefellers to discuss productions in their Radio Center theatre; he is a thorough Broadway showman; and he would trade Shakespeare, Molière, Congreve, Hauptmann and Shaw any day for Cole Porter, and throw in five dollars.

Lee Shubert frequently invests in meritorious plays — *The Green Bay Tree* and *The Children's Hour* are two more recent examples — but leaves their production and direction to outsiders. The plays he produces under his own name are generally the hoped-for box-office kind. His interests often lie wholly outside the theatre and reach out to hotels and even night clubs. Laurence Rivers is the *nom de théâtre* of Rowland Stebbins. Mr. Stebbins was a Wall Street broker who took a fancy to the work of George Kelly and deserted Wall Street to become Kelly's producer. When Marc Connelly took *The Green Pastures* to him, Connelly had a tough time persuading him that it was worth a try. With many sighs and misgivings, Stebbins finally and reluctantly gave in — and the show made a fortune. Anything even remotely approaching symbolism in drama scares Stebbins half to death.

Dwight Deere Wiman is a fashionable young blade given to modish evening dress with large white blooms in the lapel. He inherited the larger part of a big Mid-Western plow works. The theatre is a lot of sport to him, yet he actually reads most of the manuscripts that are submitted to him. His taste is for the so-called popular species of play. He is gifted in the art of the modern dance and is the fanciest private hoofer among the New York managers. John Tuerk, of Bushar and Tuerk, was born into the theatre as pet office-boy to William A. Brady and, with his partner — whose full name is George Bushar Markle — gave O'Casey's *Within The Gates* its chance when no other producer would risk his money on it. Markle plays all known varieties of musical instruments; he has a good baritone voice; he owns rich coal properties in eastern Pennsylvania; and both he and Tuerk read eagerly any promising play manuscript that comes their way. But their judgment is often decidedly faulty.

Harry Moses, producer of *Grand Hotel* and *The Old Maid,* still owns part of his old interest in a lingerie factory; John Golden came into the theatre via song-writing (he was the author of *Poor Butterfly* and many another popular hit of the yesterdays) and is a fiend for golf; and Crosby Gaige is a collector of valuable first editions, runs a small *luxe* printing press and turns out good-looking brochures on the side in his spare time, and has devised a signal system for hospital use which gives him a nice yearly profit. Delos Chappell is a dilettante from Denver who inaugurated the annual dramatic shindig in Central City, Colorado — subsequently superintended by Robert

Edmond Jones — and whose gambling taste preferably runs to plays with one set of scenery and a minimum of characters; Guthrie McClintic, husband and sponsor of Katharine Cornell, is a former bit-actor who has shown a very considerable and desertful discrimination, both as a producer and director, in the matter of play manuscripts; William A. Brady, aside from looking out for the bookings of his Playhouse, does little any longer in the way of productions; Herman Shumlin, who was once associated with Jed Harris and who is not without a measure of Harris' former good judgment, at least tries sincerely to do the best things within his restricted range; and Brock Pemberton, once a Western newspaper man, has a particular yen for light risqué farce-comedies.

Put your script into an envelope and take your pick.

The Casting Complaint

Last year's loudest complaint on the part of the producers had to do with the impossibility of casting many of their plays properly because the movies have stolen the good actors and actresses of the theatre by the carload. Who, may we ask, are all these rare actors and actresses that Hollywood has pilfered? That Hollywood has cabbaged many of the pretty ones, male and female, is perfectly true, but that it has laid its claws on any clearly discernible number who can actually act, not even the movie directors themselves, those guardian angels of art, are wholly persuaded. Nine-tenths of the great acting favorites of the screen were duds on the dramatic stage. And the figure *nine-tenths* isn't tossed off carelessly, as one tosses off, for example, such quantitative phrases as " by a jugful," " oodles and oodles," etc., but after some statistical exercise and deliberation. For every George Arliss that the pictures have kidnapped, you'll find nine Ann Hardings, Bette Davises, Fredric Marches, Lionel Atwills, Barbara Stanwycks, Sidney Blackmers, Ralph Forbeses, William Powells and Edmund Lowes who, to be excessively generous about it, hardly set the stage on fire when they were on it. For every John Barrymore whom Hollywood has snatched from the drama, you'll have no difficulty in naming nine Grant Mitchells, Ralph Morgans, Conrad Nagels, Vivienne Osbornes, Herbert Rawlinsons, John Boleses, Joseph Schildkrauts, Robert Warwicks and Verree Teasdales who never made Mr. Brooks Atkinson, Mr. John Mason Brown or anyone else sit on his hat in an excess of critical enthusiasm. And for every other first-rate player that the movies have bribed away from Broadway you'll be equally able to count off nine Ruthelma Stevenses, Ralph Bellamys, Greta Nissens, Bela Lugosis, Helen MacKellars, Wallace Fords, Lee Kohlmars, Hale Hamiltons and Minna Gombells.

The great majority of actors and actresses that Hollywood has cabbaged from the theatre wouldn't help out the alleged current casting difficulty in the least. They'd not improve plays so much as they'd hurt them. All the really competent actors and actresses that Hollywood has stolen would just about fill a single play, and one with a cast of not more than eight players at that.

Let the producers and managers quit their yowling and experiment with some new and young players. Let them follow the plan that the movies, often with success, have followed in the same direction. That the new, young players often aren't any particular shakes as actors will not matter much more on the stage than it matters on the screen, as very few persons, including critics, know real acting when they see it. The Theatre Union has got away with murder in the way of new, young actors, and the Group Theatre, in the same way, has got away at least with manslaughter. The Theatre Guild built up its reputation at the beginning with some new, young players who knew less than nothing about acting, but who nevertheless got by all right. And the Civic Repertory Theatre of Eva Le Gallienne drew wonderful press notices with a set of obscure players who would have made even Corse Payton laugh. The difficulty lies not in the good casting of plays, but in the finding of good plays to cast.

If the managers and producers are right and if we are wrong and if the movies are actually a hidden gold-mine of available actors for the casting of plays, let us consider some of the more recent instances where the stage has drawn on Hollywood for players — and let us see what happened. Rod La Rocque was called to play *Domino,* was greeted with derision, and the play was packed off promptly to the storehouse. Miriam Hopkins failed to do anything with or in *Jezebel*, and Katharine Hepburn was a dismal failure in *The Lake*. James Kirkwood got nowhere in *House of Remsen*, and the piece in which Bebe Daniels and Ben Lyons appeared wasn't even brought within hailing distance of Broadway. Melvyn Douglas and *Mother Lode* collapsed forthwith and Herbert Yost, Lila Lee and Herbert Rawlinson did nothing for the several plays they came back from Hollywood to help out. Peggy Shannon in *Page Miss Glory*, Conway Tearle in *Living Dangerously*, Lillian Bond in *Little Shot*, Eric Linden in *Ladies' Money*, Joseph Schildkraut in *Between Two Worlds* and *Tomorrow's A Holiday*, and Robert T. Haines in *Allure* didn't cause either the reviewers or the few paying customers to hurry their entr'-acte drinks in the adjacent taprooms, and Frank Shannon in *Geraniums in My Window*, Louis Calhern in *Birthday*, Hedda Hopper in *Divided By Three*, Vivienne Osborne and Tala Birell in *Order Please*, Alan Dinehart and Mozelle Britonne in *Alley Cat*, Philippe de Lacy in *Strangers at Home* and Jean Arthur in *The Bride of Torozko* disturbed only the slumbers of the watchman at Cain's warehouse.

Olga Baclanova in *Mahogany Hall* registered zero. Montagu Love as Jakob Eisner in *Birthright* was a howl. Conrad Nagel was something more than an alexipyretic in *The First Apple*. Robert Gleckler, one of Hollywood's favorite tough-mugg actors, fell flat in *The Drums Begin*.

Guy Bates Post as Professor Fritz Opal in *The Shatter'd Lamp* was plain ham. And Claude Rains has been getting progressively worse and worse on his periodic returns to the stage.

The day that they bring on Garbo and Gary Cooper as a Lunt-Fontanne combination, Joan Crawford to understudy Ina Claire, and Warner Baxter to play some of John Drew's old rôles, or even Walter Hampden's, I resign.

Myth

If a producer puts on a funny and successful play about this or that subject, all the other producers firmly conclude that any other funny play on the same subject will not stand much of an immediate chance, owing to the fact that it will be called an imitation and to the further notion that the public is temporarily satisfied with one such exhibit. The producers consequently produce only follow-ups of unsuccessful unfunny plays, as witness the succession in late seasons of dismal radio lampoons, all quickly interred in the storehouse. A really funny play, however, may easily and prosperously be followed by any number of other funny plays on exactly the same subject. The subject matter has nothing to do with it. A. H. Woods some years ago made a mint of money putting on exactly the same comedy about a girl and a bed season after season (sometimes, indeed, two or three times a season) and merely changing the bed into a chaise-longue or a hayloft.

Audiences do not care what they laugh at so long as they laugh. There are no so-called definite cycles for laughter. Thus, *Once In a Lifetime* no more spoiled the chances of *Personal Appearance* than *Personal Appearance* spoiled those of *Boy Meets Girl,* though all of them were Hollywood travesties. What is more, if all three were produced on successive nights, all three would doubtless succeed just as happily.

Shakespeare

There seem to be two favorite production ways to approach Shakespeare. One is to depart from theatrical tradition so greatly that he becomes indistinguishable from Percy MacKaye turned Harry Thaw, and the other to be so professorially cuddling to him that all the life is squeezed out of him. Obedience to the Bard is right and proper enough, but the obedience should not be that of a submissive slave but of a valiant soldier. Otherwise the result is the usual result of unimaginative humility and timorous acquiescence.

Erwin Piscator

Erwin Piscator belongs to the German producing school, exiled for still an additional reason by Hitler, which entertains the conviction that all you need for a really great theatre is, first, a stage director who can so alter a dramatist's manuscript that the dramatist has difficulty in recognizing it and, secondly, a scene designer and electrician who can so trickily embellish and illuminate it that the stage director himself has even more difficulty in recognizing his own handiwork on it.

M. Gest

It has always been Mr. Morris Gest's weakness as a producer that he gives such a good show before the opening-night curtain goes up on one of his productions that the show itself seems pretty weak in comparison. Morris' latest stage offering was Dr. S. I. Hsiung's *Lady Precious Stream,* a pleasant enough little Chinese paraphrase but one that suffered uncommonly from the preliminary performance of Morris and his press *agents provocateurs.* Morris seems never content to produce simply a play. He must, along with and ahead of it, produce a college course of instruction in the whole history of the drama of the particular play's nation, eight or ten big luncheons and banquets in order to introduce the author to Thomas W. Lamont, Johnny Weaver and Beatrice Lillie, a ball at the Waldorf-Astoria with everybody dressed in the costumes of the play's period, a list of patrons and patronesses embracing everyone in the Social Register, the Directory of Directors and the charge account at Jack and Charlie's, a series of large photographs showing him kissing the arriving playwright at the steamship dock, and a fine letter from the President regretting his inability to attend the opening. In the wealth of such anterior circumstances, even *Hamlet* might subsequently seem a little phewy.

Aside from the big pier kissing photographs and the gala No. 7 banquet at which Dr. Hsiung, with Morris' friendly aid, enjoyed the great honor of sharing a specially prepared dish of *Apfelschmarrn mit Aprikosensauce,* to say nothing of some *Mürbeteig-törtchen mit frischen Erdbeeren und Sahne,* with such eminent Chinese scholars as Hiram Bloomingdale, Tallulah Bankhead and Congressman Dickstein, the most fetching item in the prefatory ceremonies was Morris' public educational course in the Chinese drama, conducted by Dr. Hsiung and the quorum of press-agents. *Lady Precious Stream* being a play of the regulation two-hour length and with its Chinese authenticity accordingly in some doubt on the part of Westerners whose conviction it is that a Chinese play usually begins at noon on Washington's Birthday and lasts until two o'clock in the morning of the Fourth of July, Morris prevailed upon Dr. Hsiung, who must be an ingratiatingly easy gentleman, to salve the situation and at the same time placate the doubts of the criticians. Mounting the platform, Dr. Hsiung (with Morris hidden in his cutaway tails) issued the following proclamation: "This is a mistaken idea! A Chinese play is no longer than a Western one — seldom longer than *Strange Interlude* and *never* longer than *Back to Methuselah.*"

As a born and bred Chinaman out of Fort Wayne, Indiana, I hope I do not unduly pain my august Chinese colleague, Dr. Hsiung, when I say *lichee,* or in other words, nuts. At Morris' behest, the Dr. talked through his hat. While it is true that certain recent-day Chinese plays, all poor imitations and cuckooings of the modern European drama at its shabbiest, are not unduly long plays, the older and authentic Chinese drama, as everyone pretty well knows, makes *Strange Interlude* and even *Back to Methuselah* look like a couple of curtain-raisers. Even when this drama is very liberally cut, as it generally is in modern days, it runs — as any visitor to one of the permanent theatres in Hong Kong, say, will find — from eleven in the morning, with but a short intermission, until midnight. Dr. Hsiung, who, incidentally, is a very humble figure in present-day Chinese letters, of course knows all this as well as you or I, but he should take Morris and his press-agents aside and, out of hearing of the deluded public and critics, instruct them privately in the length differences of the Cheng-Pan, or historical, Chu-Ton, or domestic, and Ku-Wei, or farce, drama.

Morris has something else wrong with him. Give him a play from the Icelandic, for example, and it is a dollar to a slug that he will cast the leading Icelandic woman's rôle with someone like Anna May Wong or Josephine Baker. When he introduced the Russian Ballet to America some years ago, he engaged the Winter Garden hoofer, Gertrude Hoffman, no less, for the leading ballerina rôle. And now, with a Chinese play, he hired for the leading rôle an American actress who had been appearing in Jane Austen's *Pride and Prejudice*. And all the time, close to his hand on the stage of his exhibit, there was beautifully available for

[133]

the rôle of his daughter of the House of Wang Yun the infinitely lovely, silver-stream spoken and most delicately graceful daughter of the Chinese ambassador at Washington, Miss Mai-Mai Sze.

The Theatre Guild

It is the only too clearly observable intention of the once finely ambitious and hopefully experimental Theatre Guild to play more or less safe in the future by having recourse to the old-time star system. It is rumored that the Guild was not any too fortunate in making money with many of its productions in the two seasons preceding this last and this circumstance, combined with the unmistakable influence of the Hollywood philosophy upon several members of its board of directors, has undoubtedly propelled it toward the decision in question.

With Alfred Lunt now added to its directorate by way of making certain not again to lose the profitable Lunt-Fontanne combination to some outside management, the Guild has indicated plainly the way its sails are heading. It abandoned Robert Turney's worthy *Daughters of Atreus* as one of its last season's productions in favor of the Lunt-Fontanne starring team in their second venture in the same season, to wit, Sherwood's *Idiot's Delight*. It has signed Miss Ina Claire to a contract running for a number of years, and with a guarantee of twenty weeks a season, and it last season placed her at the head of one starring venture and, when that failed, at the head of another in the same season, to wit, Behrman's *End of Summer*. It abandoned its option on *Winterset*, of all scripts, and on such commendable experiments as Tilman Breiseth's *As We Forgive Our Debtors* and other manuscripts by young American playwrights to offer, instead, Philip Merivale and Miss Gladys Cooper as a starring combination in a snide English script, *Call It a Day*, by the author of *Autumn Crocus*, that august Piccadilly art work. It is praying that Miss Helen Hayes will return to the Guild fold, to add to its starring force, and it has its hooks out for other stars for this season.

All this is sad news. One had hoped, often against hope, that the Theatre Guild would continue as one of our more exploratory, independent and more or less uncommercial American producing organizations, and that it would devote itself, at least in part, to reputable new American dramatic manuscripts, whether they called for star actors and actresses or not. But one begins to despair. Aside from the O'Neill plays, which are generally no longer in the field of commercial experiment, and save perhaps for a face-saving gamble at rare intervals, all that we are apparently to expect from the Guild in the future are echoes of the old Frohman and current Louis B. Mayer star-spangled showmanship and the drama appropriate thereunto. When the Guild imported Elisabeth Bergner in association with Charles B. Cochran it first publicly took off its falseface and revealed itself in its true commercial whiskers. And now that it has, with *Call It a Day*, gone into business partnership with Lee Shubert and Lee Ephraim, it has taken off its pants.

Something appears to be wrong with the Guild internally and the malaise threatens, unless soon and fortunately checked, most unhappy consequences. As a sympathetic critical physician, I venture without fee and solely in the interests of the Guild's future physical well-being a diagnosis of the aforesaid malaise — and leave it to the patient to figure out its own cure.

The first and most dangerous schizomycetic organism lately infecting the Guild is the bacillus *canalis capsulatus,* more commonly known as the Hollywood bug. Three of the original six executive directors of the organization have already, at least for a spell, suffered from its effects. Miss Theresa Helburn, the Guild's head and shoulders, last year signed a contract with the moving picture people that kept her in Hollywood for something like six months, thus practically making her association with the Guild only a part-time job, and one presumably of secondary consideration. Philip Moeller, the Guild's best stage director, who has already capitulated to Hollywood to the extent of at least two motion pictures, asserts his enthusiasm for the great Chloroformia art center and has confided to his friends, they tell me, that he is itching to get back and devote at least a share of his energies to making the world safe for illiteracy. And Miss Helen Westley, one of the Guild's forthright board intelligences and one of its most telling actresses, has lately been spending most of her time on the Hollywood lots, three thousand miles removed from the Guild playhouse and the art of the drama.

With this valuable trio straddling Hollywood and Fifty-second street, be it actually or only emotionally, who are the three other directors upon whom the Guild enterprise must in major part lean? One, Lawrence Langner, who has not yet cinematized himself, in recent seasons has shown an increasing interest in affairs theatrical divorced from the Guild. His operation of the summer theatre at Westport, Connecticut, true enough, hardly interferes with his Guild concerns, as it consumes time that does not much conflict with his Guild time. But his personal attempts at playwriting, together with his independent productions and his associations with outside producers of his own work — producers who have no connection whatsoever with the Guild or with what are held to be the Guild's aims — assuredly, and quite naturally, must rob the Guild of his fullest fealty. Certainly his independent production in the last few years of *The Sidewalks of New York, Chrysalis, The Bride the Sun Shines On* and *Die Fledermaus,* the outside productions of his own *The Pursuit of Happiness* by Laurence Rivers, Inc. and *On To Fortune* by Crosby Gaige, his writing of still other plays, and his mothering of plays originally produced in his Westport theatre and subsequently brought into the Broadway theatres, intrude seriously upon his Guild enthusiasms.

We thus have but two remaining figures of the original

Guild supervising sextette who still support the Guild singly, seriously and undividedly: Lee Simonson, who does the scenery for certain of its productions, and Maurice Wertheim, a banker who looks after its finances. Both are proficient men, but what of the future of a dramatic organization of some ideals that must rely most greatly for its internal artistic health upon a scene designer, however talented, and a business man, however gifted a financial squire?

That the confusion resulting from the peculiar diversity of such recent interests as those noted has doubly confused the selection of plays for Guild presentation has lately been made sombrely evident, as it is to be remembered that the plays are selected by a vote of the aforementioned six members of the governing board — Lunt's ballot now added — and as it is also to be remembered that, in the event no unanimous decision on a recommended manuscript can be arrived at, a compromise must be reached on some other and lesser one in order to give the subscribers their guarantee of six new productions each season. It is unquestionably this compromise arrangement that has resulted in the puzzling oddity of numerous Guild choices. And it is unquestionably a falling-off in the directors' old wholehearted and vigorous concern for the Guild's welfare that has similarly resulted in a wearily unanimous approval of certain manuscripts that in other days would have been more harshly dealt with. How, otherwise, in both instances, are we in the last few seasons to account for the approved acceptance or the production of such things as Bruckner's *Races,* Denis Johnston's *Storm Song, The School For Husbands* (written in part by a member of the Guild's board, despite an original Guild rule that no plays by Guild directors would be produced by the Guild), Dawn Powell's *Jigsaw,* John Haynes Holmes' *If This Be Treason,* Fodor's *Love Is Like That,* an Owen Davis dramatization of a Pearl Buck best-seller, George O'Neil's *American Dream* (which, after agreeing upon the manuscript, the Guild subsequently had to play backwards!), and Bridie's *A Sleeping Clergyman?* How, too, are we to figure out the failure either to accept for production or in one way or another enterprisingly to get hold of such plays, produced elsewhere in the same period, as *Winterset, The Children's Hour, Within the Gates, Men in White, The Green Bay Tree, Tobacco Road, Richard of Bordeaux, Stevedore, Yellow Jack, The House of Connolly* and a half dozen others all of much greater merit — at least relatively — than much of the stuff half-heartedly produced by the Guild? How, finally, are we to account otherwise for the desperate last minute taking over of the Messrs. Selwyn's and Franklin's booking of the Charles Cochran production of *Escape Me Never,* and the sudden affiliation with the Messrs. Shubert and Ephraim?

It is clear that the Guild has a problem on its hands that calls for some quick thinking if it is to continue in its older tradition and flourish reputably. Let it, in this, its apparent pickle, deeply ponder the fate of a somewhat similar organization, the present Abbey Theatre, and reflect what has happened to it under somewhat similar circumstances. The Abbey, like the Guild, has lost a number of its outstanding and most successful players. The Abbey has found that, with the dispersal of its original guardians' interests, it has had to rely for direction upon a relatively minor talent within its playwriting and directorial ranks. The Guild may soon find itself in the same position. The Abbey, like the Guild, furthermore, due to internal differences of opinion has had to compromise upon certain second- and third-rate plays and to dismiss such available manuscripts as Padraic Colum's *Thomas Muskerry* and *Grasshopper,* Lady Gregory's *Aristotle's Bellows,* and the work of Dunsany in favor of such things as Brinsley Macnamara's *Look At the Heffernans* and Lennox Robinson's *Church Street.* And the Abbey Theatre, as a consequence, has come to be but a decrepit and pitiable ghost of its original self. Let us hope that the Theatre Guild will not follow suit.

CHAPTER VII

New York

Give Your Regard to Broadway

Picture a great boulevard whose million dazzling lights outshine the stars of night and evening, whose gay restaurants and brilliant theatres are crowded with celebrities in the world of fashion, *belles lettres* and public affairs, whose glittering hotel lobbies are thronged with distinguished men and women from the four corners of the earth. Picture a great thoroughfare gleaming with the sheen of countless Hispanos and Rolls-Royces, its large, attractive shops and window displays the envy of merchants from the thitherward towns and cities, its life, by day as by night, a veritable merry-go-round of glamourous activity. Picture the most romantic street in all America, the most electric highway in all the metropolises of Christendom, the street, in short, of streets. And then open your eyes, wake up, and fall with a loud thud out of bed.

Fiction and legend, working their wicked will upon those innocents living in the farther reaches of the land, have converted what is one of the ugliest, cheapest and most thoroughly unromantic streets in the whole world into a *luxe* avenue of fairyland. In order to give you its true, unvarnished and realistically accurate picture, I herewith escort you, block by block, through that part of it — the best known and most typically Broadway part — which extends from Forty-second to Forty-seventh streets.

We will move, first, on the east side of the street. In the first block, from Forty-second to Forty-third streets, we successively find a small United cigar store, a little store selling cheap shirts, a diminutive Fanny Farmer candy shop, a cheap shoe store, the once famous George M. Cohan theatre now a movie " grind " house showing stale fourth-run pictures for from ten to twenty-five cents, a Coney Island orange drink and nuts stand, a sixty-nine cent shirt sale, a dwarfed hat store, and Gray's drugstore, where cut-rate tickets for unsuccessful plays are handled.

Between Forty-third and Forty-fourth streets, we encounter a Schulte cigar store, a little shop where you may have your photograph snapped for a dime, a dinky store selling forty-seven cent women's stockings, another cheap haberdashery, a Mirror candy store, a cheap cafeteria, a theatre ticket speculator's stall one side of which offers for sale cheap jewelry, a sixty-nine cent women's stocking sale, an upstairs chop suey dance hall (Chin's) with a dinner costing eighty-five cents, another cheap cafeteria, a small haberdashery offering ties at fifty-five cents and shirts at a dollar, a shoe repair booth, and a Nedick orange stand.

In the next block, between Forty-fourth and Forty-fifth streets, where once stood the Criterion theatre, home of many celebrated Frohman stars, and — adjoining it — the New York, scene of great theatrical triumphs and on the roof of which Ziegfeld first displayed his famous *Follies,* we now lay eyes on a two-story tax-payer movie house fronted by puny little merchandise shops.

From Forty-fifth to Forty-sixth streets, we pass in succession a small cigar store with a cheap lunch counter, another sixty-nine cent women's stocking shop, a skimpy men's hat store, Loew's State theatre, covered with flashy posters and showing small-time vaudeville acts and second-run movies, a jitney millinery shop and a jitney jewelry shop, a sale of women's dresses at $1.98, a cut-rate drugstore, a Childs restaurant, a cheap cafeteria (the Silver Dollar), Simpson's pawn shop, and another orange drink stand.

Across the street, from Forty-sixth to Forty-seventh, I escort you past an I. Miller shoe store, another sale of cheap dresses, a sale of " jewelry " with gems priced from nine cents up, a sale of twenty-five dollar men's suits, a nut stand, a news-reel theatre (admission a quarter), a B-and-G sandwich shop, the once famous Palace theatre, the greatest of vaudeville theatres, now a second- and third-run movie " grind " house, and a Whelan cut-rate drug store.

We are now at the top of what is known as Longacre Square. The once romantic Longacre Square, at this particular and most thrilling point, consists today of a men's and a women's toilet, a triangular plot of concrete peopled day and night by disreputable tramps and bums in collarless disarray, a news-stand, and — across the way — four scrubby two-by-four stores: one selling men's hats for a dollar, another selling cheap pink lingerie, a third offering cheap millinery, and the fourth another men's hat emporium.

We cross to the west side of Broadway. Moving back downtown in the block between Forty-seventh and Forty-sixth streets, we have a Florsheim shoe store, a small movie house showing two-year-old films, a cafeteria, next door to which is an Automat restaurant, the famous old Globe theatre, once the home of the late Charles Dillingham's brilliant musical comedies and now a cheap movie house — it also covered with flashy posters, and, at the corner, another Childs restaurant.

Between Forty-sixth and Forty-fifth streets I have the honor to point out to you, in succession, a small cigar store, an orange drink stand, a shabby " burlesk " theatre (once the celebrated Gaiety, where Klaw and Erlanger held forth), a stunted hat store, a hole-in-the-wall selling sheet music and cheap " novelties," a pigmy haberdashery, a " Fudge Shoppe," a cramped room where an " auction " of nondescript articles is loudly going on, a shop offering " Doughnuts and Coffee, 10¢," the once proud Astor theatre, home of Wagenhals and Kemper productions, now serving as an inferior movie parlor, a theatre ticket agency, and a store in which a doughnut machine is demonstrated.

The Astor hotel occupies the block between Forty-fifth and Forty-fourth streets and is fronted by the following: a cut-rate drugstore, another sixty-nine cent women's stocking sale, a small men's hat store (hats at $2.50), an undersized flower shop, a $1.65 shirt sale, another little hat store, a small women's dress shop, and the Astor cafeteria.

Across the street — between Forty-fourth and Forty-third streets — you find yourselves enchanted successively by a Walgreen cut-rate drugstore, its windows full of ninety-eight cent alarm clocks and twenty-nine cent toy pistols, another Childs restaurant, a one-dollar shirt sale, a sale of low-priced women's hats, a cut-rate chain book store, another hat shop, the Paramount movie theatre plastered with Coney Island signs and fronted by a loud Coney Island barker, and a theatre ticket agency. This, on the whole and in the aggregate, is the visible part of the Paramount Building, of which you have heard much.

Once again crossing the street and strolling from Forty-third to Forty-second streets your eyes are massaged by still another cafeteria, another catchpenny " auction," a Chinese restaurant (dinner fifty-five cents), another Childs, another nut stand, and another second-rate movie house.

There, my deluded hearties, is the main section of beautiful, glamourous Broadway, the street of song and story!

Many of the gimcrack buildings that we have passed are only two or three stories high, some of them but one story high. The sidewalks in each block reveal several small soap-boxes which serve as newspaper stands, and there are two or three vendors of ten-cent " novelties," to say nothing of six or seven beggars, to each block. Chinatown sight-seeing buses, with barkers ballyhooing the wonders of a Chinatown that passed completely at least a decade ago and each containing bait in the shape of a couple of bedizened women to inveigle the male sucker trade, stand at various corners. And soiled Fords, full of the élite of the Bronx, congest the traffic.

Broadway in its other aspects, that is, below Forty-second street and above Forty-seventh, is not much different. Below Forty-second, it is indistinguishable from almost any second-rate business street in any sizable American city. The same kind of small shops and stores, without variation. Only the dirty Metropolitan Opera House at Fortieth street and the Empire theatre across the way to break the monotony of cafeterias, clothing stores and cheap lingerie booths. The Empire, incidentally, is the sole remaining recognized legitimate theatre on the entire length of Broadway. All the others have been torn down, or are closed, or have gone over to second, third and fourth run movies, or are in receivers' hands. Wallack's, Daly's, the Weber and Fields Music Hall, the Bijou, the Knickerbocker and the Casino have long since passed out of existence. The Criterion and the New York are no more. The Astor, Globe and Centre have gone over to the movies, as noted. The Gaiety is now a mean burlesque

house. The Manhattan, which became the home of a jazz
night club, is in the hands of the WPA. And only the
Winter Garden remains available for musical shows.

On all Broadway today, from Thirty-fourth street on
the south to Fifty-ninth on the north, there is not a single
first-class restaurant. As to hotels, the Astor is the only
remaining one of even the slightest pretension. The rest
are either gone or have become identical with the average
small town hotel.

From Forty-seventh street northward, Broadway is
practically a duplicate of that part of it which extends
from Forty-second street to Forty-seventh street and which
has been described. In this upper section are found much
the same paltry shops, peewee stores, delicatessen restaurants, orange drink stands, cheap lunch counters and so
on that we encounter in the other section. The Capitol and
Rivoli movie houses, along with the Strand, all plastered
with honky-tonk advertisements, are surrounded by a
welter of chop suey parlors, cheap little dance halls (each
advertising fifty or one hundred " beautiful hostesses "
and disclosing to the curious nine or ten pathetic and
frowsy females), Brass Rail feederies, shooting galleries,
snapshot booths, and quick lunch rooms. Upstairs at the
corner of Forty-eighth street and upstairs at the corner of
Forty-ninth are the Hollywood and Paradise restaurants
respectively, the features of which, aside from the intermittent appearance of a blues singer or a fan dancer, are
floor shows consisting of peroxide hussies in various stages

[147]

of undress, and all, always, going through exactly the same venerable chorus girl routine.

The widely heralded electrical display of Broadway by night is noteworthy chiefly for its consuming ugliness. G. K. Chesterton once remarked that it wouldn't be so bad if you couldn't read, but even that is doubtful. Just how a lot of badly mixed green, yellow, red, orange, lavendar and white electric bulbs assembled to spell out the name of a chewing gum suddenly become relatively beautiful if you dismiss the name of the chewing gum, or whatever the advertised commodity may be, is a problem in æsthetics that evades the penetration of this particular professor. What adds further to the eyesore quality of the electric signs is the philosophical theory of the people who pay for them that, if the names of the commodities move, the signs become even more attractive and even more lovely than if the names stand still. You are thus entertained and presumably enchanted by several dozen multicolored electrical advertisements which resemble nothing quite so much as the back advertising section of a magazine which has been printed in an Easter egg dye factory, has been seized with delirium tremens, and has been placed on sale on newsstands in an earthquake belt.

In the Broadway of today there is no touch nor hint of the Broadway of yesterday. There is no faintest equivalent of Rector's, that gala supper restaurant of other years where the world of fashion and sport was wont to forgather in an atmosphere of truffles and champagne.

Truffles have disappeared from Broadway altogether and beer and bad gin have substituted for champagne. The place of Rector's has been taken by Childs and the Automat. There is no faintest equivalent of Browne's, that celebrated chop house where the world of journalism and the theatre gathered. Its place has been taken by Lindy's delicatessen. You will find no Considine's, where once the heroes of the ring and turf convened, no Knickerbocker bar with its King Cole panel, where the wits of the town congregated, no Churchill's, presided over by a former popular captain of police, where until early dawn newspaper and magazine headliners sat quietly and at ease and settled all the problems of the cosmos. There is no longer a theatre "carriage trade," resplendent in jewels and furs and top hats, on Broadway, because there are, aside from a single remaining dramatic theatre and a single remaining musical theatre, no theatres. There is little or no so-called night life because all the better night clubs, dance places and supper restaurants have long since moved over to the east side of the city. There are, during the height of the season, few fine automobiles to be seen by night because the traffic regulations forbid Broadway turns and because the automobiles, carrying their gay occupants, have to move through the side streets either west from Sixth avenue or east from Eighth.

So common and vulgar has Broadway become that various owners of property on the street not long ago held a meeting to see if ways and means might not be arrived at to get rid, at least in a measure, of its growing Coney Island atmosphere. But the ways and means have apparently proved baffling and the Coney Island look and smell grow apace. The sound of tin pianos echoes out of twopenny-halfpenny music stores, the smell of frankfurters and hamburgers exudes from dinky lunch counters, the hoarse, loud voices of sightseeing bus steerers and movie parlor ballyhooers are heard in every block, panhandlers crowd the pavements, scrubby orange and pineapple drink stands abound, and the clamor of jitney jazz orchestras comes down the stairs and through the upper windows of taxi dance halls.

From Thirty-fourth street to Columbus Circle, poor, down-at-the-heel, pathetic remnants of manhood seek to earn a livelihood soliciting five-cent shoe shines, their home-made bootblack kits under their arms. Blind beggars, many of them long since unmasked as frauds, still tap their canes along the sidewalks and drone their appeal for coins. Peddlers of handbills bump and jostle the passers-by. And the riff-raff of the town litters the thoroughfare, for all the vain efforts of the street cleaning department, with cigar and cigarette butts, banana peels, bits of paper, peanut shells, sandwich ends, and junk generally.

Despite its pretentions to metropolitanism, the Broadway of today is essentially and encompassingly hick. Let one of the larger moving picture theatres, at the showing of a new film, put a couple of flood-lights atop its marquee and shine up the street a little and a large crowd will gather for hours. Let a man with a telescope — there are usually four or five in evidence — advertise a peep at the tower of the Empire State building for ten cents and the telescope will soon be worn out by peering customers. Let it be heralded in the newspapers that some second-rate celebrity will attend this or that establishment on a certain night and a mob of half-wits, most of them with autograph books, will descend upon the scene. A calliope covered with placards advertising something or other and tooting an old circus tune will congeal traffic, and a small Negro boy executing a *pas seul* on the sidewalk will force a policeman to clear a path for pedestrians.

You have heard, doubtless, about the brilliant Broadway theatrical first nights and about the brilliant movie openings. Inasmuch as only two non-movie theatres remain open on Broadway, as I have pointed out, first nights of any kind, whether brilliant or not brilliant, are a Broadway rarity. What is more, the Empire premières, which years ago had color and a certain dazzle, have in recent years been more or less commonplace affairs. Now and then, when a producer like Gilbert Miller is in charge of the proceedings, a touch of the old color comes back. But more often than not the productions — many of them speedy failures — attract a desultory and routine audience, wholly undistinguished in every particular. And openings at the Winter Garden are not much different.

Even in the theatres in the streets off Broadway the

brilliant first-night audience has become a slice of fiction. The late Charles Frohman once remarked that, if he could have his way about it, he would always open his plays on the second night. Since that was more than twenty-five years ago the disparagement of the mentality and manners of the present-day first-night audiences is nothing startlingly novel. But although it isn't novel it is doubtless even more loudly called for than it was in the Frohman era, when the European dramatic art that the enterprising Charles imported found its initial performances faced by a jury composed in large part of such outstanding connoisseurs of the higher æsthetic as skirt-chasing wine agents, shyster lawyers, ladies who didn't find it necessary to pay their own rent, and the more indefatigable customers of the Holland House bar.

Just why the theatre should alone and almost invariably be the patsy whenever it throws its doors open on a new adventure is something of a riddle. Certainly no other institution suffers in the same way. When a baseball park opens on a new performance it naturally attracts lovers of baseball. When a church offers a new visiting man of God it naturally attracts persons more or less interested in the heavenly arts. And so with all other pursuits. But when a theatre puts on a new drama it seems to attract far fewer persons interested in drama than in making elaborate monkeys of themselves. The present first-night audiences thus continue to resemble in the aggregate nothing quite so much as a zoo, minus only the peanuts and a small measure

[152]

of the smell. These audiences do not go to determine what effect a play has on them but to determine what effect they have on the play, and to demonstrate it in such a loud, vulgar and generally offensive manner that the more sensitive and intelligent ushers promptly consider throwing up their ignominious jobs and entering the somewhat more delicate and less self-insulting profession of sewer repairing.

With negligible exception, what are the constituent elements of the New York first-night congress? Eliminate the professional reviewers and a few honest drama-lovers who always impress one as having got in by accident and who don't seem to belong, and you behold a group infinitely better suited to the consideration and judgment of Asbury Park bathing beauty contests, Paris peep shows and night club floor-shows than of drama in any form. There are Broadway hangers-on, resplendent in the latest haberdashery fashions inaugurated by delicatessen restaurant Brummels; members of the pseudo-*haut monde,* full of cocktails, audible chatter and impatience to get the play over with that they may not lose any valuable time in getting to the latest thing in night clubs and more liquor; moving picture scouts loftily derogating any kind of play that can't be converted into Hollywood gold; indeterminate females, dressed up like floats in a New Orleans Mardi Gras parade and hopefully employing the poor dramatist's occasion as a means to horn themselves in on anything that promises a sufficient financial return, whether theatrical, radio, cinema, or amorous; celebrity chasers and demi-celebrities who crave public notice; booking agents and "artists' representatives" with eyes alert for new suckers among the lesser actors and actresses present; rival managers and producers, momentarily down on their luck and muttering sour cracks at the expense of the playwright and his impresario; and any number of other such doses of malignant variola. In such as these does the fate of a new play largely repose. Upon such as these does the immediate future of the American theatre rest.

It is the common habit to allude to this first-night audience as the death watch. The allusion is faulty. It constitutes a wake. It presupposes the corpse and devotes itself to having itself a high old time. It is its own show, which it hugely enjoys, whatever the nature of the show on the stage. It — not the play — is, in its own consideration and actions, the show of the evening.

There are persons who protest that you can never truly generalize about anything. Such persons believe that there is something violently defective in any argument that contends that all dimes are round, that all water is wet, and that the binding on all derbies gets shiny much quicker than it should. To these the above generalization about New York first-night audiences is idiotic. There are, as has been hinted, mild exceptions, but in the main those audiences fit snugly into the picture frame. Down in Fourteenth street, where the art of the drama is considered woefully deficient unless it contains at least two bombs and three ringing tributes to Communism, along with one nostalgic reference to the superiority of the beds in Moscow boarding-houses to those at the Ritz, the first-night audiences may be, and are, quite different. And up in Fifty-second street, where the Theatre Guild makes its pretensions to Kultur and where a torturingly wearisome play by George Bernard Shaw is considered to constitute much more praiseworthy dramatic art than a vastly amusing one by George M. Cohan, the first-night gathering may be, and is, also quite different. But up and down Broadway and in and out of the theatre of Broadway the first-night audience is precisely the mob of pathetic hanswursts and obstreperous mountebanks that it has been described to be. Its taste is the taste of half-wits; its manners are the manners of bounders; its intelligence is the intelligence of shoe clerks; and its smell, despite all its expensive perfumes of Arabia, is the smell of dead and dying brains. It is the fatal curse that our managers and producers, in their carelessness and lack of foresight, have laid upon themselves, upon the drama, and upon the American theatre. It is but another item in the book of a debased Broadway that, in its entirety, calls for a covering of chloride of lime or, better still, a quick vermin extinguisher.

As for the brilliant movie openings they, too, are of the stuff of fairy tales. Perhaps not more than two or three times in an entire year are the flood-lights hereinbefore alluded to put up to signalize a theoretically gala event. The new movies pretty generally open up shop at ten o'clock in the morning and their premières are accordingly attended mainly by stragglers of one sort or another, the house being not more than one-quarter or one-eighth full.

The typical Broadway crowd, presumably a gay and sporting lot, is similarly a figment of the imagination. It is made up almost in its entirety of small merchants, vaudeville actors out of jobs, sightseers from the smaller suburban towns, nondescript, styptic females, panhandlers, racing hand-book weasels, operators of so-called " concessions," professional loafers and other such specimens of unpicturesque humanity. Its habit of congregating at street corners has become so disruptive of sidewalk movement that a police ordinance has had to be put into force making it a misdemeanor. But even so, such corners as Forty-seventh street still resemble cattle chutes.

Herald Square, once the diocese of the younger James Gordon Bennett and the publishing center of his famous journal, now sees the old Bennett duplicate of a Venetian palace occupied by a clothing store. Times Square, once the home of the New York *Times,* has seen its flatiron structure given over to a drugstore and small business offices, for the *Times* has moved away from Broadway into a side-street. Columbus Circle, quondam scene of bright theatres and flashing cafés, is now a desolate ring housing cafeterias and chop suey restaurants. One by one all the old landmarks disappear, or suffer a sorry conversion. The Broadway of Frohman and Dillingham, of George Kessler and

Diamond Jim Brady, of Richard Harding Davis and Fox-hall Keene and James Regan, of Weber and Fields and Finley Peter Dunne and Nicholas Biddle, of Jim Corbett and Tod Sloane, of Lillian Russell and Irene Castle and Lillian Lorraine has passed into the shadows. Linoleum in quick-lunch joints has supplanted the deep red carpets of leisurely dinner and supper places, and chow mein signs have been substituted for the old-time green griffins, signifying the realization of gourmets' dreams.

George M. Cohan no longer sings *Give My Regards To Broadway,* no longer dolorously laments that he is *Forty-five Minutes From Broadway.* No new Raymond Hitchcock sings proudly that he is *The Man Who Owns Broadway.* Even the omnipresent Jimmy Durante has stopped singing *Broadway, The Heart of the World,* and proclaiming, with lordly emphasis, " That's *my* Broadway! " Song writers no longer compose lyrics announcing that *The Stars Shine Brighter Over Broadway* and that *I'd Rather Be a Little Bulb On Broadway Than a Searchlight In Buff-a-lo.* Balladmongers no more melancholiously beseech their listeners to *Carry Me Back To Old Broadway.* Even the slogan, *The Great White Way,* has been dropped into the wastebasket.

Broadway is dead.

New York Goes Parisian

New York's attempt to put on a Parisian falseface has become increasingly evident in the last few years, to the disconcertment of the few remaining residents possessed of a lingering desire for happy comfort. The attempt takes on various forms, chief of which, perhaps, is the outdoor sidewalk café. In the recent warm months there were so many of these outdoor sidewalk cafés in New York that a civilized visiting Frenchman, accustomed in his native Paris to dining peacefully and quietly in a good old-fashioned cozy restaurant, had to search high and low for some place where he could eat without the distraction of overly affectionate pigeons, obtrusive newsboys, gasoline vapors, and several ounces of dust per course.

The sidewalk restaurant café is designed not so much to provide pleasure for its patrons as to provide amusement for the passing yokels. Just what added delight there is in eating one's *filet de bœuf Rossini* to the accompaniment of the stares of a lot of curious pedestrians up from Bleecker and East Houston streets eludes the perception of the savant. Yet so determined is New York to masquerade as a Continental city — in which determination it fools no one — that it is rapidly becoming almost impossible in the fair weather period to get a cup of consommé without discovering when it is half consumed that several leaves from nearby trees, to say nothing of a caterpillar, have fallen into it, or a cup of coffee that doesn't contain a Fifth Avenue bus transfer, a migratory bird's souvenir, and maybe a geranium.

The difference between most of the sidewalk cafés of Paris and the majority of the New York imitations, the local impresarios seem to fail to appreciate, is that in Paris they are generally merely stopping spots on the way to lunch or dinner, where a man may sip a Byrrh or a Dubonnet, whereas in New York they are offered as the main show. But so oafish is the New York public in its longing to identify itself, along with the *al fresco* establishments, as Continental that it will apparently suffer any inconvenience, from a mere passing chill to double pneumonia, for the theoretical great pleasure of having its drinks and meals on damp gravel or concrete — and off a table covered with dust, soot, stray fragments of the *Evening Journal,* ants, ladybugs and various species of worms.

The passion to be Continental has assailed at least three-quarters of the formerly dignified and intelligently conducted New York restaurants. The smallest Italian spaghetti joint, which erewhile was content to do its business in the bosom of the house, has taken the garbage-can out of the two-by-four backyard, hung up a paper Chinese lantern, installed a couple of tables and christened itself either a Venetian Garden or, if it is large enough to hold three tables, a Grand Venetian Garden. The little French restaurants in the side-streets have laid in a pair of small rubber plants, installed them at their doorways, placed a table behind each of them, and announced themselves on new awning signs to be so many Cafés de la Paix, Rôtisseries Périgourdine and Auberges du Vert Galant. Hotels like the Fifth Avenue, Brevoort, St. Moritz and dozens of others have succumbed to the prevailing itch and have moved the cab starter ten feet closer to the curb and filled in the intervening sidewalk space with boxed shrubs, tables and chairs. Even the little snack bars have put flower boxes in their vestibules, moved one of the tables out from the barroom and tried humbly to follow in the general monkey-business. Things have come to a pass, indeed, where summertime New York will shortly have to do all of its eating on the sidewalk and all of its walking in the dining-room.

The zeal to go Parisian in a big way does not, however, stop with the outdoor cafés. High stools have been installed at the indoor bars for women who imagine that it is vulgarly American to guzzle a glass of schnapps standing up but mysteriously Parisian and recherché to do the same thing sitting on a tall chair. The spectacle of ladies, still unused to the high stools, endeavoring nonchalantly to sip Sidecars and simultaneously juggle their cigarettes without tumbling off the stools is one of the present leading sources of amusement to visiting foreigners.

Then there are the so-called Frenchy cabaret and floor-shows. It is very difficult these days to discover a night club that doesn't offer a pale, carmine-lipped hussy in a tight-fitting black velvet gown who touchingly sings *Un Peu d'Amour* every time the lights go down and who sighs through *Parlez Moi d'Amour* every time they go up again. And it is equally hard to find a floor-show that doesn't try to evoke a Gallic atmosphere by trotting out a dozen or so semi-nude girls and causing them to sing something about

April in Paris or their overwhelming longing to get back to that gay Paree. One of the cabarets goes to the extent of heralding itself boldly as the French Casino and its show as the *Folies de Femmes,* living up to its name chiefly by trotting out similar semi-nude girls who sing about the chestnut blossoms in the Booze de Boloney and who conclude their performance with the regulation number of oo-la-las. For good measure, there is also an Apache dance. (The last Apache dance actually seen in Paris was in 1922.)

Thus far about the only non-Italian restaurants that haven't gone Parisian are Childs and the Automat, although the former have caused considerable trepidation by beginning to get a little Frenchy on their bills of fare. After that, it is only a short step to the singer in the black velvet dress.

In the matter of menus generally, almost all the old favorite American dishes have disappeared and have given way to French *pièces de résistance*. It has got to be so that you can't locate a dish of plain corned beef and cabbage or a steak with fried potatoes at more than a handful of places north of Fourteenth street. Bills of fare are solid masses of *châteaubriand, canard à la presse, foie de volaille en brochette, gigot, noisette d'agneau, ris de veau, aubergine* and *petits-pois*. Each restaurant employs an interpreter for its customers, the larger establishments sometimes as many as two or three. The waiters carry vest-pocket books of French-English translations for their own secret use. As a consequence, it often takes from two to two and a half hours to get through one's meal. This, however, is held forth as an added attraction as — according to the managements — it helps to contribute to the air of Continental leisure. Irish head-waiters in the men's chop houses have been made to decorate their necks with silver chains and thus have been metamorphosed into *sommeliers*. Hatcheck booths are presided over by old French women in black alpaca who understand no English save that printed on American money.

About the only thing in New York, in short, that hasn't gone French — as yet — is the German consulate.

CHAPTER VIII

The Mob S' Amuse

☙ ☙

Tastes in Diversion

There are people whose idea of rich amusement is to go to
a pleasure park, enter into the aperture of a large barrel,
have the barrel revolve rapidly and be made so dizzy that
they are no longer able to retain their balance and are dejected with painful thuds upon their respective behinds.
There are others whose idea consists rather in listening to
radio crooners tonsilizing psalms to the isle of Capri, the
Hawaiian moon and the amorous effect of smoke getting
into one's eyes. There are still others whose idea is wrapped
up with the movies and who experience an immense satisfaction in contemplating Mr. John Boles' moustache, Miss
Shirley Temple in turn contemplating Mr. John Boles'
moustache, and witticisms like " Thirty days hath Septem-
ber, April, June, and Kentucky." And there are others still
— eccentric as it may seem — whose idea of satisfactory
entertainment lies in going to the theatre and giving ear to
such prose as " A few more moments of time, and Spring'll
be dancing among us again; dancing in golden and purple
pavilions of laburnum and lilac; the birds'll be busy at

building small worlds of their own in the safe and snug breast of the hedges; the girls will go rambling around, all big with the thought of the life in the loins of the young men; but those who are gone shall sink into stillness, deep under the stillness that shelters the dead."

As you see, there is no accounting for tastes. What is one man's meat is another man's poison, and there is no good in waxing critically snooty about it and telling him that he should leave off corned beef and devote himself to caviar. If you did, he would probably retort — to his own perfect conviction — that, as one of his favorite screen comiques puts it, "Caviar is just buckshot covered with grease." Nevertheless, it is always a little difficult for me to understand why certain people are entertained by certain things that, in my own way of reaction, engender only an alarming scordinemia. And I should like someone to explain the phenomenon to me. It isn't always a matter of relative education and culture, as the professors like to assure us. Some of the most intelligent men in the world admire cheap detective fiction, and some of the most intelligent women admire men who admire cheap detective fiction. Gladstone's favorite form of diversion was trying to balance an egg on a toothpick, and Napoleon had a great penchant for cock-fights. Thomas Hardy disliked the theatre and went to it only if there was a leg-show on tap, and Woodrow Wilson had a particular passion for vaudeville shows, particularly German acrobats.

Nevertheless, as I say, I'd like to know why. While per-

sonally I can find no amusement, like Gladstone, in trying
to make an egg stand on a toothpick or, like Woodrow, in
German acrobats, I can still understand Hardy's pleasure
in leg-shows and Napoleon's in rooster bouts. And, at that,
not more than several million of my regular reading customers believe that I belong in a lunatic asylum. But why
anyone should derive more honest pleasure from looking
at a photographed version of a play, whether good or bad,
than at the play itself, or how, on the other hand, anyone
can get more æsthetic satisfaction in going to the theatre
and looking at a pie-faced actress who can't act than in
going to a movie and looking at a beautiful one who can't
act either, I wish some psychological doctor would take me
into his back parlor and tell me.

I don't wish to attitudinize as a superior mentality, but
it is my guess that the philosophical confusion about people's tastes results from mistaking the forms of entertainment they often indulge in for the forms which they actually admire. In addition, it must not be forgotten that a
person is constantly on the search for the kind of entertainment that will satisfy him and that the mere circumstance that he is often observed in the presence of trash indicates nothing more than that he has been defeated in his
search. It certainly doesn't indicate, despite his presence,
that he relishes the trash. If a lover of fine drama goes to
the theatre one hundred times and sees ninety contemptible plays for ten worthy ones, it doesn't mean that he has a
wonderful time at the ninety doses of rubbish.

Again, simply because a person goes to a moving picture showing Mr. Leslie Howard for thirty-five cents when Mr. Howard is playing in a theatre across the street for three dollars and eighty-five cents it doesn't necessarily signify that the person in question loves the movies and hates the theatre. It may conceivably simply signify that he hasn't got, or can't afford, the extra three dollars and fifty cents. Still again, if a man sits at home and listens to Amos 'n' Andy on the radio, it doesn't entirely argue that he wouldn't rather his wife didn't have to do all the cooking, that his eight children had shoes without holes in the soles, and that he himself might be downtown with three juleps under his shirt, sitting in a good orchestra seat and listening to Gilbert and Sullivan. We are sometimes entertained, so to speak, by what we are forced to rely upon and even suffer as entertainment.

The difference between people is that one class employs diversion to forget themselves and the other, an infinitely smaller class, employs it to remember themselves. The great majority of folk are unhappy and miserable and what they crave are means to take them, as the phrase is, out of themselves. Amusement in their case is an opiate, something to deaden their consciousness of their sad lot. The great minority of folk, on the other hand, which embraces the intelligent, the meditative, the philosophic and hence the relatively contented, seek in entertainment that which will give rebirth to and stimulate their finer emotions and finer reflections. The first class, accordingly, seek radio wise-cracks that evoke empty momentary laughs, Coney Island roller-coasters that turn their stomachs upside down, Frankenstein movies that scare them out of what may magnanimously be alluded to as their wits, tearful blues singers who make their own lots seem by contrast relatively merry, hot dogs with enough hot mustard on them to burn their tongues off, jazz bands that wreck their eardrums, and other such doses of psychic, mental and emotional hop. The second class seek the sentiments of noble drama, the rememorations of fine music, the stimulating solace of great literature, and the nostalgic pleasures in delicate vintage wines. Sometimes, true enough, there happens to be a dash of the one class of person in the other, which accounts for the simultaneous lover of Beethoven and S. S. Van Dine and the co-existent taste for Shakespeare and Laurel and Hardy. But that only adds to the puzzle of the whole question.

It is a well-known fact that two critics, both of them intelligent, experienced and sensitive, will at times disagree as to the merits of a certain play, piece of music, book, or what not. One will hold it first-rate, while the other will denounce it as second-rate, or even third-rate. One, accordingly, sees in it admirable and meritorious entertainment, whereas the other sees in it defective entertainment. Thus, considering the presumed equal intelligence of the two parties, the aforesaid puzzle becomes still deeper.

What, last year, did America vote tops in the way of

entertainment and amusement? The statistics disclose the following: a moving picture based on a novel for juveniles written in 1868; a novel of the Pollyanna type written by a semi-clergyman; a radio comedian whose act consists in a dialogue of rapid-fire wisecracks with his wife; a musical show about a timid comedian who is mistaken for a desperate gangster; and a prize-fight in which neither contender struck a blow hard enough to knock out even the late Tom Thumb. I refer, of course, to *Little Women, Green Light,* Jack Benny, *Anything Goes,* and the Braddock-Baer fight.

Night Clubs

One of the things most difficult for the layman who has the price of a pair of pajamas to comprehend is what pleasure people can find in sitting up in a night club until two o'clock in the morning listening to antiquated French-women singing of their yearning for love and looking at the hardboiled female offspring of naturalized Swedes, Polacks, Wops and Brooklynese walking around the floor clad only in brassières and diapers. Yet the statistics show that in New York, Chicago and the various other larger American cities, along with some of the smaller ones, something like two hundred thousand idiots nightly en-chant themselves by doing that very thing.

The night clubs, which a year or so ago suffered a marked decline, are now again doing a land-office busi-ness. And they are doing that bonanza business in spite of the fact that the entertainment they purvey continues to follow a pattern noteworthy only for its complete lack of variety and for its staleness. The same old duo or trio or quartet of " Boys," collectively naming themselves after some yacht club or fashionable suburb, retail the same old pseudo-naughty ditties about amorous dowagers, sugar papas, Turkish eunuchs, and the deposits of cows which are mistaken by young ladies from the city for chrysanthemums. And the same old masters of ceremonies periodically interrupt the general cobwebbed vaudeville with the same old intimate and theoretically slaying facetiæ about the pickaninny who that afternoon came up to the orchestra leader on the street and called him daddy and about the acute embarrassment of Mr. Rosenbloom (or Mr. Schultz, or whoever the best regular customer present happens to be) when he got home the night before, pulled his handkerchief out of his rear trouser pocket, and found that it was a pair of silk scanties.

The night club routine, save for an occasional new gown on the lady pianist who sings in a Flatbush-Dixie accent about the demure country miss from Mississippi who missed nothing the mister from Missouri had, year in and year out changes just about as much as the climate of the Mojave desert. The girls in the floor-shows still throw little white cotton balls at the ringside tables and the cut-ups at the tables throw them back again at the girls. The two comiques still retail the query, " Do you know Nance O'Neil? " along with the retort, " What's his first name? "

The couple known as Society's Favorite Dancers — there are no less than fifty or sixty of them — still negotiate the same old dreamy waltz, along with the galloping fox trot culminating in a dozen dizzy twirls. And you will have to search far and wide to discover an establishment whose band isn't led by a " Rhythm King."

For all the supreme banality of the night club stuff, however, its popularity, as noted, has spread to such a degree that even small restaurants and cafés in the side-streets which hope to capture some of the midnight trade have had to install some kind of analogous entertainment. It is thus next to impossible these days to locate a place where one can get a simple after-theatre liverwurst sand-wich unaccompanied by a clog dance on the part of a pair of darkeys, a blues singer's lamentations over the fact that love must one day wither and die, and a Bahama carioca danseuse.

The humorous lengths to which this mad catering to the public's passion for midnight amusement goes are borne in upon the student who makes even a cursory survey of night club topography. He will, taking New York as an example, discover in the lower reaches of the city an establishment called " Balyea's Dickens Room," presumably dedicated to the memory and art of the eminent literatus and relevantly featuring " Johnny and George, the Parisian Sensations." He will find " The Old Roumanian," down in Allen street and advertised as the East Side's pet night club, which offers as its chief

Roumanian feature a " Broadway spectacular revue." And he will even discover a night club, known as " The Holland Tavern," situated close to the Holland Tunnel, of all places.

In the larger and more expensive night clubs the entertainment is often made up of the same singers and dancers whom the patrons have seen not more than an hour before in the theatres they have just attended. The singers sing the same songs and the dancers dance the same dances that the patrons have dished out their money for earlier in the evening, but if you think that that makes any difference to the patrons you are mistaken. At least judging from their antics. The current most successful program for a night club appears to be one that the customers have just left in some other place. Some day a night club impresario will put on one that the customers have already seen *twice* before in the same evening and will make millions.

A standard act in night-clubdom is the accordionist. Usually dressed up to look like a chromatic chorus man in a beer garden performance of *The Bohemian Girl,* he moseys around the tables and, after a relatively *piano* rendition of Cole Porter's *Night and Day,* suddenly lets go the bellows with such a thunder-shake that all the glasses are knocked off the table into your lap and you yourself have to grab hold of the table to keep from being knocked to the floor. He is customarily followed by a platinum blonde in green velvet décolleté, a young thing of forty-two or thereabout, who after singing one song in the center of the room gradually edges her way to your table and, while vocalizing something about her overwhelming yen for a tall, handsome, dark, strong man, coyly fingers your back hair, thus hypothetically flattering your ego and driving you so crazy with joy that you forget all about the exorbitant cover charge and order up another chicken sandwich costing $2.50.

In the night clubs that go by Spanish or Argentine names the big kick is usually a brunet male in tight black satin breeches and with a spangled maroon cape insouciantly flung over his left shoulder. He is billed either as a world famous toreador or as the favorite matador of the late Queen of Spain. He is in his present job, it appears, because he was once gored in the thigh by a particularly ferocious bull and hence, because of the injury which impeded his movements, had to give up the bull-ring. So now he is a tango dancer.

The Tyrolean and Bavarian cabarets have even less variety, if that be possible, than any of the others. In all of them one encounters the same fat blond Germans in the same short leather pants, white shirts and green suspenders all yodeling hi-lee-hi-lo or playing zithers. The Negro night clubs annually change nothing but the name of the stellar naughty dance which, in itself, remains identical year after year. And the Russian cabarets haven't changed even the ventilation since they first opened up shop.

The whole night club panorama will in all probability look just the same ten years hence as it does today. There will be the same colored " Snake Hips," the same ladies and gents billed as " America's Foremost Ballroom Dancers," the same " Singing Boulevardiers," the same " Ambassadors of Fun," the same Hawaiian Trios dressed in red and white blouses with necklaces of white onions, the same " Hottest Spot in Town," the same " Glamourous Importations from Europe's Gayest Amusement Capitals," the same " Meadowbrook Boys " and " Yacht Club Boys," and the same Rudy Vallée.

And the same suckers.

The Music Goes Rand and Rand

It was Mark Twain's stout asseveration that he would rather look at Lillian Russell stark naked than at John Philip Sousa in his full uniform. That there remain a number of men today who concur in old Mark's philosophy, the record of stage revues, night club floor-shows and the like duly testifies. But that the generality have experienced a change in taste, not only in America but in Europe, becomes increasingly evident. Feminine nudity, to tell the truth, has become something of a bore. It has also become refractorily comical.

When, not long ago, the Paris police prosecuted the dancing girl, Joan Warner, for performing in a night club in her birthday clothes, the old guard didn't have to be told which way the wind — nay, the hurricane — was blowing. There was some talk, of course, of public morals, even Paris public morals, but the connoisseurs of metaphysical phenomena appreciated perfectly well that behind the moral question lay nothing more nor less than plain downright ennui. The French cops had simply got sick and tired of looking at hussies in the nude and, in their infinite wisdom and in the high service of public amusement, acted constructively in behalf of the public good and the public pleasure.

For more years than one can remember, the picture of Paris theatrical entertainment, as I long ago recorded, was as follows:

8:30 p.m. Enter chorus in cloaks, hats, long gowns, lingerie, shoes and stockings.

8:50 p.m. Enter chorus in hats, long gowns, lingerie, shoes and stockings.

9:30 p.m. Enter chorus in long gowns, lingerie, shoes and stockings.

10:05 p.m. Enter chorus in lingerie, shoes and stockings.

10:20 p.m. Enter chorus in lingerie.

10:30 p.m. Enter chorus.

Things were at such a pass, indeed, that if one wanted to see a woman with clothes on after half past ten one had to go to the Comédie Française, beforehand making doubly certain that they were doing something by Racine. And, outside of the theatre, it was next to impossible to go to a supper restaurant or night club and eat a simple plate of scrambled eggs with truffles without having to look at a girl, or a squad of girls, cavorting around in the altogether. For twenty-five years the Paris health statistics accordingly showed a greater percentage of acute inflammatory stomach trouble than those of London, Berlin, Buda-Pesth, Vienna, Rome, Madrid and New York all rolled together. It was well that the police came at length to the aid of the health authorities. There was hardly any room left in the Paris hospitals, and as for the American Hospital, just outside at Neuilly, it was getting so that you had to buy admission tickets from speculators.

That New York, Chicago and other large cities in America were in need of their police taking similar action if we were all soon not to be put to bed with serious attacks of indigestion and worse became only too evident. With travel to Paris getting to be less and less and with the local numskull entrepreneurs catering to the imaginary desire of Americans to gaze upon the female form unadorned, the condition that prevailed in Paris began to prevail here to such a degree that when one ventured out at night in search of entertainment one couldn't tell whether one was in a night club or a nudist camp, in a burlesque theatre or a girls' reformatory shower room, in a movie house or an anatomical clinic. And, as nothing is so conducive to morality as a public display of female nudity, particularly in a wholesale dose, the business became at once trying to equanimity and very depressing.

Some years ago, when a lass named Faith Bacon first

[175]

brought it home by revealing herself to the amusement trade as bare as the late Chauncey Depew's pate, there was locally still some pop to the proceedings. For such Americans as had never left the farm to take a look at Paree, the spectacle of Miss Bacon without any clothes on was something of a novelty. But no sooner had Miss Bacon proved a drawing-card than our impresarios of nocturnal culture began rushing madly out onto the highways and into the byways and rounding up girls to emulate her. A few months later not so much as a chemise was visible on the revue stage and not so much as a brassière in the floor-shows. Mrs. Carrie Chapman Catt was one of the very few women in public life who could be observed after night-fall with a skirt on.

The warning of the popular and profitable amusement places became not " Keep Your Shirt On! " but take it off. Miss Sally Rand, who up till then had never been heard of, became nationally famous through the simple device of giving all her clothes to charity and appearing in public clad, at widely separated moments, only in a feather fan. Strip girls in the burlesque shows, such as Ann Corio and Gypsy Rose Lee, made names and wads of money by slowly disrobing for their clients. Restaurant and night club floor-shows reaped a harvest with regiments of wenches who paraded in front of the ringside tables, banked with table d'hôte corned beef hash, adorned only with miniature fig-leaves. Nudist camps sprang up behind

every third rural hot-dog stand, and " art studies " magazines, full of photographs of ladies *nature,* crowded the
Atlantic Monthly and the *Woman's Home Companion*
into the back reaches of the newsstands. Moving pictures
revealed girls with less and less on, until it got to the point
where you could tell the star from the extra girls only by
the somewhat larger diamond ring on her finger. The
revue stage, under the guidance of Mr. Earl Carroll, took
on the aspect of a Bali bathroom, and it was difficult to
find a popular novel whose heroine didn't strip at least
once in every chapter.

Came the revolution. To argue that it was based on
moral grounds is silly. It was based purely and simply on
surfeit. On surfeit and on æsthetics. The sight of so many
women without clothes on made one regret Sousa's death.
And the arrest of Miss Warner — an American girl, mind
you! — by the Paris gendarmes became, for Americans
no less than Parisians, the revolution's battle-cry. That
battle-cry was and is, " Give me lingerie or give me
death! " The reason why men contentedly and happily
stay home these nights and listen to the radio is that you
can't, whatever its other defects, see naked women over the
radio. The day that television finally comes in, they will
be driven from home back into the pool parlors.

The era of nudity for entertainment's sake is rapidly
passing. Men, in profound relief, are now actually going
to fashion shows. Plays razzing strip girls are finding their

place in the theatre, albeit briefly, as men, fed up, do not wish even to be reminded of the tedious business. The theory that such imported movies as *Ecstasy* are primarily being refused licenses because they disclose a woman without anything on is nonsensical. They are being refused licenses because even the censors are bored by such spectacles and, like the Paris censors, wish to spare the public a similar boredom. The burlesque girls are putting on skirts again to recapture trade, and the three biggest and most successful revues produced in the theatre last season had choruses fully clothed. Some of them, in certain numbers, even wore furs. The " art studies " magazines have practically disappeared, and plays like *Victoria Regina* and *Pride and Prejudice* are capturing their erstwhile subscribers in droves.

Miss Mae West, the pet of all cinema sinners, has the sagacity to put on more clothes than a war-horse. Will Hays, shrewdly appreciating the bad effect on the movie box-office, has ordered Hollywood actresses to refrain in the future from having their photographs taken displaying too much of their anatomy. The nudist camps are rapidly going broke and, in their extremity and alarm, are giving away with every admission fee a fancy long flannel dressing-gown. Earl Carroll, sensing the trend, is reported to have under consideration as his next theatrical offering a musical version of the old play, *Siberia,* with all the girls swathed from head to foot in woolens and bearskins, and slowly freezing to death. Sally Rand has already put on

[178]

clothes and played *Rain* in a summer stock company and will doubtless presently and permanently exchange Nils T. Granlund's fan for Lady Windermere's.

It is cause for rejoicing. With the girls once more all dressed up, men will have *some* place to go.

CHAPTER IX

The Theatre Turns He

〽 〽

Those who for some time past began to fear that the drama's masculinity was in serious doubt and that it would not be long before women disappeared from it altogether found, with the advent of the season before this last, that their concern, happily, was groundless. Once again, after a protracted and disconcerting period, the drama returned to normal and proceeded, as in the good old days, to chase after the girls. Green bay trees were forsaken and designs for living forgotten, and the tenets of Eadie, who was a lady, and of Frankie and Johnny, those naturals, again prevailed in the land. Nor could all the hundreds of hideous nude women in the countless restaurant floor-shows divert the drama's course back to 1933 and the season directly before. The good old times were here again.

After the dose of dramatic queerdom in which we had wallowed, the relief was comparable to a carload of bicarbonate of soda. It was again possible to go to the theatre without donning a red necktie with one's dinner jacket. Plain white linen handkerchiefs, worn in the pocket, once more came into fashion. Here and there in the audiences a bass male voice was now and again heard. It all seemed too good to be true. The better gangsters could again attend first nights without feeling that they were losing their social status. And the critics went back to straight whiskey.

The very first play of the new dispensation, *Kill That Story,* displayed encouraging signs. Not once during the whole of it did a single male character so much as glance at another male character without implying clearly that he thought him to be in the way of the woman standing behind him, and, to boot, that he considered him something of a louse. Although the play itself was poor stuff, the enthusiasm of the relieved customers on the opening night when they failed to observe a slender vase of lilies next to the shaving mirror was so great that the authors were deceived into imagining that they had a big hit on their hands. But, meditated the customers on the way out, maybe this was only a canard, a dodge on the managers' part, and doubtless the very next play would disclose at least a couple of *prisonnières* and perhaps two or three anatomical tenors. But, *mirabile dictu,* no! The very next play was *Too Many Boats,* in which a male character was actually killed for interfering with another who was after the same woman.

Small wonder the excitement and pleasure of the public were such that, though *Too Many Boats* was too weak otherwise to stampede the box-office, the Cunard Line promptly considered adding two extra ships a week on the western run in order to take care of the English trade which, after the ceaseless displays of abnormal drama on its home stages, was starved and hungry for a little of the good old-fashioned normal sex stuff. And when the third play, *Lady Jane,* came along shortly afterward and didn't have in it a single scene wherein young Basil Twickenham broke down utterly and cried his eyes out because young Pincus Rippingill had not only stolen his tennis racquet but had been seen out with a woman, the glee was deafening. Strong men began to shout for joy. And weak women shouted with a joy even louder and more significant.

As if adding bounty to bounty, there followed in rapid succession *Tight Britches,* a Carolina hill-billy exhibit — and who ever heard tell of a hill-billy with a depilatoried chest?; *Judgment Day,* which was propaganda for shooting down any man who devoted his time to politics instead of to the girls; *The Bride of Torozko,* which contained Jean Arthur; *Strangers At Home,* that didn't have even a suspicion of either a violet or a green carnation wearer in it; and *The Red Cat,* in which a woman was " made " not only, strangely enough, by her husband but also by a man who looked like him. Bonfires were lighted up and down Broadway. Hotsy-totsy prevailed through the nights. And the Commissioner of Police considered the advisability of adding several thousand cops to the force to take care of the oglers of women and the mashers who were once again appearing on the town's sidewalks. Then something happened.

[182]

The ninth play of the season was *First Episode,* an importation from London. The public's heart sank. For no sooner had the first curtain gone up than it beheld, with all the old disquiet and trepidation, an assortment of young Englishmen — there was nary a girl in sight — who started off the evening by fondly pinching one another's cheeks and otherwise indicating that they considered 50,000,000 Frenchmen not only wrong but extremely vulgar. Could this be an omen that the cerise drama was on its way back again? Woe and lamentations resounded on the night air. But lo! So loud were the aforesaid woe and the aforesaid lamentations that the management of the exhibit, smelling the storehouse before the second act even got going, promptly went into a huddle and decided upon immediate and drastic action. Telephones got busy and by the time the first act was through and two of the young men characters had affectionately hugged each other for the twenty-fourth time the electricians had already changed the title of the play on the marquee to *College Sinners,* the leading lady had had a scene quickly written for her second act in which she succeeded in winning the affections of the juvenile away from the leading man, and all the boys in the cast had been made to sit directly in front of electric fans between the acts, catch colds and speak for the rest of the evening in at least contralto voices. The first nighters' gratitude could be heard down to the Battery.

The producers had learned their lesson and the other

producers had learned *their* lesson in turn, the latter without having to lay out any money for the experience. Thereafter, there was nothing to fear. The very titles of the succeeding plays indicated their wholesome, old-fashioned fornicatory nature: *Errant Lady, Alley Cat, The Distaff Side,* etc., etc. More, immediately following *The Distaff Side* came *Small Miracle,* in which a woman actually was going to have a baby (audiences of the previous season would never have believed such a thing again possible); *Merrily We Roll Along,* in which a woman got so sore at another woman for stealing her man that, like the good old romantic heroines, those lovely and desirable creatures of the past, she threw vitriol in her face; *Spring Song,* in which another young woman was also going to have a baby (the audience could hardly believe its ears); *The First Legion,* in which there were no women but in which the men devoted their passions not to theoretical male images of God but to God himself; and a variety of other exhibits that from first to last were all that the members of the Hollywood Athletic Club or Mr. Max Baer could ask for.

American actors and actresses were as tickled as the audiences. Having been periodically compelled in various English importations to comport themselves physically with what may delicately be alluded to as a cockney accent, they expanded under their returned privilege to go straight and to break the seventh commandment as honorable men and women have broken it for centuries.

[184]

Lynn Fontanne and Alfred Lunt, given the welcome opportunity by a reformed Noël Coward to abandon the peculiarities of *Design For Living* for the lusty normalities of *Point Valaine,* found the nightly natural sex delights so happily exhausting that the management had to call the play off long before a Coward play is usually called off. Judith Anderson's dramatic satisfaction in being allowed two regular lovers in *Divided By Three* in place of one eccentric poetry quoter in *Come Of Age* was as evident as was Tallulah Bankhead's in not having to settle down with a feeble doctor in *Dark Victory* and Vermont and in getting into the good hot stride of Maugham's Sadie Thompson. Even old George Bernard Shaw who, in *Too True To Be Good,* vouchsafed his leading actress the questionable thrill of going to bed merely with an actor representing A Germ, rolled over completely, to the great astonishment of everyone, doubtless including himself, and permitted his leading players in *The Simpleton of the Unexpected Isles* — four of them, no less — to go out into the woods for purposes other than a study of forestry. The transport of the members of the Lambs' Club was such that some of them began paying their dues again, while the happiness of their histrionic sisters of the Twelfth Night Club took on the concrete form of triple Daiquiri cocktails, with double Sidecars for chasers.

The critics, an immoral lot though they are, as is sufficiently known, joined in celebration of the renaissance. Any play in which a man worked his wicked will upon a woman in the healthy tradition of 1915 got four stars, and any in which a woman, as in *Personal Appearance,* demonstrated her birthright all over the stage got twenty or thirty. The outstanding critical successes of the season, as a consequence, were the aforementioned *Personal Appearance,* in which normal sex showed a blood pressure of 670; *The Farmer Takes a Wife,* in which the farmer didn't, despite the title, wait for the clergyman; *The Children's Hour,* in which the mere whisper that a couple of women were sexually bizarre caused such a stage indignation as hasn't been seen hereabouts since the days of John McCullough; *The Petrified Forest,* in which the young heroine offered herself gratis to the hero, and threw in a little money and a good square meal as an extra inducement; *Fly Away Home,* in which a group of children showed that they were growing up in the way that Only A Boy and Only A Girl should grow up; and *Three Men On a Horse,* in which the Rabelaisian humor of the lavatory figured prominently.

After the fleeting concern induced by the young English actors in *College Sinners, née First Episode,* had disappeared, the theatrical scene took on all the sexual comfort of an Atlantic City hotel. And the comfort lasted throughout the year, save for one slight and entirely negligible interruption. That was an English importation called *Prisoners Of War,* in which another set of young English actors again went ups-a-daisy and quickly to the storehouse. What is more, this last season went in for dramatic virility on an even greater scale.

The present season, judging from the advance reports, promises to be a still more satisfactory one. A. H. Woods, who was driven from the theatre for several years because of his inability to find the necessary and called-for play manuscript wherein a young woman died of a broken heart because her fiancé married another man, announces that he will produce three plays, all laid in old-time St. Louis bawdy houses and each containing a cast of two hundred and fifty people. Max Gordon during the year will present two exhibits, one of them a chronicle play based on the lives of the chorus girls in the Earl Carroll *Vanities* series, the other with exactly the same plot but laid in Hollywood. Max Reinhardt's long delayed production of *A Midsummer Night's Dream,* a possibility for the Spring, will see the elimination of all the fairies, and we are promised the beginning of a Eugene O'Neill cycle of nine full-length plays containing forty-six seductions and three hundred and two illegitimate babies, including seven sets of sextuplets. There will also be a production of a revised version of *The Captive,* in which, in a trick O. Henry last scene, the other woman will be unmasked, to the consternation of the Lesbian heroine, as Julian Eltinge.

CHAPTER X

Fallen by the Wayside

ﻭ ﻭ

To any critic with the interests of the American drama near to heart, the collapse of so many initially promising talents during the last dozen or so years is a matter for rueful speculation. During the period in question, we have seen writers come into our theatre with what appeared to be genuine gifts, only to see them not long afterward either in a light that threw those gifts into glum and disconcerting shadow or disappear from contact with the medium of their first high ambition. Names occur readily: Vincent Lawrence, Harry Wagstaff Gribble, Maurine Watkins, Zoë Akins, Arthur Richman, Ben Hecht, Charles MacArthur, Edwin Justus Mayer, Gilbert Emery, Laurence Stallings. There are others, but these represented, perhaps, the cream of potentiality. Let us consider them.

Vincent Lawrence was, before the advent of S. N. Behrman, by long odds the one younger American writer of finished comedy who might someday be expected to figure importantly in the records of native comedy. His plays, true enough, often slowly expired in their last acts, but even in those last acts, as in the meritorious acts that preceded them, he disclosed what was generally agreed to be the sharpest and truest ear for the kind of speech associated with his various characters that we had engaged, up to his time, in American comedy writing, along with an intelligence, a cutting light social philosophy and an originality of viewpoint that we all too seldom had been privileged on the local stage. These plays, however, despite the faith that Mr. William Harris, Jr., long and steadfastly maintained in their author, got a very short distance in a box-office direction, and it may or may not have been because of this that Lawrence succumbed to the blandishments of Hollywood. Since Hollywood laid its hands on him, he has written but one play, *Washington Heights,* a miserable caricature of his original talents. Otherwise, he seems to have vanished completely into the bog of Hollywood surrender. Although a few months ago one read a rumor that he was preparing a new play for the theatre, one may pardonably finger one's ear in doubt, for all his old pride and ambition seem to have deserted him and reports have it that he has been devoting the larger part of his time in the last year or two to thinking up bits and gags for various Paramount moving pictures, at so much gold per week.

Maurine Watkins, who stormed into the American drama with that best of boisterous satires, *Chicago,* and paved the way for such elixirs as *The Front Page,* quickly went to pieces after her first excellent achievement, producing nothing that approached it in quality. And Hollywood similarly reached out and caught her in its coils. She has tried to do things for the theatre since that have aspired to some repute — I have read two of her manuscripts and portions of them reveal a mild echo of her first promise — but the results on the whole are woefully defective. Yet here was a young woman who, though the deceased and eulogized Prof. George Pierce Baker urged her, after he had read the manuscript of *Chicago* (she was one of his pupils), please to conceal the fact that she was a member of his class, lest the play, if produced, embarrass him, Yale, and certain rich contributors to that university's funds — yet here, as I say, was a young woman who appeared to have something very real and very fine to contribute to the future stage of her nation. What happened, alas, was just one play — then a poor dramatization of a novel, then a misguided original manuscript that got nowhere, and then the California movie lots.

Harry Wagstaff Gribble came to notice with the celebrated *March Hares* and thereupon promptly blew up. Numerous other plays followed it, but in none of them — save *Revolt,* and then only in spots — was there even a faint trace of what he had encouraged his critics and public to expect of him. The reason for Gribble's apparent total eclipse is only to be guessed at. He, also, has monkeyed with the movies now and then, but the major part of his time has been spent in and around the theatre, whether in one capacity or another, so Hollywood may not properly be asked to shoulder all the blame. He has, furthermore, indicated a measure of sincerity and honesty in his effort to write other plays of some merit, but out of that measure of sincerity and honesty utterly nothing worth-while has come. It is possible, therefore, that his too close contact with the commercial theatre itself, as producer, director, play-tinker and what not else, has turned much of his blood into grease-paint and that, as a consequence, he has found himself able to turn out only grease-paint drama. Or it may be — and this seems sadly likely — that he is and was simply a one-play man. But, whatever the reason, he appears at the moment to be capsized.

We come to Zoë Akins and to one of the most initially original and hopeful talents that the dawning better American stage of her day had engaged. In her earliest play, *Papa,* though the Viennese influence was discernible, she contrived a work so fresh, so intelligently humorous and so completely different from the routine American playwriting of its time that it brought to her celebration the voices of any number of leading critics. But this *Papa* was not all. In a succeeding manuscript — *The Magical City,* which, incidentally, was a forerunner of the *Winterset* rhythmic prose modern theme idea — she showed a still further originality, a pretty invention, and a gift for felicitous expression that promised much. Several plays followed, among them the very successful *Declassée,* which amounted critically to little although even here there was sufficient evidence that its author was far from being a dramatic cheapjack. Then — forgetting the box-office — came *A Texas Nightingale* (first known as *Greatness*), a first-rate comedy of the musical temperament and one of the really estimable plays of the theatre of the period. And there followed *A Royal Fandango* which, while it left a great deal to be desired, still revealed something of the original brave Akins spirit. From this point on, however, we had nothing but empty pretence, as in *The Furies* and *The Varying Shore,* nothing but a series of box-office adaptations and dramatizations, nothing but — let us politely omit the obvious and painful adjectives — *The Greeks Had a Word For It* and *O Evening Star.*

Is Hollywood, for Miss Akins made the trek some years ago and installed herself there permanently, it would seem, again responsible? Without venturing specifically to answer, one nevertheless places in evidence a recent interview in which Miss Akins rather alarmingly betrayed herself. In this interview, published in the Sunday theatrical section of the New York *Times,* she observed that anyone who went to Hollywood simply for the money to be got out of it and not with a great faith and pride and artistic belief in movie writing should be booted out of the place instanter! Fancy that. Fancy a once staunch believer in the art of the drama so compromising her intelligence and, worse still, her sense of humor. Therein we find the Siamese twin Miss Hyde murdering the twin Mrs. Dr. Jekyl. And more's the pity, for just before this accomplished and ingenious dramatist took to the movie lots she had in mind and in preparation, I happen to know, two plays (one of them a beautifully sardonic and wickedly witty New Deal for Socrates) that might have been a large credit to native playwriting, though they probably could not have brought a nickel from the movie masterminds.

One dislikes to take the easy way out of conventionally and rather tiresomely attributing the decline of such dramatic competences to Hollywood, but if there is another way to get at the root of the trouble I do not seem to be sleuth enough to ferret it out. Surely Hollywood must bear a considerable share of the burden in the instance of three of the other promising talents that have been noted: Arthur Richman, Edwin Justus Mayer and Gilbert Emery. These three sold their souls to the great Chloroformia art center soon after they had written their widely commended plays and nothing that any one of them has done since has, up to the moment that this sentence is being put down on paper, been worth the firecracker to blow it up. The Richman who wrote *Ambush* and even *Grounds For Divorce* is no longer even vaguely discernible in the plays he has manufactured since Hollywood laid its paws on him, nor is the Mayer who wrote *The Firebrand* and *Children of Darkness,* nor is the Emery who began so encouragingly with *The Hero* and who went on to *Tarnish.*

The doubtless irritating Hollywood motif appears again — though here by no means so obstreperously or so cacophonously — when we contemplate the situation of the

Messrs. Hecht, MacArthur and Stallings. Although all three of these charming rascals have also gone over to the moving pictures and although the writing of all three of them has shown a very visible and sad decline since they went over, it is doubtful, despite the fact that they seem at present to have fallen by the wayside, if the fall will be permanent. All three have proved themselves superior to the muckworm spirit of the Hollywood factories and their overlords; all three have retained a basic contempt (whatever their public face) for those factories and over-lords; all three have in the last two or three years insisted upon doing their movie jobs in the neighborhood of New York, three thousand miles safely removed from Beverly Hills Spanish-Yiddish villas, illuminated swimming pools and purple and orange Rolls-Royces; and all three have been pretty frank in admitting that they haven't the intense aversion to mere money as money that most of the pure writing artists of Hollywood loudly proclaim *they* have. Stallings goes even farther. I asked him about a year ago why in God's name he didn't give up his movie work (in his case, it consists in editing news reels) long enough to give us another sample of his old first-rate dramatic writing — *What Price Glory?* for a single example. " I'll tell you why," he answered. " I've written everything I had to say and I'm not going to write anything when I haven't got anything more to say. I'm different from some fellows that way." There, at least, is complete honesty for you — and maybe a little too much modesty.

As for Hecht and MacArthur (about whom more anon), though they, like Stallings, have done nothing in recent years to compare even remotely with their first work for the theatre — Hecht began brilliantly on his own with *The Egotist,* and his collaboration, much later, with Mac-Arthur on *The Front Page* needs no recalling — there is still hope for them, as they are both mettlesome and independent fellows and, pictures or no pictures, have not lost their original decent interest in the drama. They are, let us hope, only temporarily in the discard.

But what of some others whom I omitted in the first list? Much lesser figures, true enough, but still writers who once showed a flash of something promising? What of the Frederick Ballard who wrote *Young America* and then abruptly went down the chute into *Ladies of the Jury,* etc.? What of Bartlett Cormack who wrote *The Racket* and then disappeared? What of Hugh Stange who wrote *Veneer* and then collapsed? Have they and some few others like them also been caught in the quicksands of Hollywood — or in the swamps of the " one-play man " legend?

CHAPTER XI

The Recluse of Sea Island

୬ ୬

If there is one thing in all the world that is utterly and completely distasteful to the foremost figure in the American theatre it is the theatre. He ventures to enter one not more than once in every seven or eight years and each time loudly and indignantly swears off for the rest of his life. Something seems always to happen to him when he goes to a theatre that increases doubly his prefatory misgivings. When he went eight years ago, in Paris, to see a production by the eminent Russian director, Tairov, of his own *All God's Chillun Got Wings* — in the new and modernly equipped Théâtre Pigalle — he went upon the invitation of Baron Rothschild, whose interest and liberality had made the reformed Pigalle possible. Arriving in the box that had been set aside for him, he was cordially received by two gentlemen, both of them charming in the warmth of their manner and reception. To one of them he took, as he subsequently expressed it, an immediate "shine," though he is by nature notoriously a very aloof person and one given to few acquaintances and even fewer friends. To this one, he devoted his whole attention for the evening, listening with close and genial interest to everything he had to say and periodically and impatiently shushing aside the other, who from time to time would seek, timidly and politely, to edge in with a suggestion or passing word. As he was leaving the theatre, he addressed a sotto voce query to his companion of the evening. " Who *is* that other guy? " he demanded. " That — why that's your host, Baron Rothschild," replied the other. A look of grieved concern seized O'Neill's countenance. " Good God, then, who are you? " " I," returned the other, " I'm Jack Campbell, a reporter for the Paris *Herald.*"

It took O'Neill a week to recover his equanimity. " That's what happens," he subsequently said to me, " when I go to the theatre."

A year ago — seven years after the contretemps noted — he again took a chance on the theatre, this time in New York. The exhibit was the *Continental Varieties* and the motivating force behind his excursion was the presence in the show of Escudero, the Spanish dancer. (It was an enthusiasm for the dancer's art on the part of his wife, Carlotta, that on this occasion weaned him from his theatrical prejudice.) He sat glumly through the first part of the program, hoarsely muttering to himself, and finally succeeded in persuading his wife to get out of the place as quickly as possible. When he got back to his hotel, he discovered that he had left his favorite muffler in the theatre, and the next day he began sneezing with a terrible cold. " You see! " he told me. " Never again! "

O'Neill's whimsical annoyance with the institution that has made possible his eminence and his great worldly success has become such that, during the long period when he is engaged in the writing of one of his plays, he has struck a bargain with his wife never under any circumstances to allow the theatre or anything in any way connected with it to be mentioned in his hearing. Any letter that may come to him containing any news of things theatrical, whether directly concerning him or not, is not to be shown to him. Nothing in newspapers or magazines having to do with the theatre is to be read by him or to him. " It wouldn't be so bad if the theatre was any good," he argues when reproached for his isolation, " but as it stands — outside of Russia, maybe — it only gets in the way of your temper and any serious attempt you want to make toward good work." Whereupon he grunts, slowly lights a cigarette, gazes with wrinkled brow at its tip for a full minute to see that it is burning properly, moves to a chair in a far corner, deposits himself therein, and maintains a grim and majestic silence until he feels certain that the subject is safely changed for the rest of the day.

But the theatre is not the only thing from which O'Neill remains steadfastly sequestered. He elects, in these years, as in many of those that have gone before, to lead an existence completely removed from what the rest of us are pleased to allude to as " life." The major part of his year is spent in his lovely house, walled in from the outside world, on that little plot of land off the coast of Georgia known as Sea Island. There he lives with devoted Carlotta and a few servants — notably Mlle. Edna, a colored cook of uncommon virtuosity; there he works and broods from nine in the mornings until ten at nights, with time out only for meals, a bit of gardening, a solo swim in the sea and a run up and down the deserted beach; there he has his entire being. Two months in the year, when the weather gets bad on the island, he spends in a quiet Adirondack camp, many miles away from the nearest railroad station, or in some other such isolated spot. Perhaps a week in New York then — incognito in a closely guarded hotel suite — to consult with his dentist, to steal off to the six-day bicycle races, for which he has had a long-standing affection, to guzzle some of Luchow's Edelbräu, and to repeat endlessly to me that he simply can't understand how any man can live in New York and not go crazy — and back again promptly to Sea Island.

On his last year's visit to New York, he, Sean O'Casey, the finest of the Irish playwrights, and I lunched together in his hotel rooms. O'Casey and I, before joining him, had coached ourselves in a plot to take him to task, with a great show of indignation on our parts, for his burial of himself from all contact with the world and his fellow-men. Slowly and, we thought, with a pretty histrionic skill, we edged against his self-defence with lush arguments as to the necessity of an artist's — and particularly a dramatist's — mingling with the stream of life if he is to comprehend it and interpret its depths and mutations. As the hours passed, O'Neill began to indicate, first, a mild restlessness, then a growing mood of irritation, and finally an open, hot rebellion. Jumping out of his chair — and if there is any previous record of his ever having got out of a chair with an alacrity greater than that customarily displayed by a stock company Richelieu, no one who knows him is privy to the fact — he confronted both of us and, his face flushed, made what is the longest speech that he has made in all the many years I have known him.

"What you fellows have been saying," he exploded, " is damned rot! That mingling with people and life that you talk about, far from giving anything to an artist, simply takes things away from him, damned valuable things. If he hasn't everything in himself, he is no good. The life outside him can steal from him but it can't contribute a thing to him, unless he is a rank second-rater. You talk of the thrill of cities, as against the so-called loneliness and stagnation of the country. What is the thrill? A lot of meaningless noise, a lot of crowding bores, a lot of awful smells, a swirl of excited nothingness. You talk of the thrill of a city's beauty. Well (pointing out of the window), look at those skyscrapers! What are they; what do they stand for? Nothing but a lot of children's blocks! Do you mean to say that they've got anything to do with the great soul of humanity, with humanity's deep, underlying essence, and hopes, and fate? You're both bughouse! "

Whereupon he bestowed upon each of us a black and completely disgusted look, turned his back on us, and abruptly left the room. O'Casey and I exchanged a significant and self-congratulatory wink. In about ten minutes O'Neill returned, resplendent in some newfangled slacks that he had bought that morning. Immediately O'Casey and I launched into a lavish encomium not only of the slacks but of his general sartorial taste and even magnificence. A forgiving grin spread over O'Neill's features. The admiration of his slacks tickled him. But suddenly he caught himself and the frown again stole over his face. " Just the same," he informed us, " about that other stuff, you're both nuts! "

His thorough and firmly rooted belief in the value of isolation, indeed, is such that already he is beginning to show signs of finding his lonely island too close to the borderland of the American world and is beginning, with his wife, to study the atlas for some more distant and less penetrable hideaway.

It is not to be gathered from all of this, however, that O'Neill, despite the legend that has come to be attached to him by persons who haven't the faintest inkling of what he is really like, is not an enviably happy and richly contented man. Of all the men who are near to my knowledge and friendship, he seems to me the most happy and the most contented, and by far. The legend to the contrary has its tentacles in a variety of vacuums. First, because his physiognomy happens to have been cast by God in a tragic mould, like Henry Irving's, and because, like Groucho Marx, his expression happens naturally to be grave and even melancholy, he is held to be a tragic, grave and melancholy man. The truth about him is that, while hardly a persistently jocund one, he is fundamentally a cheerful and at times even a waggish fellow, with a taste for low barroom chatter, bordello anecdotes, rough songs and other such forms of healthy obscenity. Secondly, his complete isolation of himself has given rise to the theory that he is a misanthrope, one who hates his fellow-man and is just this side of being an eater of babies. While it is true that he cares nothing for people in the mass and goes to extremes to avoid having anything to do with them, he likes nothing better than to be with one of his few close friends, on which occasions he is as happy and sportive as a small boy. Every now and again, further, he will encounter, either by accident or in the course of what may be timidly alluded to as his public life, a stranger — like the Paris reporter referred to — toward whom he will wax warmly friendly and sympathetic. H. R. Lenormand, the French dramatist, is one such; Vincent Youmans, the American song writer, is another; and George Boll, a Southern real estate operator, is still another. Such men, although they do not penetrate deeply into his existence,

[202]

are highly agreeable company to him, and he is very fond of them.

A third source of the legend of his persistent misery is the memory of the theoretical very hard time he had of it when he first began to write plays and the extreme difficulty he encountered in gaining a hearing for his work and the slightest recognition of his talents. This, for all the popularity of the legend, is utter nonsense. While he was studying at college and shortly thereafter, he wrote a number of plays, both short and long, but, appreciating that they were not worth a hoot, he promptly destroyed all of them and would not, before their extinction, allow even his closest cronies to read them. All, that is, with one exception: a three-act farce-comedy which he rather fancied for a spell — lasting approximately three or four months — after which period he read it again, concluded that his first opinion of it was deplorably uncritical, and burned it instanter. When he began to write plays in real earnest, he experienced, the theorists should know, no lack of outside sympathy and even enthusiasm. It is true that the professional theatre was not interested in those earliest plays, for they were one-act plays and the American professional theatre has never been much interested in one-act plays, whether O'Neill's or anyone's else. But he did not lack an immediate production of these one-acters in the little theatre, notably the Provincetown, which promptly grabbed up any and everything he turned out. And it was not long before little theatres all over the land

[203]

were playing his one-acters, and the more intelligent and receptive editors were eagerly buying them for magazine publication.

What is more, the moment he turned to the longer form of drama, the professional theatre at once opened its doors to him. John D. Williams read the manuscript of *Beyond the Horizon* just two hours after it was put into his hands, immediately telephoned to O'Neill that he liked it enormously, and told him that he would produce it as soon as he could gather together a worthy cast, which he duly did. This *Beyond the Horizon* was his first long play, if we omit those he wrote and himself destroyed, and the very first professional theatre man who read it quickly accepted it for production. Both *The Emperor Jones* and *The Straw,* which followed it, were produced by the Provincetowners, but it must not be forgotten that O'Neill was a member of that producing group, and a very enthusiastic member, to boot, and that he gave his plays to it in both friendship and pride. *Gold,* which, like the two plays cited, was also produced in 1921, received its professional theatre presentation by the same John D. Williams who gave *Beyond the Horizon* a hearing. And, as in the other instance, Williams was the first producer to whom the manuscript was submitted. *Anna Christie* was produced in its original draft (known as *Chris Christopherson*) by the veteran professional manager, Mr. George C. Tyler. When it failed after a very brief showing in Philadelphia, O'Neill rewrote it. Edgar Selwyn, of the then conspicuous Selwyn firm, read the revised script — it was sent to him first — and reported that he could see no play in it. The same afternoon it went to Arthur Hopkins, who immediately accepted it for production. All of which is the true, if not generally recognized, story of O'Neill's " difficult early days " and the " awful time he had to get any sort of a hearing."

The paradoxical aversion of the first among American playwrights from the theatre is equalled only by his similarly paradoxical aversion from actors. While he freely allows that there are some competent members of the profession — he has an affection for George M. Cohan, a very considerable respect for Walter Huston, and a tender memory for the late Louis Wolheim, all three of whom have acted in his plays — he has only a large and raucous snort for the overwhelming majority. In this respect, he shares with a certain school of criticism the conviction that an actor is a creature who has missed his profession. One of O'Neill's most acute sources of embarrassment with actors may be expressed in his own words. " A lot of them seem to get away with it all right during the early part of a play, but then — pop! — out comes the fairy touch, the falsetto voice, the fancy little gesture, the roll of the hip — and the play goes blooie."

One of O'Neill's sorest spots is the criticism that is made in certain quarters of his fondness for the use of masks in his plays and the allegation that they only confuse matters and make his plays doubly difficult for an audience.

His favorite answer is: " Well, I used them in *The Great God Brown* and it seemed to confuse matters so much and to make the play so doubly difficult for an audience that the play ran for eight months in New York alone! "

For his fellow playwrights, O'Neill has little respect, save for three — or maybe four: Lenormand, Maugham and O'Casey — and, lately, Maxwell Anderson. He confesses that the greatest influence upon his work is Strindberg. " He is the greatest influence on any playwright who is worth anything today, whether the playwright admits it or not," he adds. It is torture to him to write a letter. He will shy from the task for days and then, more often than not, will entrust the job to his wife who, incidentally, is no mean literata in that department. He is not at full ease and at peace with himself unless he can live near the sea. Most of his life has been spent either upon it or at its borders. When he is removed from it, he must have at least a river, a lake, or some body of water near by. His present work-room in his house on Sea Island is built to resemble a cabin on a schooner; its windows look out upon the Atlantic and it is full of ship models and records of the sea and of the ships that have sailed the seas. Yet never once, in all the years I have known him, have I ever heard him use so much as one nautical term in conversation. That discourse, as the reader has doubtless ere now perceived, offers in general a distinct contrast, as is so often the case with writers, to O'Neill's literary self. As against the formality of his writings, with their frequent poetic overtone, it is free, easy, colloquial, and often négligé, which makes him the surprised delight of any interviewer who, approaching an audience with him, foresees a painful session with a gloomy pundit. And as the cast of his spoken words denies all of the usual pretensions of *homo literarum,* so his private reading pleasure, self-critically confessed, indicates his unaffected simplicity. O'Neill reads every mystery and detective novel immediately it appears on the stands.

A last word and we drop the curtain, for the time being at least, on this strange, this oddly self-sufficient, this genuinely engaging fellow. Just as he detests every phase of public life, so he detests — as one such phase — being written about. That is, as a person apart from his work. When I wrote to his wife that I was going to confect this chapter on him, she replied that, while it was agreeable to her to have someone who knew him well dispel " the school-boy legends that have gone their ridiculous and dull way into print " and to have him pictured somewhat more faithfully than one who, at the age of fifteen months, leapt directly from his perambulator into a barroom, where legend has had him remain ever since, nevertheless " Gene doesn't at all cheer at the idea!! " The two exclamation marks are hers. O'Neill, in short, the most widely discussed figure in the American theatre, finds such discussion, including this, gratuitously obnoxious. He wants, dammit, to be left alone.

CHAPTER XII

The Renegade Duo

∽ ∽

If, in one of those guessing games currently so popular
the country over with men and women who, as small
children, promised to reach maturity with no such disconcerting symptoms of abnormality, the question was as
to the identity of the two most publicized scenario writers
of Hollywood, it would probably be a backward moron
indeed who would not promptly either write down or
speak up with the names of Hecht and MacArthur. For
these twain, though they have composed fewer movies
than dozens of other literary refugees in the California
art center and though they see less of Hollywood than
any dozen dozen of the others, have become in the more
sophisticated cinema, theatrical and post-speakeasy consciousness the symbol of whatever it is that they and their
adopted profession stand for. Which symbol, incidentally,
has been carefully manufactured, with considerable sly
humor, by none other than Hecht and MacArthur themselves.

Originally two Chicago newspapermen who, by virtue
of brilliant impudence and reportorial derring-do, per-

formed the journalistic phenomenon of keeping their city editors on the water-wagon lest, if they fell off even briefly, the duo would in the meantime wreck the newspapers with wild monkeyshines of one sort or another, the boys individually — and Hecht in elaborate particular — soon brought themselves to wider public attention by such extrinsic performances as publishing and writing almost all the copy for a weekly literary review that stripped the pantaloons off every belletristic stuffed shirt within two thousand miles of Michigan Avenue, confecting as many as seven or eight short stories for a single issue of the old *Smart Set* magazine, writing ironic periodical fiction based upon the various gruesome contretemps in Chicago jails and death-houses, fabricating Frenchy sex comedies for the New York stage, and making loud love nightly to nine-tenths of the bartenders in Chicago. It was this last-named mutual peccadillo that led some years later to their equally collaborative efforts in other and somewhat more punctilious directions.

The first of these other collaborations, which put the limelight on them, was the well-known play called *The Front Page,* in which they paid their sardonic left-handed compliments to their old Chicago city editors and to certain other former newspaper colleagues who, to their way of looking at it, would benefit richly from a ribald kick in the slats. A second collaboration was the equally well-known play called *Twentieth Century,* in which they paid more sardonic left-handed compliments to certain theatrical personages who, for one reason or another, had disturbed their equanimity. Hecht then took a few months off and composed, solo, a novel — *A Jew In Love* — in which he abandoned mere sardonic left-handed compliments and gleefully and very painfully stripped the hide off the ego of a well-known theatrical producer who had got under his collar. More recently, Ben and Charlie (they are Hecht and MacArthur only to people who owe them money) jointly manufactured a talking picture, written and directed by themselves, which bore the title, *The Scoundrel,* and which ripped up a New York publisher for whom they retain a memory that may hardly be described as sweet. If they don't care for a man or, caring, consider him something of an ass nonetheless, they invariably sit themselves down and take it out on him in the form of a novel (Hecht has written another that drove its poet prototype wailing to the mountains), a play or a movie. They have, in a word, capitalized to good returns the kick-'em-in-the-pants art.

As collaborators, they are also highly adroit in another direction. Hecht himself describes it in the following ingratiatingly forthright manner. " You see, I'm something of a son-of-a-bitch when it comes to dealing with people, especially people who in my high and flattering opinion of my own self don't seem good enough even to eat in the same country with me, and naturally, when we've got a deal to put through, I'd make them sore and gum things up. That's where Charlie comes in! Charlie, as you know,

just swims in charm and, at the critical moment, just
when everything seems to be going to hell, in he comes
and squirts it all around the poor guy until the poor guy
is sunk and we get what we're after."

As Hecht hints, MacArthur is his complete personal
opposite. If Hecht thinks or feels a thing — and his thinking and feeling are usually contemptuous of the metaphysical and emotional processes of ninety-nine out of
every ninety-eight persons with whom he comes into contact — he lets go with a vocabulary that lifts the ceiling.
Meeting even an old friend after an interval, his very first
remark is generally to the effect that the latter shows
every sign of having decayed both mentally and physically
and that he is in all probability ready for the ash-heap.
MacArthur, on the other hand, never fails affably to tell
everyone that he meets up with, whether friend or complete stranger, male or female, eighteen or eighty, that
the one in question never looked better in his life, looks
twenty years younger than when he last saw him, has
such pink cheeks as would bring envy to a dairy-maid,
and certainly has never done such good work (even if the
person, unknown to MacArthur, is out of a job at the
moment) as in these last two or three weeks. He then
invariably puts the candied cherry on the marshmallow
by warmly assuring the individual that he is his favorite
person, by buying two rounds of drinks, and by urging his
vis-à-vis to have lunch with him on any day that the
vis-à-vis selects, Charlie insisting that, whether the *vis-à-*

[211]

vis wishes it or not, he will send a motor car to fetch him. And if you don't think it works, just you get the statistics from Hecht!

This MacArthur charm hose, delightfully turned on and off at its régisseur's will, has not only been responsible for most of the partners' popularity and business success, but without it Hecht would doubtless long since have been taken for a ride by the Hollywood poobahs whom he has flouted and outraged, and MacArthur would still be a bachelor. It may be that his numerous talents and other estimable qualities might have persuaded Helen Hayes to marry him, but one has a feeling that the very first words he ever spoke to her, on their casual meeting at a party in New York, exercised their charm effect upon her as similar verbal delicatessen has exercised its upon the magnates of Hollywood. Not having been introduced to her, observing her alone in a corner, and flustered at the spectacle of her, Charlie — with an admirable performance registering shyness — approached her and pulled out of his coat pocket — with an even more admirable performance registering boyish hesitation — a bag of peanuts. Proffering the bag, he spoke. "Have some?" Miss Hayes smilingly took a handful. "I'm only sorry," whispered Charlie, "that they aren't pearls!" A short time afterward, they were married.

Hecht informs everybody that his partner has more sprays of all descriptions in his bathroom than you could find in a boulevard of drugstores and allows that Mac-Arthur, though he insists they ᵣre for use after cold, grippe and influenza attacks, unquestionably employs them, much like an opera singer, to keep his larynx at the proper degree of mellifluence.

In the first days of their joint Hollywood incumbency, they were the essence of tractable, even honeyed, agreeableness, but it was not long afterward that it got to be all the diplomatic MacArthur could do to keep his partner from being deported. The Hollywood masterminds, as everybody knows, have long been used to a slavish concurrence in their opinions and ideas, if any, and presumption on the part of mere writers even faintly to doubt their oracularity constitutes high treason. Hecht proceeded with but slight delay to change all that. One of his earliest business meetings was with the head of one of the three largest studios. Without stopping to shake hands, much less remove the hat from his head or the large cigar from his mouth, he opened up. " Now let's get this straight, you old blob! " he announced. " I'm here at your request to do a story for your God damned movies; I'm a writer and you're not and, what's more, I'm a writer who knows his business. So I don't want any of your imbecile horning in. If you want me to do the job, and have got the necessary dough ready, I'm set to begin. If you have any other notions in that thick head of yours, spit them out now so we can call it a day and I can clear out! " The movie magnifico looked at him and blinked. " Say," he purled, " why get sore about it? " Hecht got the job and the " dough " without further ado.

The Hollywood adventures of Hecht and MacArthur are replete with such garlics, Hecht having insulted — to very satisfactory financial returns — almost everyone out there but Shirley Temple, and MacArthur having subsequently mollified everyone and saved the firm's reputation for being at heart two all right boys. Hecht alone and Hecht and MacArthur together have been particularly trying to the Holywood bosses in the matter of declining to travel out to Hollywood to do the work periodically commissioned of them. " If you want us, come to us," has been the frequent telegraphic reply. Two years ago, Hecht absolutely refused to accept a handsome offer to prepare a scenario unless the Hollywood director-producer came to New York, hired him a suite at the Park Central Hotel, had all the telephones ripped out, and guaranteed that he himself (the director-producer) would stay away and not bother him. Last year Hecht accepted a contract to make a scenario of *Barbary Coast* for Samuel Goldwyn, whom for two solid years he had made writhe with his tart sarcasms, only on condition that the director assigned to the job, along with his associate, come to New York and play a newfangled Hollywood marble game with him and MacArthur in the spare time. Mr. Goldwyn duly arranged for the two men to come East and play the marble game.

A couple of years ago the boys concluded that, while it was all right for them to write scenarios now and again for the Hollywood studios, it would be a better idea, instead of arguing constantly with others how they wished their pictures to be made, to make them themselves. So they worked out an arrangement with the Paramount and Erpi companies to take over part of the studio at Astoria, Long Island, and promptly installed themselves there in an office which, in turn, they promptly and waggishly decorated with more nudes than the Minsky brothers ever dreamed of and with a large sign reading: "If it's good enough for Metro-Goldwyn-Mayer, it isn't good enough for us!" Their next move was to arrange for two-hour daily lunches, with imported dill pickles, and to requisition the studio automobile to be at their command at twelve-thirty each day in order, if they so willed, to hasten across the bridge to New York and fetch back one or two pleasant guests to adorn the table and help eat the pickles. Their third move was to have large photographs taken of themselves — for advertising purposes — displaying them huddled over typewriter and writing pad with furrowed brows, working themselves to death. Then they began, after a protracted and well-deserved period of rest, to ruminate, now that they had the studio, the elegant office, the lunches with dill pickles, the automobile and the photographs, what they were going to do about a movie.

Crime Without Passion was their first. They wrote it,

cast it, directed it, edited it and even press-agented it personally. By hiring for the leading male rôle a New York stage actor who at the moment was at liberty, by engaging for the leading woman's rôle a young girl who had been dancing on the Waldorf-Astoria roof-garden and who had hitherto had no acting experience — and by playing a couple of the minor rôles themselves — they managed to turn out the completed picture at the low figure of $172,000. It grossed slightly less than half a million. "Which," they observe, "is considered a stinking failure in Hollywood."

The principle which they followed in this initial picture venture has been followed by them in the several pictures which they have made since. "Cut the costs to the limit, cut out as many exterior scenes as possible because, if it rains and you can't shoot, it sets you back at least $1,100 a day, cut out expensive actors or, if you have to have one, make him work on a percentage arrangement and gamble with you, write pictures with an eye to a somewhat more intelligent public than the Hollywood boneheads believe exists, forget moonlight swimming pool parties, stick to dill pickles, and trust in God!" That is their expressed policy. And that, whatever the success or failure of their pictures, some of which have been pretty awful, there is a marked and healthy sagacity in their article of war must be apparent to anyone who is not deceived by the juvenile overtone of cocky independence and arch-snootiness.

This cocky independence and resolute snootiness often

take on, in both of the boys, but in Hecht especially, some strange and grotesque forms. While MacArthur's is more or less *piano,* Hecht's is generally *fortissimo.* When O'Neill's *Strange Interlude* made its great success in the theatre and became the subject of wide critical acclaim, Hecht disdainfully and derisively proceeded to indite a scathing denunciation of it. "But you haven't even seen it!" he was reproved. "See it? Why should I see it?" he yelled. "I can smell such herring a mile off without ever going near it!" Not long ago, a moving picture exhibitor in the Middle West wrote to the boys and told them that one of their movies which he had shown drove all of his customers out of his theatre. Hecht confected a long letter to the fellow which began: "Louse. This is probably the first time you have ever received a letter with a three cent stamp on it," and which went on, at voluminous length, to apprise the exhibitor of his numerous grievous mental, anatomical, hereditary and other shortcomings, including his inability to operate a movie theatre and get anybody into it. Vastly proud over his great epistolary performance, Hecht had copies made and forwarded them to the various trade journals, thereafter sitting back and pleasuring himself with a rich and contented chuckle on his devastating triumph. Several days later he got a reply from the exhibitor. Very briefly, it ran: "I can get people into my theatre all right, but with *your* pictures I'll be damned if I can *keep* them in!"

Of the Albertina Rasch girls, Martha Graham choreographic artistes and other such exponents of the art *moderne* of the dance, Hecht observes that they always suggest girls who have jumped straight from Appleton's First Reader to Proust. He attributes his fancy for heavy rainstorms in his pictures to his opinion of the generality of movie actors. " I like to see them catch bad colds." When MacArthur tries feebly to say something good about Hollywood by observing that it may be Babylon but that Babylon had some good points to it after all, Hecht sniffs, " So had the Roman sewers."

They work out their scenarios at strange hours and in strange places. In his house up the Hudson, MacArthur has had built for himself, at a very considerable outlay, a room that is not only sound-proof but the wall panels of which may be slid across the windows, so that nothing may distract the eye of its occupant from his profound meditations and labors. If there is any record of MacArthur's having used the room even once for working purposes, no one thus far knows of it. Hecht has a house not far away, at Nyack, and there is a record of his having worked there at odd times, but more often he may be found battering away at one or another scenario in some out-of-the-way room in New York. The preliminary conferences of the collaborators are almost invariably held either in Jack and Charlie's booze parlor in West Fifty-second street or in Tony's, a few doors up the block. They are rapid workers. It is related that on one occasion Hecht got an order for a scenario from one of the Hollywood studios and rejected a flat sum of $15,000 for the job, insisting that he wouldn't under any circumstances touch it for less than $1,000 a day for each day he spent at the task. After much bickering back and forth, the $1,000 a day was agreed upon. Hecht subsequently found to his acute dismay and chagrin that it took him only ten days to finish the scenario.

The boys' directorial technique at their Astoria studio would give the average director in Hollywood something only mildly to be described as fits. When they hired Margo, the attractive Waldorf-Astoria roof dancer, for the leading feminine rôle in *Crime Without Passion,* she began at the outset to go in and play the rôle like a Broadway actress on the grand histrionic loose. "Hey, sweetie, stop it!" shouted Hecht. "Don't act. There's thousands of lice who do that — and look at 'em!" Margo stopped acting and duly turned out to be one of the screen's most winning and effective personalities. While looking at "rushes" of *The Scoundrel* in their projection room, Noël Coward, who played the central male figure in the film, protested against the hideousness of the dress that Julie Haydon, the leading woman, had on in the big dramatic scene wherein the hero bluntly tells the heroine that he is sick of her and is leaving her for good and all. "But, of course," politely allowed Coward, "it's too late now for us to do anything about it." "Not at all!" drawled Hecht and MacArthur. "We'll put in a line saying he's leaving her because of the dress."

The boys have been putting various paraphrases of that line into their life and work from the first day they entered into collaborative harness. And they will doubtless continue to do so when, at length and perhaps very soon now sick of pictures (or vice versa), they return to their early love, the theatre.

CHAPTER XIII

The Playwrights

ᄽ ᄽ

Clifford Odets

Clifford Odets has been hailed by the critics as the most sensational discovery that has come over the horizon since the *Santa Maria*. The hailing in point, whether sound or not sound, indicates, if nothing else, the American theatre's continued lack of good playwrights and, to boot, the pathetic critical intoxication when even a first-rate second-rater comes along. That Odets is, on the record of what he has thus far disclosed to us, more than such a first-rate second-rater no critic with less than thirty-two Stingers under his belt can intelligently argue. What he has given us are just four exhibits: one, *Waiting For Lefty,* the best of the lot, a mere prolonged one-acter utilizing the audience-actor device familiar to popular audiences for several decades but with the kick of a new passion in it; the second, *Till the Day I Die,* still another prolonged one-act play with two effective melodramatic situations but generally, by common consent, an inferior job; the third, *Awake and Sing,* a study of Bronx Jews containing some interesting character drawing and some snatches of sharp dramatic dialogue but on the whole a play at once defectively composed and toward its conclusion not a little bogus; and, most recently, *Paradise Lost*.

This *Paradise Lost* has caused his votaries some faint concern. It is, it seems, hardly what they expected of him, although their disappointment is couched in terms that seek slyly to conceal their previous overwhelming critical exuberance. There is no need, however, for any undue disconcertment on their part. In this new exhibit of his, Odets again clearly demonstrates the possession of all the unusual qualities which he demonstrated in his antecedent efforts and which evoked their ecstasies. The simple critical fact is that, together with these unusual qualities, he again also clearly demonstrates his weaknesses and defects which, in their uncontrollable ebullition, they neglected to perceive in those other plays and which now, somewhat belatedly, they have become uncomfortably conscious of.

That Odets has a share of real talent no one can gainsay. But that it is as yet insufficiently mastered and orchestrated into sound drama should be obvious. His faults were every bit as plain in *Awake and Sing, Till the Day I Die* and even in *Waiting For Lefty* as they are, now, in this *Paradise Lost*. He can write sharp, true, electric dialogue; he can feel passionately and he can convey that feeling; he has a good sense of character; he has eloquence; and he has that attribute so vital to the true tragic dramatist, pity. But he can also — and at times close upon heel — write counterfeit theatrical dialogue; he can feel and convey a grease-paint passion; he can sophisticate character to stage ends; he can be spuriously eloquent; and he can smear pity like mustard on what is essentially dramatic ham.

In *Paradise Lost* he admittedly attempts some Chekhovian dramaturgy, but Chekhov is as far from him as Pirandello was to B. M. Kaye a short time before in the equally admitted effort called *On Stage*. He pursues the Chekhov elliptical method and futilitarian scheme with such a vengeance that the ellipsis and the futility get the better not only of him but of his characters and his play, and in desperation at the end he struggles vainly to gather the threads together and achieve a last-minute-to-play centrifugal goal with a suddenly tacked-on panegyric to the future of man that sounds like an O. Henry twist brewed from Shaw's *Too True To Be Good* last-act curtain by Chekhov's Trigorin. Here and there, a scene attests to Odets' independent vitality; here and there, a passage of dialogue attests to his fine fire; and here and there, despite the banality of his radical utterance, his old passion sings its ringing song. But the amateur still goes arm in arm with the man who may one day possibly be a sound dramatist.

The growth of propaganda drama has been one of the most significant things about the past two theatrical seasons. Its chief accoucheurs, following upon the heels of Mr. Elmer Rice, have been the Theatre Union, down in the Luchow diocese, and the Group Theatre, up in the Automat and Rudy Vallée belt. It has inveighed against every-thing from the Nazis to labor conditions in the West Virginia coal mines and has whooped it up for everything from the oppressed southern Negro to Communism. Communism, of course, whatever the embellishing doodads, has been generally the main show. Sailors of Cattaro, stevedores of the American docks, amorous Russian movie directors on trans-Atlantic liners with an eye to the possibilities of colored wenches, New York taxi drivers, it matters not how first acts have started out, have one and all wound up in red union suits.

Odets is the best of the young propaganda playwrights, if not the best of the propagandists. As has been noted, he is the young man whom the gentlemen of the press have especially singled out as The Works. No such critical tributes have been read hereabouts since the Shuberts some years ago stopped sending out cases of Haig and Haig at Christmas. But Odets should not despair, even though he may meditate that one Martin Flavin was once, and not so very long ago, hailed with a similar enthusiasm after *Children of the Moon,* that one Cleves Kinkead, some time before that, was touted as a genius *par excellence* on the score of a dish called *Common Clay,* that Dan Totheroh, more recently, was anointed with the semen of pêche Melba because of *Wild Birds* and *Distant Drums,* and that, in short, it is a rare year that doesn't bring forth its dawning American Ibsen, or at least its potential Hauptmann. That Mr. Odets seems to have a considerable talent for the theatre is, as already stated, true, but that he is as yet the white-headed and purple-whiskered boy he has been confidently announced to be is a horse of another color. While he reveals an aptitude for the melodramatic tricks of the stage that William Gillette might even in his prime have envied, while he can write dialogue with a glint of lightning to it, and while he indicates an integrity above the average, he is still, as a dramatist, much like a pianist who has learned much more about the loud pedal than he has about harmony.

As a propagandist, moreover, our promising friend has an equal amount to learn. Expert propaganda consists in a sleight-of-hand shuffling of the deck and a sharky dealing out of the cards from the bottom, with the sucker artfully persuaded that he has detected nothing wrong and duly hornswoggled. Odets stacks the deck so obviously and deals out his cards so awkwardly that he gives himself and his purpose away. In the theatre I, for one, despite all my public pretensions to an immaculate and unassailable critical sagacity, may readily be nousled by a sufficiently wily playwright into believing, at least for the moment, almost anything. I have thus, in my time, been bamboozled into a sympathetic metaphysical liaison with everything from the invincible goodness of God to the doctrine that all bachelors possessed of a dress suit are romantic guinea pigs and from the theory that the American Indian invariably planned his attacks on white settlements and military garrisons strictly after the cumulative third act dramaturgical formula of Sardou to the sanctity of love. I have been, in a word, as I remain, a come-on for any skilful playwright, be he however otherwise an idiot. But bust my britches if propaganda playwrights like Odets, for all their other virtues, can hocus me into their way of thinking by hitting me over the head — soft theatrically as it is — with the sledge-hammer of their stark prejudices. I am perfectly willing to be converted to Communism if need be, or to Fascism, Nudism, or even the Hay diet, but the job can't be accomplished by Odets boys who argue that Stalin is the only true redeemer and that everybody else is cheese because New York taxi drivers aren't paid enough by their villainous capitalistic bosses to buy even one evening shirt, much less a top hat, at Brooks Brothers (*vide Waiting for Lefty*), and because Hitler, like Franklin Roosevelt and Frances Perkins, is partial to means to frustrate Communism that might be frowned upon by Emily Post (*vide Till the Day I Die*).

Odets' propaganda, in short, is for those who are already convinced of its subject matter before the curtain goes up. And Odets' drama is like the late Huey Long in that it has a world of extrinsic vitality with a minimum of intrinsic equilibrium. That is, so far.

Nevertheless, unlike the other Little Red Writing Hoods who seem to believe that true literary and dramatic art consists solely in crying *Wolf!* at capitalistic society for a couple of hours, Comrade Odets, though likewise not niggardly with his lupine ululations, realizes that a little

[226]

ability isn't a bad thing to have around at the same time. What is more, he has that ability, even if he is as yet apparently unable to discipline it and make it serve its best ends. He has, further, all the limitless vitality and bold eagerness of a Scotch terrier trying to leap up at an aëroplane, all the dancing glow of a far fire against the distant sky. But he is still sometimes in a general way like Shipwreck Kelly in that, though he deposits himself cockily atop a high flag-pole and though no one will gainsay his dexterity in thumbing his nose at the bourgeoisie below without falling off, it all occasionally seems, despite the spectacularity of the act, to be just a little gratuitously nutty.

In *Paradise Lost* his climbing ambition has brought him, as recorded, to tackle a Chekhovian play. But all that he has succeeded in confecting, aside from two or three ably contrived short episodes, is an exhibit that mistakes the constant aimless wandering in and out of actors for Chekhov's inner psychological and philosophical wanderings, that confounds theatrical meaninglessness with Chekhovian dramatic futility, and that confuses exaggerated external eccentricity of character with the uncertainty and chaos of the Chekhovian dramatic soul.

But while it is not deplorable to fail in so lofty an ambition — it is better to write third-rate Chekhov than first-rate Samuel Shipman any day — it is discouraging to observe several new and extra-measure shortcomings in Odets that one had not anticipated. One of the most discouraging of these is the amateurish transparency with which he maneuvers the injunction of certain lesser modern dramatists to the effect that all human beings have a good side to them as well as a bad and that, to make even a deep-dyed villain with a black moustache and patent leather riding boots real and convincing, you have to show at least once during the evening that he kicks only big dogs and loves his mother. Odets goes about the business with the comprehensive assiduity of a beaver in heat. By the time his play nears its finish his gunman taxicab driver who has seduced his best friend's wife and has been a hellion generally has been shown to have a heart as contrite as a repentant Salvation Army sinner, his ignoble embezzler has been revealed as a creature possessed of such delicate sensibility as would shame the hero of *The Passing of the Third Floor Back,* his old Gus, the family friend, who has been a sponger and who has lasciviously monkeyed with young girls in the subway has been disclosed as the very soul and essence of generosity and honor, and so on. All that is lacking at the eleven o'clock curtain, in point of fact, is a grand transformation scene in which everyone who hasn't already been shot and who isn't already there is shown going to heaven at the end of gold wires. Even as it is, the transformation scene is at least metaphorically present, what with Old Man Gordon standing whipped and beaten amid the wreckage of the world around him and yet delivering such a lush panegyric to the future bliss of mankind as makes the ordinary happy

ending of the commercial Broadway drama look like the
finish of *Othello*.

Another thing about our Comrade that worries us is the
self-confusion that has worked itself into the body of his
writing. It is sometimes hard to know whether he is doing things with a straight face or not. When, for example,
he pulls the old joke about the woman who sleeps with
cats (Mrs. Katz), we can't be too sure that he is doing it
knowingly, even though he puts it in the mouth of a
tedious gabbler, just as we find ourselves disquieted when
a line or speech which he seems to regard as literate and
even slightly poetic suddenly goes oh-yeah on itself. His
Communist allusions and challenges, furthermore, while
assuredly not criticizable in themselves, are couched in
terms of the utmost banality, which is somewhat surprising from a writer who can speak his mind on other subjects with some eloquence and freshness. In this, however,
he shares the common fault of most of the other local
Little Red Writing Hoods. What they say may have sense,
but it also has such an utter weakness and poverty of expression that it resists — as one's palate grudgingly resists
cut and watered whiskey — an otherwise conceivably hospitable surrender to it.

Odets is too precious a talent not to listen attentively to,
and profit by, the harsh criticism that is being widely written of him at this apparently befuddled stage of his career.
Its very harshness indicates the esteem in which it holds his
future, for critics seldom exert their severity in the case of

hacks. Let him forget that some of my colleagues prematurely and very foolishly, when he had just barely begun to sprout, proclaimed him a full-fledged genius and let him now read the misgivings of those deluded ones not with an arrogant, if rather justified, snort, but with a humorous humility and reinduced modesty that will put him safely back on the path that may lead him ultimately to glory.

What concerns us in the meantime, however, is a dubiety as to young Mr. Odets' preparation and working background. This dubiety is predicated upon nothing less than Mr. Odets' own innocent and artless self-confessions.

Having announced that his latest work was influenced by Chekhov and that it reflected the Chekhovian technique, it was, for example, none too reassuring to learn from a subsequently published admission that he had never read and knew nothing of Chekhov's finest play, *The Cherry Orchard*. Indignant over criticism of his dramaturgy in *Paradise Lost,* it became further apparent that, struggling to defend himself, he was completely unaware of the good point for the defence to be found in Strindberg, notably *The Spook Sonata*. Attempting in a public statement to confound his critics in other directions, it became painfully obvious that his desire to have people think he knew something about music was based upon sheer affectation, and that his musical knowledge must have been gained either from loose and casual reading or at bogus second-hand. Surely some kind friend should

[230]

have prevented him from issuing such absurd statements as those concerning Mozart and Beethoven. Consider, in example, this: " For as the established social order breaks down, the same process is working out in the artist's forms. Blithely, and with great talent, Mozart is able to spill twoscore or so symphonies on paper. Beethoven, a few years later, in a period of social flux, is able to write only nine, which means that the symphonic form was sufficiently stabilized for Mozart to keep minting out coins from the same mold, while *his distinguished pupil* had to make a new mold for each of his gold pieces."

Even when it comes to the present-day theatre and drama, Mr. Odets displays an equipment of information hardly more copious than that exercised by him in the direction of music. " Even a cursory examination of serious American dramatists' work shows serious craft problems. It is easy to see that for them the slick synthetic plot play is an outmoded form. *The fourth act has long since been delivered to the ash-heap.*" Mr. Odets will perhaps not deny that Eugene O'Neill is a serious American dramatist, yet O'Neill's very last play was in the four-act form. And there are other instances that might equally embarrass the profound Mr. Odets.

" Even where the three-act form is retained, ' third act trouble ' is general instead of exceptional," he continues. This is simon-pure bosh. What of O'Neill's excellent third acts, *e.g., Ah, Wilderness!*, etc.? What of Maxwell Anderson's? What of the admirable third acts of our most serious American writer of comedy, S. N. Behrman? What, to make the dramaturgical argument more general, of the third acts of the outstanding present-day European dramatists?

Mr. Odets goes on to instruct us in his ignorance. " The final truth is that Chekhov's people are not imaginative characters, but spring from the social impasse around him. . . . He knew that to imprison them in plots would be to do violence to the deepest truths of their lives and social backgrounds. O'Casey in the bulk of his plays knows the same thing about his people." O'Casey knows nothing of the sort. Mr. Odets should acquaint himself with O'Casey's work. There is enough so-called plot in the drama of O'Casey to satisfy even half a dozen Owen Davises.

A few months ago, in addition, I am told that Odets actually wrote a letter to Bernard Shaw, insisting that Shaw pay attention to him on the ground that " I am your playwriting son! " — assuredly as ridiculous critically as it is sophomorically belated. Playwrights of all kinds have been writing that vainglorious twaddle to Shaw for the last twenty-five years.

These are but a few symptoms of one's worry over Odets. They hardly indicate the solidity under him and under his writing that his enthusiasts had believed was there. Let us hope that he will henceforth study, take careful stock of himself, remain silent apart from the speech of his dramas — and slowly and safely grow up.

Maxwell Anderson

The late Avery Hopwood's chief and most vociferous hate on life was the valuable time that he, like every other practitioner of one or another of the arts, had to waste daily in bathing, shaving, brushing his hair, cleaning his fingernails, dressing and otherwise making himself unnecessarily presentable to a public for not more than three or four members of which he cared a faint hoot. While the dramatic critic in active practice feels much the same way about it as Hopwood, he has an additional and even more uberous grouse, to wit, the valuable time he is forced to dissipate nightly digging into the rubbish-can of the theatre in the fond hope of finding therein, at belated intervals, something fair and fine and just a little golden.

It is a notable season that, out of a hundred or more productions, disgorges — aside from musical pieces — even ten plays that come within hailing distance of the taste of the kind of man who, soon after meeting an attractive woman, doesn't inquire of her how much she weighs, or of the kind of woman who, soon after meeting an attractive man, doesn't ask him to let her see his hand and who then takes it in hers, gazes intently at the palm, affects a very occult and inscrutable look, and gives a silent show of detecting in the lines thereon something excessively portentous. The great majority of the exhibits which the critic has to attend in the pursuit of duty fall into either one of two categories: the downright and splen-

[233]

diferously fecal, or the well-intentioned but sadly middling. The plays in the first group, aside from the precious hours he has had to throw away in seeing them, do not otherwise pox him, as he may peremptorily dismiss them with a line of copy, consisting mainly of variations on the thematic word *junk*. But the plays in the second get in his hair. He cannot thus quickly dismiss them, for they honestly try to get somewhere, and he cannot treat of them at sober length because, despite their good intentions, they don't get there. So he has to waste additional time figuring out how to say the same old thing about them in some fresh and original critical manner. He knows that he can't go on holding his customers and getting editors to lay out handsome honoraria by constantly mouthing the venerable, if perfectly accurate, observations that the achievement is not up to the intention, that the materials are better than the execution of them, that while the plays are superior to the average they are still a very far cry from really reputable drama, etc., etc.

Maxwell Anderson's *Valley Forge* is such a play. It is honest; it is superior to the average but still a very far cry from really reputable drama; its materials are better than the author's execution of them; its achievement is not up to its intention, etc., etc. So much for the old critical rubber-stamps — and my publisher may deduct a dollar and a quarter from my royalty check for setting them down here. And now, *manibus pedibusque,* to try to earn the dollar and a quarter back again.

Mr. Anderson, who is one of the most gifted and endorsable writers for our stage, on this occasion has not written a drama so much as a recitation. From first to last, save for an intermittent and fleeting episode, his account of Washington's tribulations tries to talk its way, rather than to act its way, into drama. It is largely declamation that essays to warm itself into theatrical life with periodic mild echoes of the gross locutions of *What Price Glory?*, with snatches of physical rough-house, and with a dozen or so musket shots. And the manuscript's general air of dramaless declamation was heightened by the stage direction, which had evidently instructed the actors to refrain from the slightest indulgence in the histrionics commonly associated with "undignified" melodrama. As a consequence, we had an essentially heroic manuscript played — much as Percy MacKaye's *Washington* some years ago was played — as if it were just a little ashamed of and superior to a theatre stage.

Nor does the play do much credit to Mr. Anderson's powers of original dramatic invention. One already begins to fear the worst, indeed, when in the very first scene he trots out that seemingly inevitable hokum character in all plays dealing with soldiermen and war: the delicate and sensitive young boy, weakened and sickened by the cruelties and hardships of combat, who nevertheless is bravely determined to carry on and who, in the end, dies beatifically and proclaiming lofty thoughts the while the General himself — or at least a lieutenant-colonel —

[235]

stands in moist and heart-touched sympathy over his ex-
piring form. These initial qualms are doubled when, not
long afterward in the first act, the heroine makes her way
through the enemy lines by dressing herself up as a boy.
And they are tripled — if not dramatically then certainly
historically and biographically — when our own George
Washington, that hot papa, thereupon abruptly declines
the little beauty's thinly veiled invitation to spend the
night with her on the ground that an old, old man like
himself (Mr. Anderson apparently is unaware that Washington was at the time not yet forty-six) is beyond any
such sports! Even had Washington been seventy-six, Mr.
Anderson's dramatic-psychological equipment would be
leaky, for is it not true that a man defeated — as Washington at the moment was — arbitrarily seeks the nepenthe
in a woman's arms that he has small immediate wish for
when crowded success is shining upon him?

With the subsequent production of *Winterset,* it still
remains a matter of doubt to me if Mr. Anderson has entirely made up his own mind whether he wishes to ad-
dress his plays to literary critics or to drama critics. In
the case of this, his latest play, the two stools are again
in evidence, with the literary critics sitting somewhat
easier than the drama critics. More than ever with *Winterset* I find myself thinking back to 1914 or thereabout and
to the first time I heard of Anderson. Louis Sherwin, at
the time drama critic for the since deceased *Globe,* came
one morning into the office of the old *Smart Set* maga-

zine, of which I was co-editor, and told me that there was
a first-rate editorial writer on the paper who was writing,
on the side and in addition, some very good verse. Sherwin
suggested that I get into touch with him and ask to see
some of the verse. I did, found it good, as Sherwin had,
and published some of it. I also began reading the fellow's
editorials on such topics as politics, justice, etc., and likewise found them good. That combination talented newspaper editorial writer and poet was Maxwell Anderson
and it is my conviction that the present-day dramatist
Maxwell Anderson remains, after these many years, still
part editorial writer and part poet and that the two are
not as yet either properly differentiated or convincingly
synchronized and orchestrated.

In *Winterset,* accordingly, we have, for all its other un-
deniable high virtues, a vacillating pendulum swinging
uncertainly now toward the forthright melodrama of a
son seeking to avenge the murder of a father and then
toward a semi-mystical, semi-philosophical blank verse.
Gorki tries to dance with Maeterlinck, and O'Neill with
Stephen Phillips, both couples bumping embarrassingly at
times into Robert Sherwood and the late Paul Armstrong.
Sharp and true direction is periodically missing. The intention was doubtless a tale of Sacco-Vanzetti vengeance
seen synchronously through the eyes of the Gorki of
Night Refuge and the Gluck of *Iphigenia,* with minor
variations by Schubert, and much of the intention is
dramatically realized, but there is also a suggestion of

Maeterlinck and Sam Leibowitz after a brief holiday in Russia with Jehudi Menuhin. However, there is in some of his lines authentic song; in some of his scenes the flame of beautiful drama; and in all of his intention dignity, and high aim, and courage. And there is one thing else. We had, in the last theatrical year, plays of slick and fancy humor, plays that have caught neatly the essence of novels, plays that have met happily the demands of lighter entertainment, but only in this *Winterset,* with all its faults, did we engage the American drama in a valiant, if not always unslipping, mountain climb toward the proud peaks of dramatic-literary beauty.

Robert Emmet Sherwood

Ever since the late William Archer wrote himself into the public awe and a considerable slice of the box-office with a 10–20–30 melodrama that contained one $3.50 allusion to Bernard Shaw, writers of melodrama on both sides of the Atlantic have tried to horn in on the technique of *The Green Goddess'* author. The result has been a succession of melodramas in which the old-time smell of gunpowder has been largely supplanted by the smell of the book-shop and which, in many cases, are distinguishable from drawing-room drama only by virtue of the fact that certain of their scenes are laid out of doors.

The latest follower in what are at least Archer's technical footsteps was Mr. Robert Emmet Sherwood. His exhibit was called *The Petrified Forest* and it improved upon

Archer's single reference to Shaw with three references to Mark Twain, Lew Wallace and François Villon. This, naturally, created a tremendous stir among the critics, one of whom was so enormously impressed that he hailed the exhibit as " wise, mature, of rich flavor and fine penetration . . . there is more in it than meets the casual eye or the midnight typewriter . . . here is a play to take and hold high . . . my hat is off . . . and if I had four hats they would all be off in general and grateful salute! " Such enthusiasm was easy to understand when one recalls that not only had Mr. Sherwood mentioned *three* authors but, improving even more greatly upon Archer, had included in his melodrama *three* machine guns. This combination of remarkable intelligence with the most vigorous boom-boom properties of old-time blood and thunder melodrama was irresistible. The show was a huge success.

Nor did Mr. Sherwood stint in other directions. As the critics rapturously informed you, he further embellished his exhibit with " some remarkably fine and profound symbolism," the aforesaid remarkably fine and profound symbolism reposing in the title of his play of which " for clue Mr. Sherwood makes the artist say that he belongs in the petrified forest with all the other dead and turned to stone illusions of a credulous society."

Then there was, too, " some deep philosophy." It was somewhat difficult to make out from the ebullient critical appraisals just what and where this deep philosophy was, but from a first-hand engagement with it I take it that an

illustration might be had in Mr. Sherwood's hero's proclamation that Mr. Sherwood's heroine was just what the
present world needs for its salvation, confidence and faith.

This heroine was a young girl working in a lunch room
at a cross-roads in the eastern Arizona desert, Gabby Maple
by name. Gabby was a free, outspoken sweet one who
offered herself without marriage to the hero and offered,
to boot, to provide him with money out of her own pocket.
When he declined the proffer, she promptly tendered herself for a moonlit roll in the grass to a husky young em-
ployee of her father's. In a word, Gabby was, one fears,
what is known in unrefined society as a pushover. This
particular phase of Mr. Sherwood's " deep philosophy " as
to what the present world needs for its salvation, confidence and faith therefore seemed to elude me. Nor was
I able to get much farther into his metaphysic arguing
that " the artist and the gangster, the dilletante and the
bully, are useless and impotent and archaic, but out of
them and this present confusion may come a world that is
fit to live in." How the world is going to be improved by
getting rid of artists and gunmen and substituting for
them pushovers with a penchant for the ejaculation
bastard, I am afraid I shall have to leave to younger
philosophers than myself to figure out.

Let it be repeated at once, however, that Mr. Sherwood's
play seems to be exactly the kind of show that not only the
reviewers but lay theatregoers are generally crazy about,
and then let it be recorded in a small and doubtless wholly

unimportant voice that it still isn't the kind that this particular critic has any taste for. It was shrewdly manufactured; it was not without a modicum of theatrical interest even so far as the aforesaid critic was concerned; and it achieved at least part of its author's purpose. But I trust that its author will not refuse to take off his hat and bow low to me when we pass on the boulevards if I write that, once you have nominated it a very smart box-office show, you have said the best about it that you honestly and critically can.

I may be doing the agreeable Mr. Sherwood a gross and rightly resented injustice when I hazard the opinion that he aimed much higher in his own mind than the mere creation of such a good box-office show and that he imagined he was writing something pretty tony in the way of a symbolical-philosophical exhibit, even though it did contain four gangsters, three machine guns and two bottles of whiskey. I hope for his reputation's sake that he didn't, although there is evidence in the manuscript that leads us doubtfully to scratch our heads. This evidence refractorily suggests that Mr. Sherwood pleasured himself with the idea that he had some profound cosmic philosophies to unload, along with some pretty fine symbolism, and that his melodrama, down in his secret heart, took second place to them. But despite the fact that the evidence in question was accepted at its face value by almost all the reviewers, who enthusiastically elected Mr. Sherwood to a metaphysical niche only a couple of inches below that occupied jointly by Plato and Socrates, I like to believe that Mr. Sherwood was fooling himself very little and the critical lads a lot, and that much of the stuff they fell for he wrote with his tongue in his cheek. If he didn't, may God and the headmaster of the Oswego School for Young Boys have mercy on his future.

Mr. Sherwood, whatever his deficiencies as a thinker and a dramatist of any bulk, is certainly not a cheapjack. There is a measure of pride in him, and a seeming resolve to try to do something better than the common run of Broadway mishmash. But he is no philosopher, and he himself, let us trust, will be the first to know and to admit it. What he is is a hard-working dramaturgical stagehand who thus far has succeeded in producing nothing of any real quality, but who is clearly so eager to and so sincere about his job that it is conceivable that someday, when he grows older and a little more impatient with himself, he may. As of today, he still betrays the youthful wish to intellectualize plays that would be twice as good if he allowed them to pursue their simple emotional and dramatic courses, and he still has not achieved the artist's contempt of mob reaction to his characters. He still relishes the sure-fire, if dramatically corrupting, laugh and he still surrenders to the quick and facile, if internally dubious, effectiveness of situation and character. Thus, in this particular play of his, though he knows as well as you and I do that his young heroine, her fancy thrillingly wrapped round his artist hero, would no more suddenly decide to

go out and roll in the grass with a hick lunchroom em-
ployee than you and I would suddenly decide to go out
and guzzle a magnum of strawberry pop, he permits her
to do that very thing merely to prick his audience. Thus,
though he is too experienced to believe for a moment that
his rich Middle-Western married woman would propose
to a gunman, whom she had just laid eyes on, that he take
her for a roll in the hay, he also permits her to do it in
order to get an easy audience laugh. And there are a sufficiently illuminating number of other such thuses. That's
not honest dramatic writing, Mr. Sherwood, as you, being
an honest fellow personally and something of a good critic
too, will agree, even if it does make a wad of money at
the ticket-till.

Following *The Petrified Forest,* our subject provided us
with a second specimen of so-called intellectualized melodrama. It bore the title *Idiot's Delight* and its technique
was generally similar to that in the antecedent exhibit.
Here, Mr. Sherwood occupied himself with the stupidity of
war. But his philosophical equipment permitted him to
get no farther than the posing of various grave questions
and the answering of them with a like number of ditties
and clog dances on the part of his central character, a
vaudeville hoofer. The success of the affair with various
critics, and also at the box-office, equalled that of his earlier
play.

Sidney Kingsley

Sidney Kingsley finds himself in the unfortunately embarrassing position of having first-rate dramatic ideas and a second-rate dramatic equipment. But he was apparently born with a rabbit's foot in his mouth, for his indifferent play scripts seem to have a way of falling into hands that are able to gloss over their incapacities and make them pass muster as something relatively gustful. Thus, two seasons ago, his *Men in White* profited from the beneficent dramatic editorial advice of Mr. Sidney Phillips, to whose attention he first brought it and who helped the author to guide it into the faint semblance of merit that illaqueated a Pulitzer prize committee. And thus, this last season, his *Dead End* profited from the visual legerdemain of Mr. Norman Bel Geddes, who — like some apt couturière with an anatomically platonic figure — laid hold of its skimpy and knock-kneed dramaturgy and gave it an aspect of seductive grace and fluid line.

As a dramatic manuscript *Dead End* suggests a virtuoso cornet solo by Jane Addams periodically interrupted by a Harry Von Tilzer nickel piano, with a mandolin attachment. Every now and again as its picture of wretched tenement urchins headed irrevocably for life's criminal sting begins to penetrate into the emotions, the author chills the effect by introducing such slices of shameless hokum as the love of a poor tenement boy (and a cripple, to boot) for a girl of the *luxe* upper classes, to say nothing of

[244]

speeches, wistfully recited in the moonlight, comparing life to a little paper boat floating helplessly down the gutter and hopeless love to a drowning star. As a dramatic poet, one fears, Mr. Kingsley is in the Eddie Guest class. What is more, while his understanding of the lowly and humble is often acute, his knowledge of the economically and socially more lofty has evidently been culled from the kind of novels that the maids of the latter read on their Thursdays off. As his play presumes seriously to contrast the life and condition of the upper and lower classes, this is hardly auspicious. There is something refractorily humorous about his bon-tons whole-heartedly accepting obvious and self-confessed kept women into their aristocratic circle, his amorous rendezvous of evening-clad feminine riches with lowly masculine rags in alleys and on slum waterfronts, and his elaborate yachting dance parties ostensibly attended — aside from two outside couples — exclusively by the occupants of his fashionable apartment dwelling, whether supposedly River House or not.

As a play, in short, *Dead End* amounts to little more than a basically eloquent theme insufficiently embroidered with the colored silks of imagination and skilful dramaturgy. But as a show maneuvered by Geddes it swept up an audience with a very considerable theatrical force and tricked the benignly uncritical into seeing in it virtues that Kingsley only dreamed of. Taking the scenario placing in juxtaposition the squalid poor and the gimpy rich, Geddes, with his art catching a note of realism plus, fattened the outline into a visual stage piece of high and vigorous thrust. So vigorous, indeed, that certain susceptible critics were bamboozled into mistaking his impressive scenery, lighting and stage generalship for an impressive sociological document.

Here and there we noted other criticians who, while admiring Geddes' realistic production, at the same time deplored it, dubbing it a throwback to the Belasco day when the ultimate in art in West Forty-fourth Street was considered to be the wafting over the footlights of recognizable coffee fumes from a pot actually boiling on a real stove in a scrupulous reproduction of a Childs restaurant. Such laments customarily emanate from those who in turn believe that the ultimate in stage art, whatever the nature of the particular dramas, are sets that look like something thought up by a hophead full of aquavit and suffering slightly, in addition, from hereditary insanity and an attack of jungle fever. Thus, a production of even *Pillars of Society* that doesn't closely suggest a free-for-all fight between Cubists and Vorticists on the one side and Dadaists and Fauvists on the other, with several designers of Norway travel-cruise posters horning in, is displeasing to their æsthetic sensibilities.

That there must always remain a place for production realism in the theatre, despite the patent fact that it was worked almost to death and became a little ridiculous in the Belasco era, should be plain. What made Belasco realism nonsensical was its constant visitation upon fake-realistic plays. It was the old maestro's habit of taking a manuscript that cheaply romanticized fact and truth and lodging it in settings that sought to conceal the sophistication that made him a critical laughing stock. All the realistic tenement streets and Childs restaurants and ranch houses that he ever threw upon his stage couldn't conceal the adulterated and unrealistic dishes of dramatic tripe that he produced within them. George Bronson Howard and Wilson Mizner did the backward criticism of the day a service when they showed up, for once and all, the Belasco fraud by writing an honestly realistic version of *The Easiest Way,* producing it without obfuscating thousand-dollar Tiffany lamps, door locks that enchanted the nitwits by clicking loudly when keys were turned in them, and cigars containing small electric batteries that gleamed in the darkness, and proving that there was a very great difference between truthful drama and merely truthful props.

Dead End, whatever its deficiencies as a dramatic script and its occasional lapses into the romantic hokum of the old House of David, is often basically honest in its realism and Geddes' production was accordingly the only right and proper kind of production for it. Now and again the wafted smell of cubeb cigarettes (surely those gutter kids would have walked a mile for a Camel) or something else of the sort invaded the authenticity of the realistic picture, but on the whole the job was a thoroughly admirable one.

Lillian Hellman

Miss Hellman's first dramatic effort, *The Children's Hour,* is a material contribution to American playwriting. The stage production, save in the final passages, was, furthermore, a credit to the text. Those final passages themselves, indeed, may have been a discredit to the stage production, for while they may be, as the author convincingly contends, in the key of truth and hard fact, they nevertheless constitute dubious theatre. People, thousands, ten thousands of them, still commit suicide when the grimness of fate staggers them, but the modern drama at its best is a philosopher or a wit or a psychoanalytical professor which credibly argues its own fate-struck children out of doing it. However, the manuscript merits your devoted attention. Its theme you already know: the ruin and tragedy that befall two young women teachers in a girls' school following a whispered accusation — on the part of a maleficent little pupil — that they are Lesbians.

In the loud insistence of several of my critical colleagues that the title of the play is unduly misleading and that the play is assuredly not for children, I fear that I cannot entirely concur. It assuredly is for children, as well as for adults, unless it be deemed expedient to bring up American youngsters in the belief that dramatic art is solely something in which all the characters are dressed as playing-cards, rabbits and walruses. Children may not like it, true enough, any more than they like castor oil, but it will be equally good for them. Nevertheless, in the pretty general insistence that the last half of the last act is defective, I can — as noted — concur fully, though it seems to me that several of the arguments advanced in company with that insistence are disingenuous. One of these is that, in this latter section of the manuscript, none of the adults involved displays a modicum of common sense. That they do not, as charged, display a modicum of common sense is true, but their failure to display it is certainly logical, and dramatically sound enough. It is seldom the gift of mortals to display acute common sense when emotion overwhelms them, save perhaps in the plays of Bernard Shaw. Common sense is rarely present on such occasions in actual life, and its arbitrary introduction into drama in emotional crises would have wrecked many of the finest plays ever written. This silly longing for common sense in drama is often part and parcel of the passion for the so-called "realistic" drama, itself frequently so largely fraudulent and bogus. There is a true romance in fuddled feeling, and true drama, and realism and logic have no place and no welcome on that side of the footlights. One too many touches of adult common sense, let such critics reflect, would make *Antony and Cleopatra*, aside from its poetry, dramatically indistinguishable from one of John Drinkwater's plays.

Another contention against the final moments of Miss Hellman's play is the re-introduction of the apologetic grandmother and the explanation of the brat's malfeasance. Here, again, truth and the theatre are critically divorced. What Miss Hellman has written is essential to the integrity of her theme, even if in stage practice it be discommodious to an audience's patience. Her show may be over and done with before the aforesaid re-introduction and explanation, but her play — that is, her manuscript in all its honesty — is not. What she has written is necessary. So we come, myself along with the others, once again to the reluctant conclusion and admission that the theatre must woefully often forego fact and truth to make good plays better than they are and to satisfy even the more intelligent audience.

George M. Cohan

It may seem odd to use George M. Cohan as an index, but I believe that in no surer way than through the changed appraisal of him may the considerable advance of local drama criticism be perceived. The critics of his early playwriting days saw in him, if they so much as condescended even to glance at him, a mere vulgar vaudeville smarty, to be listed on a level with the man who wrote Lew Dockstader's olio monologues or one of the lesser of Goldman's performing dogs. With the exitus of these critics, brought on by senility, an over-indulgence in teas with Shakespearean actresses or strainful labor on voluminous tomes celebrating the god-like attributes of Augustin Daly, there appeared a second group who, still under the influence of their critical forbears, discerned in the plays of Cohan's

middle period only a quickstep illiteracy and cheap cocki-
ness, and in the actor-author himself a presuming little
Broadway gutter-snipe. With the death, in turn, of these
gentlemen, brought on by apoplexy induced by attempts
to conciliate the Shuberts or by an intemperate gourman-
dizing of David Belasco's free dinners, accompanied by
his rare 1912 Napoleon brandy, still another and younger
fraternity came into being and it was this newer lot that
for the first time began to detect in both the old and the
new plays of Cohan something of real native humor and
merit, and in the fellow who wrote and sometimes acted
in them no inappreciable two-a-day hoofer with a penchant for talking out of the side of his mouth but the most
surefooted and proficient actor in the whole American
theatre.

I think I report history accurately, for I have lived and
operated through the three periods in question. What is
more, I recall that when, in the far days of my critical
novitiate, I somehow — either through a clairvoyance inherited from a great-uncle who occultly predicted himself
on eight different occasions into jail or through an ob-
stinacy in differing from mob opinion inherited doubtless
from the aforesaid great-uncle's pet mule — managed to
discover a very considerable virtue in Cohan and, to the
disgust of my punditical editor, put it into print, I was
put down by the first two sets of critics as even more
vulgar, more illiterate and more cocky than Cohan himself, and was thenceforth denied a bowing privilege to

all the eminentos of the craft, from William Winter and J. Ranken Towse on the one hand to Alan Dale and Acton Davies on the other.

That George M. Cohan has actually come closer to writing what is an American approximation, however occasionally lopsided, to certain of the Abbey Theatre's Irish folk exhibits, has for some time now been apparent to local criticism. And in the few instances where it still isn't apparent, the lacuna is sufficiently bridged by a recognition of the fact by various Irish cognoscenti themselves. The ubiquity in the Cohan drama of crooks, detectives in derbies and cops, the characters' alecky brashness of speech and their boozy excursions into mundane philosophy, all of which for so long offended and even outraged the pedagogic critical æsthetic on the ground that such lush academicians as Augustus Thomas and J. Hartley Manners wouldn't conceivably descend to such plebeianisms, have latterly been appreciated as thoroughly honest, appropriate and soundly integral elements in a reflection of the particular phases of American life and character with which Cohan has dealt. And so, too, has it come to be appreciated that if the materials he chooses to treat of are cheap, so are they cheap in truth and actuality. He is the humorous reporter and impudent interpreter of a droll and frivolous segment of our people. And if often the vulgar flavor of Broadway has revealed itself in his plays, let it not be forgotten that it is of vulgar Broadway he has often written, and that vulgar Broadway may possibly be as valid and acute a subject for an American playwright like Cohan as the vulgar Bronx is for one like Odets. Or, for that matter, as the doubly vulgar Boul' Mich' has been, over three-quarters of a century, for any number of French playwrights.

Cohan's latest, *Dear Old Darling,* while an unaccountable box-office failure and while it didn't measure up to his better things, still contained a sufficient measure of his sly observation of human idiocies, along with his uncommon knack of telling off character by a single foolish speech or a single vacant look, to make it decidedly amusing theatrical fare. As in the past, most of the male performers, whatever the nature of their rôles, comported themselves much in the image of Mr. Cohan himself and, also as in the past, the scenery economically harked back to the cradle days of Cain's warehouse. On this occasion, himself doubtless conscious of its deplorable antiquity and much-used aspect, Mr. Cohan sought to throw his audience partly off its guard of critical consciousness by putting in a line saying that he had inherited the house from his father. This coming year when he uses the same set in his next play we may accordingly and confidently expect him to put in a line saying he inherited it from his grandfather.

Benavente and Lorca

Jacinto Benavente, as you know, is the foremost living dramatist of Spain. He is also one of the foremost living bores in or out of Spain. I appreciate that this is no way to talk about a man who occupies so lofty a position in his native land, who has been awarded the Nobel prize, who has had countless championing pundits in various countries, who has been decorated with so many academic gold medals that he suffers from lead poisoning, and who for thirty years has had the pick of the girls in Madrid. Surely so important a fellow should be treated with proper respect and not be disparaged in so bourgeois a manner. Well, I duly and humbly apologize, and repeat that this great man is one of the biggest bores to be encountered anywhere in the modern theatre.

This momentous decision is not arrived at, facilely and carelessly, after a mere consideration of the play called *Field of Ermine,* his most recent American production. It is arrived at after reading every play that our magnifico ever wrote and after seeing a sufficient number of them played on the stages not only of this country but of his own as well. *Field of Ermine,* however, may none the less be offered as a delectable example. That it was written back in 1916 is of no immediate critical point, as it was considerably dated even then. Allowing the author a large rebate on the English translation of John Garrett Underhill, a translation patently so overawed by the sanctity of Benavente that it is as humbly and dully obedient to the original as one of Cain's storehouse horses to its driver's whip, the play yet comes into the theatre of today like a dusty ghost of a thirty-year-old corpse. And not only in its thematic content, but also in its character drawing and general literary-dramatic craftsmanship. Duly trotted out are all the stencils of the early Pinero and French problem play era: the loose woman and her illegitimate child, the aristocratic relatives of the child's presumptive father, the elderly gay Lord Quex with an eye still to the fair sex, the Cayley Drummle whom no woman has ever, alas, loved, but who is a tender, understanding and deeply sympathetic friend to the troubled heroine, the device of taking the banal edge off certain of the playwright's pet philosophies by shrewdly attributing the dullest of them to their spokesman's grandfather and the somewhat slightly less dull to his father, etc. The dialogue, replete with moist references to the human heart and soul, is generally of a Josephine Baker super-elegance and has an air of being served to the various characters called upon to speak it by a consciously recherché butler. The speeches, further, remind one of a man sending a night letter telegram who can well say everything necessary in twenty-five words but who is determined willy-nilly to get his money's worth and who laboriously works over the message until he gets in the full and allotted fifty. Poor Echegaray, a really talented Spanish dramatist, must toss about in his grave when he contemplates such stuff being still hailed by Spaniards as high dramatic art.

Close on the heels of the above nonesuch came a second exhibit from the Spanish: *Bitter Oleander*, by Federico Garcia Lorca. If additional proof were needed that the Spanish drama, with exception as rare as a steak Tartare, is no longer welcome to the American stage, here it was with a vengeance. What we got on this occasion was one of those peasant tragedies that the Spanish love and which generally seem just a bit mutinously comical to intelligent foreign audiences. They are, the majority of them, cut from much the same pattern, with everybody gay and happy and wearing bright yellow costumes in Act I and with everybody grieving over the death of someone or other and wearing deep mourning in Act III. I don't happen to be familiar with Lorca's original text, but there is no apparent reason to believe that it is much superior to the English translation which we engaged, even though that celebrated Andalusian, Mr. J. A. Weissberger, who did the translation, is seemingly not aware that certain locutions, if too faithfully and literally translated, take on a false color in alien ears. What is pretty sentiment to the Spanish thus sometimes becomes burlesque to others. The performance was something tasty to behold, with Miss Nance O'Neil, in the rôle of the old mother, comporting herself like a royal funeral procession and with Miss Eugenie Leontovich, in the rôle of the tempting morsel for love of whom two men killed each other, overacting to such an extent that the management should have paid her two salaries.

Although Benavente, as noted, is generally regarded as Spain's leading living dramatist, the American theatre, with one exception, has provided a very cool reception to his plays, and that one exception, *The Passion Flower,* produced about sixteen years ago, made what popular headway it did simply because it retailed festooned sexual pyrotechnics at a time when festooned sexual pyrotechnics were still something of a draw at the box-office. The coolness of the reception in other and somewhat more elevated directions has been, despite Benavente's eminence in his homeland, perfectly understandable and critically logical, as of all nations Spain for many years has been theatrically and dramatically, with but slight qualification, the most backward. Thus, to challenge the attention of the local stage in this day and age with a thing like *Field of Ermine* was akin to opening a shop with a stock of 1906 calendars.

Benavente's drama, almost in its entirety, is by present standards a moribund one. Its influence in the main has lain not so much in the Spanish soil — as, for example, the influences of Sierra and the Quinteros have — as in the polite and artificialized stage of the England of three decades ago and, to some extent, the French stage of the same period. *Field of Ermine* is an illuminating specimen. It remains little more than a voluble literary distillation of Pinero and Hervieu at their weakest.

John Van Druten

Plays arguing that going out and getting shot in khaki for some theoretically lofty purpose is not so appealing to the calmer intelligence as staying at home and keeping one's self happily intact in tweeds are no particular novelty, and Mr. Van Druten's *Flowers of the Forest* falls into that category. Nor does Mr. Van Druten's pacifist proclamation depart, save in one detail, from the customary dramatic treatment of the topic — and that detail, as well, is hardly to be described as excessively spick, for all Mr. Burns Mantle's curious and enthusiastic belief to the contrary. The detail in point, which Mr. Mantle designates as " a fascinatingly new philosophy," is, as he puts it, " the human radio, no less." That is, " the suggestion that things said with passionate force hang about the place in the air and can be picked up years later by a properly attuned mind." Surely Mr. Mantle, who has been covering the theatre for many years in Denver, Chicago and New York, doesn't forget the old Watson, Bickel and Wrothe act (*circa* 1899) in which the same notion was advanced as to long ago played and lost melodies whose notes similarly hung about the place in the air and might be picked up years later by a properly attuned ear.

Mr. Van Druten is one of the more deft of the younger English playwrights and in this play, as in all of his others, there is a sensitive quality that not many of the British young men display. But the piece as a whole does not measure up to his past efforts and it remains in the end weak and even somewhat addled going. It lacks sound design and, in spite of some moments of nice writing, has a disconcertingly moist and squashy quality. Perhaps we are fed up with plays dealing with the last war and a playwright starts in that direction under a handicap. We have had our fill of psychically fastidious and affectible young men, usually with a gift for poetic expression, who have been disillusioned by the hypothetical glories of the battle-field, of young women who have been with child by them and who bitterly eat out their hearts for the rest of their lives when enemy guns cut the aforesaid young men down, and of fiery addresses on the fierce wrongness of it all. And we are ready for a lot more shows with Bobby Clark in them, as a consequence. It is Mr. Van Druten's misfortune to have come along at least half a dozen years too late. The local theatre turned pacifist long before he did.

It is light comedy rather than the more serious drama that is Van Druten's forte. If there is among the present-day younger English comedy playwrights a more adept and tickling hand at that species of entertainment, I do not know his name. Indeed, I do Van Druten something of an injustice with the qualifying adjective, " younger," for among the middle-aged themselves I can think only of Maugham as his superior in that department. What is more, there is a penetration of character and an observational wit in him that are absent from the other smart young Englishmen's superficially amusing badinage. But, like some of them, he on occasion unfortunately denies his gay feathery lines the substantiality of a dramatic pillow covering, with the result that they float all about in the air and decline to settle down into a compact play for the comfort of an audience's head.

Van Druten's aforementioned considerable virtues and sometime faults are visible in his most recent comedy, *Most of the Game.* Nor, when I mention his present particular fault of doing everything for the dialogue that he does not do for the underlying play, am I even so one to complain too loudly, for I happen to be one of those bizarre criticusses who much prefer no body whatsoever in a play to the rather corpsey and slightly reasty bodies that a number of the school of lighter playwrights deem vital and necessary. The relatively greater fault here, oddly enough, is his unwonted incorporation into his otherwise smoothly humorous dialogue of several wheezes so ancient and asthmatic that they give one critical pause. Surely, Van Druten is the last man you would think of to resort to the mangy vaudeville gag about the man who orders the whole bill-of-fare and then, by way of an additional fillip, a cup of coffee. Or to the ones about Alice Foote MacDougall and Wagnerian opera.

George Gershwin

That there are several merits to Mr. Gershwin's so-called American folk opera, *Porgy and Bess,* is readily to be allowed, but it seems to me that the chief of them is ambition. As to Mr. Gershwin's ambition there can be no doubt. It is a fine and adventurous thing. But it, like certain other fine and adventurous ambitions in the American theatre, still lacks a sufficiency of soaring wings. (Paul

Green's and Lynn Riggs' ambitions in the direction of folk drama are illustrative cases in point.)

Among Mr. Gershwin's other merits is the ability to confect better than usual popular Puccini-flavored music show tunes, several samples of which are present in *Porgy and Bess, e.g.,* " Bess, You Is My Woman Now " and " I Loves You Porgy." He is also talented in humorous revue melodies and, with his lyric-writing brother Ira, offers a specimen here in " It Ain't Necessarily So," with its Cole Porter rhyming frippery like " Jonah was at home in, the great big whale's ab-do-min," or something of the sort. And he indicates on this occasion that in the loftier matter of chorals and in ingenious contrapuntal devices, albeit sometimes paraphrasings which are not unrecognizable, he has some skill. But these qualities, meritorious in their several ways though they are, are not sufficient unto the composition of a folk opera and, as a consequence, *Porgy and Bess* (based upon the Heywards' familiar play) is considerably less a folk opera in any true sense of the term than an indeterminate, wobbly and frequently dull mixture of operetta, musical comedy, drama-with-music and musical vaudeville. The recitative passages are completely nude and interruptive of the exhibit's flow. Certain numbers, for example, " I Got Plenty o' Nuttin'," " Summer Time," and most certainly the clogging " There's a Boat That's Leavin' Soon for New York " seem much more in key with something like *Show Boat* than with something that purposes being a real folk opera. There are passages in the score that flutter toward musical dignity and even some mild musical standing, but in the aggregate the enterprise is without the coherence, the compositional drive, the orchestral background and, above all, the exaltation that are the prerequisites of any kind of opera, whether folk or otherwise.

George S. Kaufman

George S. Kaufman is one of the fresh and original talents in the contemporary American theatre. George S. Kaufman is one of the most amusing playwrights in the contemporary American theatre. George S. Kaufman is one of the best stage directors in the contemporary American theatre. All of which, pretty widely agreed upon, I have no critical difficulty in concurring in. But as for the also pretty widely accepted idea that he is one of the real wits of the contemporary American theatre I find myself something considerably more than a mere noncomformist.

Mr. Kaufman can at times write some exceptionally funny dialogue — he has amply proved it in such plays as *Once In A Lifetime, June Moon, et al.* — but authentic wit is seldom, if ever, a part of it. It generally consists, rather, in Broadway wisecracks that have spent a year in college and achieved a measure of literate gloss and in saucy comebacks distilled from a journalistic sophistication and its associated feigned superior disillusion. It is comical; it is very good theatre; and it is prosperous at the ticket-

[262]

window. But, gentlemen and scholars, it ain't wit. For wit consists in something much finer than vaudeville wheezes (as in *First Lady,* his latest collaborative effort) about crêpes Suzette, George Arliss, Graham McNamee, Jean Harlow, and sweetbreads.

Mr. Kaufman's comicality, sometimes in its kind wholly endorsable, lacks any traces of the reflection, philosophical point of view and shrewdly volatilized humor that are the wet-nurses of wit. It has an infinitely greater affinity with the life reflected in *Variety* than with life lived away from the world of Tony's, Hollywood studios, the company of the metaphysical Marx Brothers, and the concomitant ferociously indefatigable repartee. It is, in short, gaggery. Lest you think, however, that this is only one man's opinion, I append fifteen samples from *First Lady* in the conviction that the opinion may be doubled:

1. " The table looks beautiful! . . . I never saw so many flowers. Looks like a gangster's funeral."

2. ". . . I can take the words right out of your mouth. Such an unhygienic phrase, I always think."

3. " An army travels on its stomach."
" Well, isn't that awfully uncomfortable ? "

4. (*Picking up a bunch of flowers*) " But surely I don't have to put *this* on ? . . . All right, if you want me to look like Arlington on Decoration Day! "

5. (*Looking at a photograph on a table*) " My dear, look! Queen Marie . . . It's signed ' Marie R.' What's the R. for ? " . . . " Roumania! "

6. " I tell you they've got a horse named after you! (*A voice rising above the noise:* " Which end of the horse was it? ") . . . He ran down in Florida today. His name is Tightwad! "

7. " In my opinion, war with Japan is inevitable." . . . " Really? Will you bring me back a kimono? " . . . " Certainly, I'll have the Mikado help me pick one out."

8. " I think his wife prefers (the court of) St. James." . . . " Yes, I suppose so, That's all those New Yorkers see in politics. Those three feathers are more important to them than they are to a fan dancer."

9. " I was just dying to ask Guilio all about everything but all through supper they kept playing music — you couldn't talk at all." . . . " That's why they have music. That's called diplomacy."

10. " Catching a newspaper reader is a very delicate operation." . . . " What do you use? Salt? "

11. " Somebody slipped up on the entrance cards for the White House diplomatic reception, and one of them — which country was it, Jason? — got delivered at the wrong door with the ice-cream or something." . . . " Oh, that was Germany. And the worst of it was that it was French ice-cream."

12. " Her nostrils positively breathed fire. You could have cooked crêpes Suzette over them."

13. " I think that was the Persian minister. No — Turkish. Anyhow, one of those rug countries."

14. "She had the most beautiful crest — a gorgeous crown, and unicorns sitting on sweetbreads."

15. ". . . Senator Keane was born in Canada, Belle, and he can't ever be First Lady. Of course he can be Queen of England, Belle, but you never told me about that."

So that is wit, is it, and Mr. Kaufman is a great wit? So *First Lady,* according to my colleague, Mr. Gilbert Gabriel, is " a fine carrier of the finest wit . . . the talk is imperishably brilliant . . . some of the lines from it ought to be engraved on the Capitol walls long after it is gone "? Well, then Somerset Maugham is a slapstick clown, S. N. Behrman a custard pie heaver, and John Van Druten simply pulls chairs out from under his characters.

First Lady, plotted by Katharine Dayton and largely dialogued by Mr. Kaufman, is plain out-and-out Broadway play merchandise, better than the average, to be sure, but still merchandise. Its comedy, excepting perhaps a couple of scenes between the two women rivals for Washington social-political eminence, is generally in the Algonquip style: the straight line followed ceaselessly and unsparingly by the inevitable wisecrack. The impression one gets, accordingly, is that the characters all talk as if they were habitués of the Algonquin Hotel who were on their way to pleasing contracts as gag writers at the Metro-Goldwyn-Mayer studios. The play has that polite aura which customarily cozens the more injudicious critics into confounding manner with matter and it offers, in addition, that filigree of suave malice which is theoretically imagined to transform any Joe Miller into an Oscar Wilde on the spot. But it remains at bottom, in execution and in the end, showy junk.

Mr. Kaufman's antecedent collaborative effort with Moss Hart, *Merrily We Roll Along,* is similarly showy junk. It attempts to impress us with the tragedy of a potentially important playwright who, compromising with himself and his early ideals, gradually becomes a cheap and contemptible hack. It fails to impress us with any trace of tragedy because the authors have been unable to invest their protagonist with the slightest evidence or symptom of importance; they insist that he might have been important through the mouths of other characters, but not one single thing that he himself says or does — aside from a moony youthful testimonial to his high aspiration — indicates for a moment that he ever was or ever might be anything more than a pitiable ant. There can be no real tragedy without a fall from the heights, and their protagonist falls merely from a lower rung of a little stepladder.

The play, in addition, is replete with such snuffy hokum as the hurdy-gurdy in the street below grinding out its gay tunes in counterpoint to the sober action on the stage (shades of *The Easiest Way!*); the mention of various prominent figures in the community by name (Lew Dockstader used to hire someone in each town he played to prepare a list of such names that would guarantee an audience nudge or laugh); the device either of sagely predicting, in a scene laid in the yesterdays, something — usually an invention — that the audience recognizes as having since actually happened, or of denying with humorous bumptiousness that it ever could happen when the audience knows that it has (*vide When Knights Were Bold, Berkeley Square,* etc., etc.); and — as God is our judge — old plush-dressed and ostrich-feathered lovable Irish Mrs. Riley, mother of the successful stage star Althea Royce, *née* Annie Riley, who comes to the big party after the opening night, gets a bit boiled, and embarrasses the snobs, to say nothing of the haughty butler, with her outspoken reminiscences and loose language (shades of a couple of hundred neo-Boucicaults!).

Edouard Bourdet

The recent failure of Bourdet's *Les Temps Difficiles,* presented locally under the title, *Times Have Changed,* causes us to reflect that, of all the various French plays produced in the last four seasons, only one has enjoyed any measure of success, and that one, Fauchois' *The Late Christopher Bean,* unquestionably owed much of its reception to the liberal adaptation of Sidney Howard. All the rest have proved either prompt flashes in the pan or briefly hopeful but vain wooers of the box-office. Look over the list: *The Sex Fable, Papavert, Wolves, Domino, Mademoiselle, Lucrèce, Best Sellers, I Was Waiting For You, Another Love, Ode To Liberty, Times Have Changed,*

[267]

Noah. What is more, none of the revivals of the older French plays has managed to capture enough public attention to make it a paying investment.

Several of the plays mentioned represent the work of the better current French dramatists, yet the American public taste seems to have altered so greatly that no, or at best very meagre, audiences have found any use for them. And no amount of theatrical hocus-pocus appears to be able to influence the audiences to change their minds about the matter. Such popular actresses and habitual drawing-cards as Katharine Cornell and Ina Claire could do nothing to avert the fate either of *Lucrèce* or *Ode To Liberty*. An excellent Gilbert Miller company could not do anything for Bourdet's *The Sex Fable*. Grace George got but a snail's distance with Deval's *Mademoiselle*. What, one speculates, is the reason? Some of the plays have been great successes in Paris. Some have been adroitly translated and ably performed here. But to no avail. The day when French drama occupied a very welcome place on the local stage is seemingly gone. The drama that helped to hold for many years the old Charles Frohman fort, among others, has turned out to be a puny little popgun.

It would be easy to take the lately offered *Times Have Changed* and from it argue a reason for the local collapse of Gallic popularity. But it would not be fair, for the play in point represents only one phase of current French dramatic writing. That phase is the painfully scrupulous technique that builds itself up into a well-made but thor-

oughly empty play. And that phase is, further, the persistent Bernstein melodramatic handling of sex, culminating
in a bedroom scene of sexual roughhouse that suggests the
activities of a troupe of Arab acrobats under the influence
of a year's output of Lynnhaven and Sea Cross oysters. But
though such stuff has long since engendered only embarrassing chuckles on the part of the local theatregoer, it is
hardly typical of the bulk of present-day French drama.
Yet it nevertheless hints at what is, in the American eye, a
more general defect. That defect is the whimsically un-
varying and unyielding preoccupation with the ritual of
sex, whether the treatment be grave or light.

With but few exceptions — Obey is one, Pagnol is another, and Giraudoux is a third — the current French
playwrights are either mildly Freudian Sardous, now and
again crossed with a little bitter Maugham, or Michodière
Schnitzlers. Like their fathers, they suffer dramatically
from the tumescent handicap of Mr. Dashiell Hammett's
thin man when he engaged in a wrestling match with a
fair one. The interesting modern dramatist is one who can
write about sex and yet at the same time nimbly forget it
once in a while. The average French dramatist, even when
he adroitly tries to forget it for the moment, constantly
gives his auditor the impression that he is utterly unable to,
and the result is either tedium or a low laugh at the unfor-
tunate literatus' expense. The modern theatre has gradu-
ated from the French dramatic kindergarten with its
elaborate sieges of ladies' private favors, its horrified trepi-

dations over the safety of maidens' corporeal honor, and its evening-long concerns with interrupted, or even uninterrupted, liaisons in Lyons hotel suites. Sex has become, at least in considerable part, an incident in drama rather than a thesis. On occasion, these French playmakers try to smile their way out of their old-fashionedness. But they can't fool grandma.

Times Have Changed, with its tale of the innocent virgin sacrificed on the altar of money to the half-wit son of a rich neighborhood family and with its routine fireworks bedroom episode wherein the half-wit demands his marital rights of the cowering and shrieking vestal, is seriocomic flubdub so far as the American theatre of today is concerned. It is the *Point Valaine* in the dramatic career of M. Bourdet.

S. N. Behrman

Since the felicitously endowed and developing Vincent Lawrence was swallowed by Hollywood, and his talent with him, Behrman has had no native competitor as a contriver of literate, intelligent and thoroughly adult comedy. There has been in him, since first he began to write, a complete and incorruptible probity and a regard only for himself — apart from all other considerations — as an artist. If he has ever thought of editorial checks or theatrical box-offices, it must have been in his sleep, and then only during the Prohibition period of bad liquor. Even his poorer work never fails of dignity. And year by year he suggests a growth visible in the instance of few of his American contemporaries. His *Rain From Heaven,* a study of present-day ethics and prejudices in fierce open clash, is a testimonial to the fellow's fine honesty, very considerable skill in drawing character in short, pithy strokes, high gift for dialogue, and steadfast avoidance of every trace and smell of facile theatrical sham. If he happens to have a theme, as he has in this case, that may best be treated with an almost complete dramatic quiescence — that is, in the Philistine critical sense — well, that is the way he treats it, and to hell with anyone, in or out of criticism or the box-office, who doesn't like it. If he feels a thing, he lets himself feel it, let audiences in turn feel whichever way about it they will, and may they go hang. It isn't that he deliberately slaps popularity in the face; it is rather that he appears never to be conscious that such a thing as popularity exists in the world, or at least in his immediate world. He is a writer, whatever he writes (which is uncritical criticism), with whom our theatre, still replete with posturers and charlatans, may be vastly satisfied.

There is one moment in *Rain From Heaven* that illustrates more nicely, I think, than any in recent dramaturgy the gulf that yawns between the new drama and the old drama of the Pineros whose influence, as Charles Morgan has lately pointed out, dominates still to no little degree the more backward and lesser Anglo-American stages. That moment comes at the curtain to the second act. The scene is Lady Wyngate's house outside of London, wherein — under her hospitable roof — is gathered a party of Americans and of German and Russian refugees. Suddenly jealous of the attention his Lady is privileging the German exile Willens, the young American hero spatters at the latter the sling, " You God damned Jew! ", which is immediately echoed by his elder brother. Willens, in the dead silence that follows, makes no move. Whereupon Lady Wyngate, taking his hand, in the quietest and smoothest of voices turns to the two others, still colored with bitter distaste and hate, and says, very softly, very graciously — and unexpectedly and joltingly enough in the case of the young suitor for her favor — " Remember, please, Mr. Willens is not only my lover; he is also my guest."

There never lived a Pinero, a Henry Arthur Jones, an Alfred Sutro or any other such exponent of the older drama who would not, to achieve a facile surprise second-act curtain, have turned that line hind end foremost.

Behrman's *End of Summer,* however, is a disappointment. That he remains, in spite of it, our most important writer of light comedy is still evident, but in this, his latest work, there is form so disordered and attack so periodically groping that the dramatic impression is of a usually very skilful pianist playing a composition that irritatingly keeps slipping off the rack. Some of the scenes, notably one between the predatory psychoanalyst and the attractive daughter of the woman who would have him as husband, are in the author's best vein, but a number of others indicate rather clearly that he has permitted a makeshift resignation and even a certain degree of auctorial despair to fill in spaces left personally unsatisfactory through the failure of imaginative inventiveness to hearken to his pleas. Some of his lines and quotations, too, are streaked with tired cobwebs, for example, the old Bismarck animadversion on the wisdom of the Irish exchanging countries with the Dutch, the collegiate jest as to who it was who psychoanalyzed Freud himself, the character who observes that he is grateful for his deafness as it prevents him from hearing bores, etc. Behrman, to repeat, for all this exhibit, remains our first comedy writer, but pride in his high position should have impelled him to spend considerably more time studiously rewriting and editing it before risking it upon his critical disciples. It is, for all its occasional virtues, a meandering and ill-considered job.

Little Red Writing Hoods

One of the confusing things about many of our more conspicuous young radicals is their apparent great dexterity in denouncing capitalism as the prime evil of the world and in accepting soft and pleasingly lucrative jobs from it at the same time. They seem, at the moment, to be unable to make up their minds whether it is better for them to go to Moscow, serve Stalin, make fifteen dollars a week, and freeze to death, or to go to Hollywood, serve Irving Thalberg, make five hundred a week, and bask in the warm sun.

To read what these young gentlemen write is, of course, to believe that nothing is so odious to them as the mere sight of a dollar bill, particularly one stamped with the image of that ignoble capitalistic Virginia aristocrat, landowner and slave holder, George Washington, and nothing so contemptible as the kind of man who, after decades of hard labor, has enough of them safely put away in the bank to pay the doctor, when he gets on in years, to look after his prostatitis. But to scrutinize the procedure of these same young gentlemen when they lay down their flaming scarlet pens is to experience some slight misgivings as to their probity.

It is, for example, pretty hard to reconcile the eloquently expressed conviction of the young radical playwright, John Howard Lawson, that the one thing that will save the world is a strict practice of the doctrines of Karl Marx with Mr. Lawson's own apparently happy and vastly contented surrender to the money moguls of Hollywood, to whom he is perfectly willing to dedicate himself at a fat and comfortable weekly salary. It is also not easy to sympathize wholly with the program for an anti-capitalistic cosmos as firmly outlined by such lads as Clifford Odets, Paul Sifton and Samuel Ornitz when we regularly find them hot-footing it on Saturday morning to a Los Angeles bank to deposit their weekly capitalist-derived movie boodle. Somehow a stout belief in and loud advocacy of Communistic or Socialistic principles doesn't seem to jibe convincingly with writing rich pent-house and Rolls-Royce happy-ending scenarios for Jean Harlow, Miriam Hopkins and Clark Gable.

John Wexley is another of the radicals who seemingly has no trouble at all in composing plays arguing vociferously that the present scheme of economics is all wrong and at the same time composing scenarios for the movies, at a gratifyingly handsome emolument, proving that it is a dirty shame Carole Lombard and Warner Baxter have to get along with only a single gold and onyx swimming pool and maybe just a couple of Hispano-Suizas and a lone private airplane, even if, in the last reel, love does conquer all.

When we hear playwrights like Albert Bein, Albert Maltz and the Messrs. Sklar and Peters flaying capitalists and capitalistic society and showing us the dire effects of accumulated wealth, we are prepared to shed a tear. But the tear somehow isn't as sympathetically wet as it should be when we read that these same young men are at the same time doing everything in their power to get a slice of the Guggenheim Foundation's mazuma so they may enjoy themselves in a whole year's repose and meditation, gratis. Is it possible that they do not know that Mr. Guggenheim is a capitalist of the first carat? Elmer Rice is still another of the boys who, in his plays and published manifestos, gets pretty hot under the collar thinking of the

atrocities of capitalism and who stakes his faith in Karl
Marx for the salvation of destitute and starving humanity.
As in Mr. Bein's and the others' cases, our comradely tears
are quickly dried, however, when we see in the newspaper
reports that Mr. Rice was recently called upon to pay an
additional $3,330 to the New York State income tax
bureau on an income of something over $157,000. It is con-
soling, at any rate, to know that, whatever his faith in
Marx and Stalin, Mr. Rice isn't exactly destitute and starving to death.

Then there is the protean Little Red Writing Hood who
calls himself Robert Forsythe. As Robert Forsythe he in-
veighs against capitalism like a house afire. His hoarse
cries of *Canis latrans!* resound not only on the night air,
but on the morning, afternoon and evening air as well.
He hochs Marx and Stalin, denounces anyone who has so
much as fifty dollars in the bank, makes mock of any
bourgeois who owns more than one shirt, and contends
loudly against the capitalist-owned press, the capitalist-
owned magazines and the capitalist-owned any and everything. That's Robert Forsythe, and when you say it, you'd
better smile! But on the other hand there is also Kyle S.
Crichton, which happens to be Robert Forsythe's real
name. This Crichton, peculiarly enough, seems to be quite
a different fellow. Covertly shedding his bold whiskers,
he emerges as a very well-paid member of the staff of the
leading humorous magazine in America, a magazine
wholly opposed editorially to everything that he believes

in, and also as a very richly paid staff writer on one of the biggest capitalist-owned American weeklies, which is also wholly opposed editorially to everything that he, as For-sythe, believes in. Recently he went to Hollywood on be-half of the capitalist-owned weekly to compose articles on beautiful movie stars at a luxuriant weekly fee, and with all expenses paid. He had the royal suite at the Beverly-Wilshire Hotel, with a valet in constant attendance, a private bartender to look after his needs, and a colored boy in uniform to take his two blue-ribbon Airedales out for their walks. As when living in his lovely apartment in New York or as when dining at the Crillon, he never missed his daily two large portions of Beluga caviar and bottle of Niersteiner Falkenkrone Auslese, 1929, served in glasses blown especially for him by the Steuben Glass Co. Title: Portrait of a Communist.

Aside from such bizarre mundane activities of these radicalissimos — I have suggested, by way of space con-servation, the many in terms of the few — we likewise engage some very fancy stuff when, sitting profoundly in their ateliers, they allow their Marxian critical faculties full rein in fields apart from economics and commerce. Granville Hicks, for example, who, when he is not march-ing in torch-light parades celebrating the birthdays of Marx, Lenin, Stalin and Michael Gold, performs as pro-letarian literary critic for the *New Masses,* lately delivered his cerebrum of the following in concluding his review of Ernest Hemingway's last book: " This is the dullest book I have read since *Anthony Adverse*. Hunting is probably exciting to do; it is not exciting to read about. I should like to have Hemingway write a novel about a strike."

There's a critical tootsie for you bourgeois blockheads!

Clifford Odets is another example. Mr. Odets, who wakes up every morning feeling like giving all the money he has made out of his Communistic plays to the Soviet treasury and who then promptly goes back to sleep again, lately confected a treatise on " The Awakening of the American Theatre " for the revolutionary *New Theatre* magazine. I quote, for the delectation of you bourgeois punks, a few morsels:

1. " In the boom days of our country, lots of young and old people slept fitfully in the night. They wanted ' art ' . . . So they finally started the Little Theatre Movement. They got their 'art' . . . All this was true of the big time Broadway theatre too. A rash of art broke out all over the street. Art was a paying proposition! . . . With the first thunderclap it was all over . . . *The Columbia Burlesque circuit gave up the ghost."*

2. " Then a curious thing occurred: certain small groups of theatre people began to concern themselves with 1929 and the years to follow. These isolated groups said art must be about something. *It must be hot and spiteful* . . ."

3. " And (then) how talented men like Lawson, Maltz, Saxe, Rice, Peters, Sklar, Wexley *and Odets* — lots of others — how they grew and developed upward . . ."

[278]

There are *three* tootsies for you ignorant low capitalistic muggs!

Noël Coward

Noël Coward's *Point Valaine* displayed once again all his many virtues as a theatrician and all his numerous deficiencies as a dramatist. As a stagewright (which seems to be a word that best designates him), he has at the moment few superiors, but as a playwright he disappointingly continues to betray all the infirmities that have been in his work from the beginning. It is the first mark and criticism of Mr. Coward as a writer of plays that not a single character which he has ever in the past contrived remains solidly in one's recollection, a fact which quickly stamps his status as a dramatist. One can readily recall the name of the actor or actress who played the rôle; one can remember a bit of business, perhaps, and maybe even a line or two of dialogue; but the name of the character and the substantial after-image of the character have vanished into the thin air directly the last curtain has fallen upon the performance. I do not mean gratuitously thus to derogate Mr. Coward upon the higher plane of drama and to intimate, needlessly, that he is not in this direction in the proud company of the first-line dramatists. What I mean to point out is that he does not, in this same direction, find himself in even the company of the second or third line. He has not in all his work devised one such recollectable character — I choose the most obvious examples possible — as even the second-rate Carroway Pim of A. A. Milne or even the third-rate and refractorily memorable Nubi of Jean Bart.

The reason for this is that Mr. Coward in the first place does not compose characters but contents himself with mere characteristics. The excellent and highly finished performances which his carefully and shrewdly selected actors and actresses give of his rôles — and there is none better than himself when he elects to play one of his own rôles — deceive the injudicious into imagining character where none is present, but what others soon discern is simply the suggestion of character given an approach to reality by lines directed upon it from without and further superficially deepened by the independent talents of very ably directed players. If anyone is skeptical of such criticism, let him have a look at one of Mr. Coward's plays when it is done by some ordinary stock company or when it is revived with an inferior troupe.

So again in *Point Valaine* we had nothing but stage marionettes (in this instance lavishly and melodramatically supplied with all the vulvovaginal and testicular glands that were lacking in *Design For Living*) who were tricked into a semblance of actuality by a handpicked and unusually dexterous group of actors and by Mr. Coward's own directorial hocus-pocus.

As for the play itself, it was the kind of thing that W. Somerset Maugham might ironically write to order for Hollywood, provided that Hollywood paid him $100,000 in advance, plus agent's commission, and provided, in addition, that he was just recovering from a prolonged jag and had a slight touch of the flu. The scene was a tropical island. The atmosphere was burdened with the customary white linen suits, rum punches, rain storms, slinky-footed servants, sultry afternoons, passenger boat that brings the gabby young female tourists in the latest Abercrombie and Fitch outfits, comical dowager who complains about her liver, green-screened hotel veranda, and all the other appurtenances of the conventional Pango-Pango drama. The heroine was the daughter of a missionary who, now in her forties, ran the hotel. The hero was a young British aviator who fell in love with her. And the villain was a mysterious brute of a Russian headwaiter whose sexual attraction for the heroine was so overpowering that she couldn't resist him. The big scene was the villain's sudden return, his discovery that the heroine had given herself romantically to the young aviator, his beating the hell out of her, and his subsequent contrite slashing of his wrists and propulsion of himself into the waters below to be devoured by the sharks. Seventy-two cheers for Sam Goldwyn!

It is impossible to believe that Mr. Coward, a fellow of some humor, could have written such zymotic bilge with a straight face. Somebody was razzing somebody. The villainous, bare-foot Russian made up like a combination Maldonado-Tarzan who crawled like a lecherous ape over window-sills into the heroine's boudoir and made such grunts as had not been heard on a stage since Thompson and Dundy's elephants last appeared in the Hippodrome spectacles, the cynical literary gent who prowled around the darkened stage (striking a match so the audience might duly identify him) and who shrank dramatically against the wall as the villain stole in to surprise the lovers, the heroine who " had never known love " until the young aviator came into her life (the other thing, ugh, was vile, just animal passion) — no one, and surely not the sophisticated Mr. Coward, could offer whangdoodle like that seriously. What he unquestionably and deliberately set himself to write was a boob hot-pants version of *The Grand Duchess and the Waiter*. Or am I mistaken?

Louis Bromfield

If Louis Bromfield never does anything else in his life he can plume himself on having made the New York play reviewers angrier than they have been since the time Lester Wallack announced an opening on the night of one of the worst blizzards in local history, got the whole lot of them to his theatre at half past eight, and then decided to postpone the show. It wasn't that Bromfield postponed his show; it was that he went ahead with it as scheduled and that the aforesaid show gave the fraternity such a critical cholera as made the late epidemic in India take on the comparative aspect of a small boy's bellyache. And Bromfield may supplement the pluming with an additional feather on having made his first-night audience, composed largely of the Social Register, just a little sorer than even the reviewers.

The occasion for all the indignation was something called *De Luxe,* made from a story by Bromfield, by Bromfield himself with some assistance from one Gearon. The something in question dealt with the queer fish who have swum and swim still in the social sewers of Paris, the international collection of more or less fashionable kept women and kept men, decayed titles, degenerate moneybags, and other such sexual rotters and general wasters. It dealt with them in terms of an incontrovertibly bad play, but it also dealt with them, as characters, in such an unashamedly honest and purely smelly manner that, like a stink-bomb, it outraged the reviewers and that first-night audience not so much because it was a bad play as because its characters assailed their nostrils with a completely true but offensive and even nauseating odor. As for a certain share of the audience, the characters doubtless also smelled a bit uncomfortably like home.

It would be pleasant, after the periodic and highly disagreeable Nathan critical practice, to argue rather convincingly that the play itself was not the desolate mince that the reviewers insisted it was, but that would take a much greater ingenuity than the aforesaid Nathan possesses. To fall in whole-souled with the procession, therefore, he lends his cuckoo note to the expressed opinions and makes it unanimous. But, having thus proved himself a polite, acceptable and brotherly fellow, a trace of

[283]

skepticism begins to steal over him as to the alleged complete badness of the play. If the play was the total loss the reviewers asserted it was, how could it arouse all the indignation and resentment that it did? Nobody grows red in the face and flies off the hot handle over anything utterly worthless or over anything admittedly negligible. To argue that it was simply the foul rottenness of many of the characters that got under the boys' collars won't do, as the characters were obviously and naturally part of the play. It would accordingly seem that moral indignation substituted for sound criticism. One believed that that had long since passed out, along with the late Willie Winter and J. Ranken Towse.

Another assigned reason for the play's badness which puzzles me was the staleness of its subject matter, to wit, the hollow tragedy of the tinsel-mad post-war generation. That we are all by now fed up on that subject is perfectly true, but we are fed up with it not because it is stale but because it is essentially bogus. The subject matter of perhaps three out of every four plays that we admire is customarily almost equally stale, but its essential truth gives it a persistent life and force. The characters in *De Luxe* were no more peculiar to the years following the late war — the war had utterly nothing to do with the majority of them and it had no effect nor influence upon them — than are the similarly befuddled, sex-ridden and degenerate characters of, say, Wedekind's *Earth Spirit,* which appeared in 1907, or of Bruckner's *Patricide,* which, while it appeared after the war, made small claim that its characters had ever heard of the war. So with most of the plays that have argued moral collapse in terms of the war. For every one of them in which the war has been blamed, it is easy to name two or three written before the war in which an identical moral collapse has been far removed from any shell shock, result of having been gassed, sexual despair, sense of life's futility, or some other such concomitant of the late great democracy preserver.

To get back to the matter of the characters and to the basic reason for the play's badness, it was not the circumstance that the characters were unpleasant and even disgusting that was properly to be charged against them, but rather that the authors lacked the skill to make that unpleasantness gratifyingly dramatic. Here we have the difference between the competent and the incompetent dramatist. The characters in *Night Refuge* are quite as unpleasant and disgusting as those in the play under discussion, as are also the characters in *Pandora's Box* and *Our Betters,* but where a Gorki, a Wedekind and a Maugham have been able to make them acceptably unpleasant and disgusting, the authors of *De Luxe* succeeded only in making their characters unacceptably so. They gave us the unpleasantness and disgust unfiltered through the art of dramatic writing. They gave us a *Tobacco Road* of Paris Ritz society, a picture of fashionable perverts, parasites, pimps and prostitutes, that amounted in sum to a dramatic stogie.

Next to making dramatically acceptable and agreeably interesting characters depicting unrelievedly boresome persons, the most difficult of dramatic feats is to manage the same thing with characters like those in *De Luxe*. The unpleasantness and disagreeable essence of such characters must be trickled into an audience's consciousness, not squirted full into its face, as in the Bromfield-Gearon technique, with a 16-inch fire hose. The emphasis on the characters' foulness must be directed not from the stage but from the auditorium back to the stage. Otherwise by ten o'clock, as in the instance of *De Luxe,* the audience is certain silently to mutter, "All right, they're bums and bastards, so now what?", and to hop around to the nearest revue theatre to look at some nice, filthy, but satisfactorily brief black-out sketches.

After which eloquent lecture on the grave critical deficiencies of the play, there remains but one confoundingly paradoxical and rather embarrassing remark to offer. That remark consists in the confession that, although the professorial phase of this particular reviewer found the exhibit full of all the flaws duly noted, the personal phase of the same fellow found some of it nevertheless peculiarly diverting and extra-dramatically interesting. Never within his recollection has a more venomous *drame à clef* been shown on the stage, and not frequently within that same recollection has a bad play, a woefully bad play, here and there triumphed over its badness, as this one did, with moments of painfully true and realistically bitter, if not al-

[286]

ways theatrically dramatic, reporting. . . . It may be that, as with the small boy who craved a bite of another small boy's apple and was selfishly discouraged by the latter with the news that it was rotten, the answer of any such ignominious and deplorable critic is that he likes rotten best.

J. B. Priestley

What the ingratiatingly resilient Priestley has written in *Laburnum Grove* is the kind of comedy that needs only a rich Irish brogue and a ten-cent interior set to serve as a likely, if minor, item in the Abbey Theatre Company's repertoire. It is precisely the sort of thing, light, inconsequential, but diverting, that we every now and again get and for some time now have got from the Emerald Free State. Its tale is a simple one; the effect upon his family of a supposedly respectable suburbanite's sudden and casual confession that all these years he has been supplying their needs from the art of counterfeiting. Although the author has found that he is not always able to sustain the story with dramatic life — it sags somewhat heavily in the second act — his humor, his easy literary skill and his amusing sense of character come to his rescue before the evening is over, and the result is a play that provides a pleasant theatrical session. Despite its weaknesses, the exhibit gives one the unaccustomed and very agreeable sensation that its author is a cultivated and what, back in the 1920's, used insistently to be called a " civilized " fellow.

The presenting company was headed by Edmund

Gwenn, one of London's most adept comedians, who unfortunately on his visit to America seemed to be infected with the common British notion that our audiences are made up entirely of Indians, cowboys and pork-packers and that it is therefore necessary to forego the more tranquil species of acting that is welcome to the more cultured English and substitute for it a cross between pogostick hopping and ballet dancing. On the stage of the Booth, Mr. Gwenn accordingly did everything with his rôle but request the audience to come up on the stage and play duck-on-rock with him.

Priestley's *Eden End,* on the other hand, was an undeniably sincere and honest effort but at the same time also an undeniably dull one. It has been alleged against Mr. Priestley that the trouble with his plays is that he thinks like a novelist. This is unfair. He does not, in certain of his plays (some others, like *Dangerous Corner* and the above-mentioned *Laburnum Grove,* happen to be meritorious), think like a novelist so much as he thinks like a poor dramatist. Some novelists — Hemingway, Malraux and Hammett are examples — think like dramatists, it may incidentally be pointed out. In such a play as *Eden End,* Priestley not only thinks like a poor dramatist but he also employs many of the devices of a commonplace dramatist. Even an expert in dramaturgy, novelist-minded or not, cannot do much at this hour with the old Sudermann scheme of the returned Magda, with the stale humorous idea of prognostication in a past period of events that the audience recognizes as having turned out in an opposite manner, and such like.

Valentine Katayev

Squaring The Circle, the much discussed Soviet comedy by Valentine Katayev which has been running prosperously in Moscow for something like five years and which has been offered as evidence of our Communist friends' ability to laugh at themselves, proves, if nothing else, that we less jocund and more grave American democrats do not share the same sense of humor. The play, in essence, is nothing more than the stale French farce about the two ill-assorted married couples who find that they are wedded to the wrong mates and who duly rectify the situation, with numerous allusions to Marx, Lenin, dialectic materialism and the petty bourgeoisie substituted for the customary Gallic sex *double entendre.* In its native land, where a four-hour performance of *King Lear* on a dimly lighted stage or a sovietized *Hamlet* on a stage that the audience couldn't make out at all had hitherto of necessity been accepted as the mediums of a hot old time, its avid and enthusiastic acceptance is readily comprehended, like a gob's first night on land after a long period at sea, a patriotic teetotaler's first swig of kerosene and door-knob polish upon the repeal of Prohibition, or a Brünnhilde's reverberating busting of a corset-string in the third act of *Siegfried.* Over here, however, things are a bit different.

Zoë Akins

Miss Akins' latest dramatic performance was derived from the fable of the life of the late Marie Dressler and again lugubriously demonstrated Hollywood's influence upon what was once one of the likely talents in our theatre. What Hollywood has done in Miss Akins' case is to exaggerate all her worst faults and diminish to the vanishing point her quondam virtues. It is true that, even before she went Hollywood, a kind of gold swimming pool quality infected her writing, but the gold swimming pool is now found to be overflowing with mush. Miss Akins' over-elaborate rhetoric is, of course, ideally suited to the penthouse literature of the screen, but in the theatre it is just a little ridiculous. Her last act Cartier death scenes, with their wistful gabble about the stars and with a stageful of actors in swallow-tails grouped about the swooning leading woman (her nose glued sentimentally to a nosegay sent to her by a past lover), take on the air of a Pinero minstrel show. Her moist allusions to feeling like a tree abloom in the snow belong to the old Garbo pictures. And surely such attempts at humor as the beset and worried leading actress' remark upon a mention of Marie Antoinette: " I hope I won't lose *my* head," are hardly suited to even the feeblest gag picture. Add to this, all present in the promptly deceased *O Evening Star*, the customary jape at Gloria Swanson, the joke about the " original " movie script borrowed from J. Fenimore Cooper, a paraphrase of the mother-son last scene out of a dozen plays from Henry Arthur Jones' *The Profligate* to Bisson's *Madame X,* and a number of other such mildewed morsels, and you get the idea. It's too bad. The Zoë Akins of fifteen years ago — even of ten years ago — was very much above all that.

The Travelogue Revue Chefs

Each theatrical season discloses at least one or two " travelogue " revues in which the scenery successively resembles a back-yard in Cranford, New Jersey, or the maple trees in front of the Atlantic and Pacific Tea Company's store in Lewiston, Pa., and in which somebody or other then comes on and sings an acutely relevant lyric about the South Sea Islands, a fiesta in Madrid, or Calcutta. These revues begin with the musical number announcing that we are to be escorted " Here and There " and thereafter show us, during the course of the evening, various backdrops purporting to be Spain, the Mississippi river, Paree, India, South Africa, Honduras, Greece, etc. What occurs before these different backdrops, aside from a yodeling of the kind of lyrics noted above, seldom varies. Pretty generally you will find that Greece (the scene being the Acropolis) seems to be inhabited wholly by Broadway hoofers, that the speech of the Andalusians in Spain sounds uncommonly like that of Mr. Lou Holtz, and that the Canadian North Woods are peopled largely by men and women who spend the major portion of their lives acting dirty black-out sketches. Then, of course, there are the dance numbers. These dance numbers customarily have even less variety than the lyrics, melodies and other elements in the exhibit. There is certain to be a dusky Harlem wench for the Mississippi, India and South Sea Island scenes who will violently agitate her rear in the first two episodes and even more ecstatically wobble her mammæ in the third. Somewhere in the show there will come a terpsichorean " fantasy," known as " The Moth and the Flame," " The Kiss of Death " or " The Birth of Passion," in which a Russian gent in a gilt loin cloth and with calves the size of watermelons wrestles for ten minutes with a semi-nude hussy, at the end of which time he grabs her around the waist, strains her lasciviously to his lips, and makes her swoon — but not before she has covertly removed a couple of hair-pins and allowed her hair to tumble down and has made certain, with a quick side-glance, that when she falls she will not land in the footlights. Also, we are sure to get, particularly in such scenes as represent Abyssinia or West Point, a trick clog or two. If the producer's suckers have enough money to spend, there will in all probability also be " At the Ballet," its elaborateness depending upon the amount of the aforesaid sucker money. It will thus be either a large chorus number with the girls in tarleton and the postures a combination of Degas and Ned Wayburn or — if there are only about one hundred dollars or so available — a duo number which differs from " The Moth and the Flame " and " The Kiss of Death " wham only in that it doesn't wind up with the lethal gum-suck but finds the woman partner still on her legs and coyly throwing a kiss to the audience.

Damon Runyon

Mr. Runyon, one of the most amusing newspaper writers in America, and Howard Lindsay, one of the most proficient gatling-gun stage directors in the same acre of God, collaboratively provided us with a farce-comedy called *A Slight Case of Murder* and Mr. Runyon remains still one of the most amusing newspaper writers in America and Mr. Lindsay one of the most proficient gatling-gun stage directors in the same section of the atlas. Their play, despite some highly amusing incidental humors, on the other hand remains largely in their good intentions.

What they planned to write was a bit of mad waggery about an ex-racketeer who rents a house at Saratoga for the racing season, fills it with his loyal old retainers, and in spite of everything makes a serio-comic effort to go straight, the effort being somewhat handicapped at the very outset when he finds that the corpses of four muggs who have been taken for a ride have been inconsiderately deposited by some unfriendly old-time competitor in one of his more recherché guest rooms. But what they finally found on paper was little more than their juicy original idea distilled into occasional guffaws but more often and for the most part struggling desperately to keep life in itself with extrinsic tonics. The purely rough-house aspects

[293]

of the evening were all that any professor of the critical art could ask for, but when the authors got to the bridge-work of their play it was a different matter.

In this respect, the play was like many of its American kind. Just as the audience had been maneuvered into a vastly jolly and receptive mood, the authors rushed in with those twin humor purgatives, Young Love Interest and Plot, and spoiled everything. Four out of every five of our farce-comedies suffer from the ailment. After their playwrights have set us to laughing heartily with nimble monkeyshines of one sort or another, someone comes on and throws a wrench into the whole business either by pulling a grave face and remarking, " Now we've got to stop a moment and think of Mary's future and best inter-ests " or by quietly drawing up a chair and entering into a depressing five-minute colloquy on how to arrange the vital loan from the First National Bank. And as if these in-terruptions of the comic mood were not enough, they pursue the routine sedative further by halting the fun every now and then with sentimental scenes between the ingénue and the juvenile.

The low burlesque slices of the Runyon-Lindsay show were, as recorded, very merry. The episodes wherein the sedate prospective father-in-law of the racketeer's daughter tried vainly to make himself heard above a honky-tonk blues singer's loud nasal moanings, wherein the aforesaid dignified old gentleman was slyly given the " hot foot " by one of the racketeer host's irrepressible old pals, and wherein the guest muggs entertained a friend lying ill in a hospital out on the Pacific coast by singing torch songs to him over the long distance telephone, at the conclusion of which one of the muggs announced, after speaking to the hospital, that " Some broad says he's running a fever," were the stuff of jocosity. But here and there the humor had traces of strain and rang with an artificiality and heavily manufactured tone as, for example, when someone remarked that something or other was wonderful and the racketeer had the out-of-vocabulary rejoinder provided for him that it was phenomenal.

Various Tyros

Something Gay, by Adelaide Heilbron, brought Tallulah Bankhead back to the plate for the third time in a single season, but once again failed to provide her with a bat. Miss Heilbron's notion of a play was to have Miss Bankhead come on the stage and then one by one bring on the other characters, have them in turn individually and separately engage her in conversation, and shoo them off-stage, again in turn, when they had finished their jobs. The evening hence resolved itself into a series of dialogues that were interrupted only on such occasions as Miss Heilbron thought it would be nobby to have Miss Bankhead run upstairs and change into something else cute, when the dialogues became monologues on the part of the deserted actors. During the monologues, the deserted actors, once they had recited their time-killing lines, were driven to consume quarts of theoretical whiskey and soda, as it was frequently apparent that Miss Bankhead's maid was no quick shakes in fastening hooks and eyes and buttoning things up the back.

The play, which the producer surely couldn't have read, was the turkey dealing with a wife who tries to win back her husband's love by making him jealous. In the last act, Miss Heilbron doubtless imagined that she had hit upon a fresh idea when she made the wife, to her husband's chuckling and self-satisfied disbelief, really go off with her young lover. But the trouble with Miss Heilbron is that, like her producer, she doesn't read plays. If she did, or if she went to the theatre oftener, she would have known that her fresh idea ceased to be fresh when Crommelynck used it sixteen years before in *The Magnificent Cuckold*. And even then Crommie had been anticipated by half a dozen other playwrights. Nor was Miss H. any more fortunate in the vernal quality of her dialogue, which consisted mainly of cracks that were already dated when Lee Shubert was still living in Syracuse. Miss Bankhead worked like a beaver to get some life into the evening and Hugh Sinclair even went to the length of laying in a new double-breasted dinner jacket, but their efforts were in vain.

In *To See Ourselves,* E. M. Delafield similarly imagined that a succession of dialogues constituted a play, but Mrs. Delafield at least enjoys a literary skill and an eye to character that Miss Heilbron was not vouchsafed by her fairy godmother. The only difficulty with Mrs. D.'s literary skill and eye to character is that they seem to be more aptly fitted to the novel form than to the dramatic. And to the slow-moving novel form at that.

In this exhibit we also engaged materials that were theatrically rococo. A middle-aged wife married to a clod of a husband bethinks herself of other days and pines for a whiff of romance. This she finds in a young Irishman named Michael Dennison (played by Earle Larimore, who possesses all the rich Celtic quality of chow mein). Apprised by her that her libido has been inspired by the Irishman, her husband incredulously contents himself with a derisive sniff, argues with her that she must be ill, and urges her to be herself. In the end we find the husband still passively sitting by the fire reading his newspaper, the young Irishman off to marry the ingénue, and the middle-aged wife sitting on the sofa with a far-away look in her eyes and meditating upon the " moment of beauty " that had come into her humdrum existence. If you've seen that play less than fifty times, even not counting the time you were last in Vienna, I am no hand at figures.

* * *

Kind Lady, manufactured from a Hugh Walpole story by Edward Chodorov, was the tale of an elderly woman who sympathetically took a presumably starving young man, along with his supposed wife and baby, into her house and then discovered, to her terror, that she was harboring a gang of vicious crooks. This obviously melodramatic theme the author invested with so inexorable an avoidance of any trace of melodrama that the audience momentarily looked for the wheeling in of a tea cart and the settling down of the characters to a spree of epigrams.

The mellowing of melodrama into something approaching polite drawing-room drama is one of the deplorable aspects of present-day playwriting. It is a mark of the spurious theatrical sophistication which has helped steadily to boost James Cagney's salary and increase the audiences of the MM. Boris Karloff and Bela Lugosi, those two great artists. When people want melodrama, they want melodrama and not Frederick Lonsdale with his shirt merely open at the neck. Starved for it under the new theatrical dispensation, they may go even to a mild imitation of it and may accept the imitation in lieu of what they are really hungry for, but the very next evening you will find them either at a movie so full of machine guns that you can hardly hear the gum chewers, or at home reading a thriller with at least six murders to a page. What the theatre box-offices cry for are melodramas that do not give the impression of being ashamed of themselves and that whoop it up in the good old-fashioned manner. " Take *that,* you cur! " and " One step nearer and I'll blow the living daylights out of ye! " will bring back to the ticket-window a lot of people who are now driven in despair to films containing Frankenstein monsters pursuing platinum blondes, G-men

[298]

plying their artillery in night clubs, and Chinamen creeping up on Ronald Colman with poisoned daggers.

*   *   *

The late Charles Frohman frequently stated that no play could richly succeed save its appeal were primarily to women. Since Frohman's time so great a change has come over the ladies that it is today pretty safe to say that it is a rare play that can richly succeed save its appeal be primarily to men. In the altered modern world the tastes of women in the various departments of life — art, morals, sport, literature, drama, sex and alcoholic liquor — have not only approached closer and closer to those of their boy friends, but in several of the aforesaid departments, to put it delicately, have exceeded them. One of the results is that what some years ago would have been regarded as a distinctly man's play nowadays finds its auditorium so full of the girls that it is all a man can do to horn in.

That women no longer generally relish plays written with a deliberate eye to a massaging of their vanities, whether actual or theoretical, is to be perceived from the mediocre reception of the various recent exhibits having that box-office purpose in view. As one illustrative instance out of a number we may point to Mr. Joseph Kesselring's *There's Wisdom In Women*. (Parenthetically, the producers of such senile drool might meditate that a certain revived classic showing a husband beating the tar out of an ill-tempered, shrewish wife and making her eat humble-pie drew more delighted women last season than all the pro-female pieces put together, just as a certain play showing a husband brusquely giving his vain, spoiled spouse the gate and making off happily with a more amiable woman the season before did the same thing.) When we were all considerably younger, the kind of play in which Miss Grace George or some other actress, symbolizing the transcendent sagacity of women, succeeded shrewdly and handsomely in putting Mr. Frank Worthing or some other actor, in turn symbolizing the pathetic doltishness of men, in his place, was a sure bet with women audiences. That was the sentimental era of woman's dominance both in drama and in the seats out front. It was best at the time described by Shaw when he observed that even in dramas dealing with military life it was, of course, usual for all army commanders to be superseded at critical moments by their daughters. But tempora mutantur, et the damsels mutamur in illis, in the drama as well as out front. So, when the grandpa Kesselrings these days belatedly again trot out the old romantic whiffle, the increased intelligence of modern women is affronted and they grab at their cigarette cases and make a bee line out of the theatre for the sidewalk, where they may enjoy the consoling and comforting spectacle, more often than not, of some gangster gentleman inducing in his girl friend a wholesome and devout yearning for him by kicking her puissantly in the slats.

The mothy sexual philosophy of the Kesselrings is even more obnoxiously silly to the observant modern woman theatregoer than the Kesselrings' romantic. When the Kesselrings note with a profound show of experience and cunning, as they do in such hackspiels as *There's Wisdom In Women,* that the moment a man gets what he wants from a woman he begins to tire of her and that the only way for a woman to win and hold a man is to keep him at an arm's length, any such observant modern woman slumps down in her seat, yawns, and politely mutters *Noisettes!* The Kesselrings belong to the past. The *There's Wisdom In Womens* which lift the curtain on a group of musical folk who, following stage tradition, indicate their possession of artistic temperament by passionately running their fingers through their hair, running hither and thither about the room for no discernible reason, and simultaneously talking about food and Bach, are equally of the past. And the *There's Wisdom In Women* plots dealing with a great pianist's patient and understanding wife who wins back her errant spouse's love by deliberately throwing him into the arms of the beautiful young girl who momentarily captures his fancy (maybe marriage isn't so bad, after all) are of the past even more so.

* * *

The MM. Brewer and Bloch put everything into *Dark Victory* but what is often described, in our wittier circles, as the kitchen stove, and even that was just off-stage in their third act. If there was anything else, whether in showshop drama or current pulp literature, that they omitted, I can't think of it at the moment. I list a number of the items, which will give you an idea of the whole. No. 1, the young woman who has only six months to live and decides to have a pungent time of it while she lasts. No. 2, the Long Island riding, cocktail-swigging set. No. 3, a paraphrase of the Lady Chatterley-gamekeeper gambols. No. 4, a soupçon of Michael Arlen's Iris March. No. 5, the Noël Coward fashionable employment of the word *bitch*. No. 6, the gay, flip, worldly young woman who, immediately after she gets married to her heart's desire, settles sweetly down like a glass of five-cent ginger-ale and begins ordering bulbs to plant in the garden and keeping household accounts. No. 7, the serious young doctor who can't understand how people can go in for cocktails and bridge. No. 8, the mad piano-pounding business from Coward's *The Vortex*. No. 9, the kindly and solicitous old housekeeper who looks out for her bachelor charge like a mother. No. 10, the nurse who silently bears an unrequited yen for the young doctor. No. 11, the scene from *The Outsider* in which the medico sympathetically examines the morbose heroine's symptoms. No. 12, allusions to the beautiful green hills of Vermont, from *Quincy Adams Sawyer*. No. 13, the melodramatic smashing of a windowpane. No. 14, the noble heroine who chokes back her grief and with brave resignation enjoins the hero to go forth in answer to the call of duty.

[302]

There is, I take it, little need to extend the catalogue; the above samples will sufficiently indicate the stale nature of the chowder. Nor did the authors display any greater departure from familiar routine in the instance of character treatment. Take a single example: the young surgeon alluded to. Here we got simply the stock figure out of plays without number: the professional man whose importance, distinction and dignity are indicated in his haughty aversion to the pleasures and gaieties of other folk, and whose substantial masculinity and general superiority to the run of the people about him are emphasized by his steadfast disinclination ever under any circumstances to wear evening clothes. That three-quarters of the eminent physicians and surgeons one knows — especially those who, like the figure in the MM. Brewer's and Bloch's exhibit, are called to more or less fashionable practice — not only are hounds for bridge but like nothing better than to embellish themselves with boiled shirts, and are anything but anchorites when it comes to the girls, is a phenomenon that seems to have eluded the over-theatricalized appreciation of the authors. And the same, in other realistic directions, with other of their characters. Their play, in short, was so much actor-paint.

* * *

Whenever I look at a program and find that the entire action of a play is to pass in a cellar or basement, I promptly turn the page to see who the author is and if it isn't Gorki I prepare myself for the worst. This, of course, is no polite way to approach the reviewing of a play, despite the fact that over a very long period of years the prejudice has been amply borne out by subsequent events. Except for *Night Refuge,* unless my memory isn't up to par, every single play laid in a cellar that has been produced here in the last twenty-five years has turned out to be pretty shabby stuff.

Nicholas Cosentino's *Moon Over Mulberry Street* further — and very handsomely — supported the prejudice. " The entire action of the play takes place in the Morello basement flat on Mulberry street " confided the playbill and, as generally follows, the entire reaction of the audience duly took place in the lobby and on the sidewalk in Forty-fifth street. It was estimated that on the opening night alone no less than 4,000 packs of cigarettes were consumed outside while the second and third acts of the play were left to consume themselves inside. For to the customers' advance trepidations in the matter of the cellar locale there were promptly added further dire misgivings when the first curtain rose and disclosed, in a niche in the wall, a small statue of the Virgin with a little red light burning before it.

There is, as in the case of plays laid in basements and cellars, surely no sensible reason why the great majority of present-day plays with niches in the wall and small statues of the Virgin with little red lights burning before them should invariably prove critical and frequently box-office duds, but once again facts seem to be facts. In the Italian theatre, where every other play reveals such a holy figure, together with the customary illumination thereof, things are different, although the critical business in Italy isn't much more bloomy than the box-office. But outside of Italy, and most certainly in America, it is a Polichinelle secret among drama critics, evidently not yet assimilated by play angels, that there is in the prop a considerable dose of theatrical hoodoo — unless the show happens to have a cast of one hundred or more, including maybe a white horse and two dromedaries, and offers a big spectacular ecclesiastical parade up and down the aisles at least twice during the evening. Or unless the Leblang ticket agency, as in Mr. Cosentino's case, gets both shoulders behind it.

Mr. Cosentino's little gem essayed to be a folk play of New York's Little Italy and ran a winning race for the Rubber-Stamp Sweepstakes. Here again were all the established morsels of the pulp wop drama, from the humorous allusions to spaghetti and the penchant for garlic to the wistful disquisitions on the humble furniture with which papa and mama began their married life and their prideful struggle to make a career as a great lawyer — " he might be Presidente of the United States some day " — for their beloved son Fillipo. This Fillipo, it seems, was enamoured, to the qualms of old Piccino and his wife Lucia, of the haughty and beauteous Helen Richards of Park Avenue. Miss Richards, whose blue-blood was indicated in that species of locution more usually associated with over-educated Negroes, was in turn attracted to Fillipo by his sexual potentialities and, though he expressed doubts that they could be happy together because of the difference in their social status, she crept into his embrace — this all occurred in the Mulberry street basement — and pulled out full distance the " Thy people shall be my people " stop. Meanwhile, Papa Piccino Morello and Mama Lucia Morello, with much headshaking, provided an obbligato with the " East is East and West is West " stop pulled plumb out of its socket. Things went on in this way for a long spell, interrupted at appropriate intervals by the entrance of little Nina Baccolini, who nursed an unrequited passion for the handsome Fillipo, and by copious doses of " atmosphere." And in the end Helen went back to Park Avenue in the person of one Grant Whitmore, a fashionable dog who always donned tails and a white tie when he visited Mulberry street; Fillipo saw the light and took little Nina unto his chest; and the day was saved for Mulberry street and race pollution.

The author's characterizations, together with the acting, were strictly and comprehensively ham. Papa Morello was the Poli vaudeville wop who couldn't eat with his collar on and who celebrated gala occasions by putting on a low-comedy tight-fitting sassafras-brown suit of store clothes and a brilliant red necktie. Mama Morello was the genial and expansive fatty in the apron who solicitously attended her chicks and, in the serio-comic moments of the evening, elaborately crossed herself. Angelo Baccolini, the neighbor, was the portly and vastly excitable wop in shirt-sleeves who moved right in on the Morellos whenever anything to eat or drink was in sight; Helen Richards of Park Avenue further indicated her lofty social position by keeping Fillipo's lowly family waiting fifteen minutes for dinner and then by being snooty about the food and general surrounding décor; and the rest came similarly out of the old wastebasket.

*　　*　　*

Miss Dodie Smith, author of *Call It a Day,* is a maiden lady and English. The theme of her play is that Spring does something to people. This is how she demonstrates its excitoglandular effect upon ten of her characters, to say nothing of two dogs.

The handsome Roger Hilton is beseeched by a young, beautiful and passionate actress to come to her flat and enjoy an affair with her. He comes, and spends the entire time chatting with her on her career. His wife encounters an attractive bachelor, is duly attracted by him, but shrinks from him with a ladylike qualm when he tries to kiss her. Vera, the young maid-servant, sneaks out several times to meet the amorous butler of a neighborhood family, but the butler doesn't show up. The Hiltons' comely young daughter offers herself to an artist Lothario, but the Lothario, after a few moments' hesitation, says nothing doing. The hero invites his stenographer to take an automobile ride with him after office hours, cheers her up no end, and then suddenly calls it off. The son of the family, a gay young blade, succumbing to the charms of a forward young minx, talks casually with her for a short time and then moseys upstairs to dress for dinner. And the two dogs in heat, one male and belonging to the family and the other female and belonging to a nearby household, merely bow politely to each other and thereafter carefully avoid each other like the plague. " Oh to be in England, now that April's here! " (*Memoirs of Casanova,* pp. 1–465.)

While it is both obvious and morally certain that Miss Smith has never seen or read her German namesake, Lothar Schmidt's, old comedy of what Spring does to folks, *Only a Dream,* it is equally obvious and morally certain that she has seen and read a great deal of old theatrical humorous hokum. No one can doubt it who listens to *Call It a Day* and gives ear to her repertoire of wheezes ranging from the one about what a newspaper always looks like when a woman gets through with it to the one about the dieting woman who has solved the problem comfortably by eating a lot between meals so she won't feel like stuffing herself at lunch and dinner. Nor does Miss Smith forget the kitchen one about the sugar being in the can marked rice, the one about the family impatiently waiting its turn to use the bathroom, the one about the homely girl followed by a masher in the park — until he gets a look at her face, and a half dozen or so others. To repeat, Miss Smith is a maiden lady and English.

Shaw

It is as ungenerous and distasteful as it is gratuitous to repeat that George Bernard Shaw, now arrived at the age of eighty, clearly indicates that he is not as spry as he was twenty or thirty years ago, but if Mr. Shaw himself persists in elaborately and insistently proving it to us there is little else for us to do. We want him to be as spry as once he was; we hope against hope that he will be; but he perversely continues to take us by the scruff of the necks and to show us that he isn't. He has been doing it now for a number of years, and we don't like it. He has, in his day, given us altogether too much delight for us to be now, in this late season of his life, ungrateful and churlish. But old age is old age, and old age is weakness, and the first who should realize the unhappy but inevitable fact is the sagacious Shaw himself. There is a greater fame in a wise retirement than in a skilless and senescent activity. If Shaw had retired ten years ago, the glory of the literary and dramatic world would still be singing its loud song in his ears, faithful in the perhaps foolish conviction that, if he had not seen fit to retire, he could have gone on endlessly composing masterpieces. But with his stubborn determination to keep at it until hell freezes and with his increasingly inept performances like *The Apple Cart, Too True To Be Good, Village Wooing, On The Rocks,* and — worst of all — *The Simpleton of the Unexpected Isles* and *The Millionairess,* the song has turned into something sadly re-

[309]

sembling a snicker, the hymn has become a cacophonous grunt, and a once great man must suffer the critical consequences of his own folly.

It is a pity that age so often fails to appreciate that the jig is up after a lifetime of notable achievement. It is a pity because big men should remain in our memory and in our faith as big men, and not spoil the show. Shaw, had he retired in time, would have remained for us the symbol of vital youth and vital wit and vital mind even if he lived to be one hundred and ten. As it is, he has become for us — though assuredly we do not for a moment forget the high brilliance of his past days — an increasingly addled and rather futile old man. *The Simpleton of the Unexpected Isles* and *The Millionairess* are the last straws. Not only have they almost unanimously been put down as two of the most supremely dull plays of their time; not only do they betray a tired old gentleman himself at least partly aware that he is a tired old gentleman; but, further, their pathetic repetitions of ideas that were fresh thirty years ago have a corpsey odor that all the sweet flowers of Malvern are unable to conceal from even those gracious and over-friendly English critics who, though realizing full well that Shaw is done for, would like to pretend for old times' sake that he isn't.